# HUNTING FOUR HORSEMEN

# HUNTING FOUR HORSEMEN

## A DANGEROUS CLIQUE NOVEL

JIM GERAGHTY

DISCUS BOOKS

ALEXANDRIA, VIRGINIA

*To everyone, wearing scrubs, uniforms, or anything else, who helped keep us upright and aboveground during the pandemic.*

# TABLE OF CONTENTS

# CHAPTER ONE

FLAM, NORWAY
MONDAY, APRIL 5

"**F**irst Atarsa, then coronavirus, now even our enemies have their ranks going rogue," Ward grumbled. "World's gone mad."

Snow stuck to his red beard. Ward Rutledge was a former Army Ranger, honorably discharged but still collecting a paycheck from the federal government. Stout and solid, bundled up tight in winter gear, including a red hat and thick blue coat, earmuffs covering his earwig, Ward resembled the puppet of Yukon Cornelius even more than usual. His teammate and best friend Alec would have joked about the resemblance, if Alec hadn't stopped telling jokes.

Two women and a man stood by Ward, watching the small, steep-roofed building on the horizon, and the light within.

The quartet stood on the outskirts of Flam, Norway, a tiny village of about three hundred residents, located on in the inner end of one of the most scenic fjords in the country. Just two years ago, the tiny village was a major tourist destination, particularly for cruise ships touring the spectacularly steep valley and cascading waterfalls.

But the cruise lines first announced they would be delayed, then would be skipping a year, and by the time the next season arrived, almost all of them were out of business or limping along with minimal staff, passengers, and schedules. Tourists were few and far between. The local rail line, one of the steepest in the world, shut down, and with it, the souvenir and tchotchke shops. The residents hunkered down for a temporary lockdown that had ended physically but not psychologically. Flam now was just a frozen, far-off corner of the world, the kind of place a man could run to if he just wanted to disappear and for the world to forget about him.

Ward and his colleagues had traveled to this frigid speck on the map because they hadn't forgotten about the crimes of one particular new transplant to the village.

"The world hasn't gone mad," Katrina Leonidivna murmured quietly. "It's just broken." She glanced over at her husband Alec Flanagan, who was as cold as the rest of them, but enduring the temperature in uncharacteristic silence. "People go mad, not worlds. Men go crazy in congregations, but they only get better one by one." Another gust of wind pelted snow against them, seeming to mock Katrina's relatively cheery assessment.

"If the man we're looking for went mad, it would explain a lot," the other woman, Raquel Holtz, whispered.

Raquel was the woman who ran the small, secretive Central Intelligence Agency team nicknamed the "Dangerous Clique" by other often-resentful agency employees. Roughly one chaotic year after 9/11, Raquel had been appointed to that position by the colorful—some would argue more accurately labeled *eccentric*—former deputy director Harold Hare.

Running the new team, Raquel quickly lost all appetite for promotion. From her perspective, her team offered maximum effectiveness with minimal bureaucratic entanglements—and, in the eyes of some other managers at the agency, minimal accountability. As the war on terror raged, first against al-Qaeda and then against ISIS and related extremist groups, the Dangerous Clique had journeyed around the world, secretly ending the careers of up-and-coming terrorists before they could get promoted to the major leagues. The Navy SEALS, Army Rangers, Delta Force, and the other military special forces units eliminated the big fish and generated the headlines and movie docudramas. Raquel's team was content to ensure that terrorists, arms dealers, terror financiers, and other enablers of threats to Americans that the general public had never heard of kept dying in "mysterious accidents" that frequently never looked that accidental at all.

As Alec, one of the team's founding members, once explained in a briefing, "we made it look like he fell down an elevator shaft, and just happened to land on a pile of bullets."

To Katrina, Alec, and Ward, Raquel was technically their boss, but of late had been joining her small team of operatives out in the field. Raquel had sufficient skills to handle herself on foreign soil, evading the watchful eyes of hostile intelligence agencies or extremist groups. She was no "modern samurai," as some managers had nicknamed Katrina, but she could hold her own in a fight and was even better at avoiding the fight in the first place. Katrina suspected that the events of recent years had left Raquel antsy and frustrated; staying back at Langley or the team's office at Liberty Campus in Tysons Corner while the rest of them were out tracking some target in some far-off corner of the world had frayed even Raquel's deep reserves of patience.

Katrina understood. Less than a year after the team's heralded success in tracking down the leaders of a cult-like terrorist group calling itself Atarsa, the country had faced another massive threat, but one that wasn't in human form. You couldn't assassinate a virus. And so, like hundreds of millions of Americans and billions around the world, the Dangerous Clique stayed home. Quietly seething with frustration, anger, sorrow, and a pervasive sense of powerlessness, they watched the situation get worse.

Scientists believed the notorious coronavirus was gone now, and most people around the world were vaccinated, including almost all Americans except the now-outlaw bands of anti-vaxxers dwelling off the grid in the wilderness. But the virus had changed everything. The number of deaths, serious hospitalizations, and lingering side effects left a scar on the world, and the associated trauma had left emotional repercussions on par with 9/11 and the Great Recession. Psychiatrists and psychologists reported an explosion of patients with agoraphobia—fear of leaving home—and enochlophobia, the fear of crowds. More than a few pointed out that based upon recent experience and the uncertainty that no other comparable viruses were still floating around out there, those were not necessarily irrational fears.

Halfway across the globe to northern Virginia, in Liberty Crossing, in the building that included the Office of the Director of National Intelligence, Dominica "Dee" Alves was connected to their earpieces and at a workstation relaying information.

"His alias credit card just pinged," Dee confirmed. "Your target just ordered a beer and set up a tab."

"Good," Katrina confirmed. "I count three doors. Ward, the back. Alec, the side. Raquel and I through the front. Ward, when I say we want him alive, that includes his ability to speak."

From a heavy bag, Ward removed a SIG Sauer MCX Rattler, which looked like the offspring of mating between the familiar AR-15 rifle and the old Uzi submachine guns. The result was a small rifle that used larger, high-velocity, powerful 5.56-millimeter ammunition but was only twenty-six inches long. Upon the MCX Rattler's debut, some asked if the easily concealed powerful rifle would become "the deadliest gun on planet earth," but it was pricey—at least two thousand dollars—and relatively rare. Gleaming black, the short rifle was an intimidating sight, guaranteed to make any handguns in attendance look mundane.

"Think of me as a motivational speaker," Ward chuckled. "One minute with him and I'll have him heavily motivated to speak."

Alec hadn't said anything during their conversation, a silence that until a year ago would have seemed unthinkably odd. Ward found his longtime friend's sudden embrace of eerie taciturnity the clearest sign that something was terribly wrong with the world. He kept setting up jokes for Alec, but his taller friend never took the bait. Since the moment they had departed the United States, Alec hadn't joked that Flam sounded like "phlegm," or called the local trucks "Fjord F-150s," declared that Norway was "occupied," made references to Tonya Harding or Nancy Kerrigan, Edvard Munch's *The Scream*, lutefisk, or Minnesota Vikings, or observed that all of the locals seemed to look like Tormund Giantsbane.

Just getting into Norway had been a challenge. When the scale of the virus's threat became clear, the Norwegian government had closed the border to all non-Norwegian citizens and expelled all foreigners without residence or work permits. Those restrictions had only gradually and begrudgingly been lifted, piecemeal and with considerable confusion and bureaucratic delay. The quartet had left the United States on unofficial cover by flying to Amsterdam and then bribing a cargo ship to make a major detour. The bad weather all over Europe provided the captain with a convenient excuse for the delays.

They had spent the past hour standing outside, watching all of the entrances to Ægir Bryggeri, a brewery and bar in a building of medieval Viking architecture, with a roof so long and sloped it almost looked like a pyramid. They managed to stay open through the village's lean times because in both good times and bad, people like to drink.

Within the bar's walls was the former Iranian intelligence official Iraj Khansari, who went by the alias "Div-e Sepid"—the "White Demon."

***

"What's it like inside?" Ward asked from outside the back door.

"*Game of Thrones,* or maybe that place where Indiana Jones met Marion," Raquel answered under her breath. She realized that with Alec now quiet, she had picked up his habit of comparing everything they encountered to something from pop culture.

Inside the moderately rowdy pub, a giant of a man spotted Katrina moments after she entered and strode right up to her. A Bukhari Jew, Katrina looked Eurasian and could blend in from Morocco to Mongolia, but in Norway she stood out as a golden-tanned fantasy of every lonely man—and even most of the not-so-lonely ones.

The giant slid his hand down her back to her tush, offering some sort of wild night of carnal delights in Norwegian, one of the few languages she didn't speak at all. Katrina's expression betrayed nothing, other than a slight squint of her eyes, as she assessed the inebriated man and his obliviousness to how vulnerable he was in that position: his eyes, nose, neck, crotch, back, and where his kidneys resided beneath his skin and the sides of his knees and his anterior cruciate ligaments.

"Here we go," Raquel sighed. "Katrina, get rid of this guy. We're here to do a job, and I don't want Eric the Red here to get in the way."

"Do you need help?" Alec's voice buzzed in her earpiece. He knew the answer but asked anyway.

"No, she's got it," Raquel answered for her.

Katrina noticed a nipple ring poking through the tight shirt of Eric the Red, just a few inches from a wet spot where beer had missed his mouth a few moments ago. She smiled sweetly and pointed at it, and Eric the Red, thrilled at her interest, unbuttoned his shirt to show it off.

A moment later, Eric the Red realized the terrible error of his ways while groaning and rolling on the floor, as his buddy tried to clot the bleeding with a napkin. Before Eric could realize what was happening, Katrina had suddenly yanked the ring out of his skin and casually dropped it into his mug of beer.

Katrina shot a look around at the rest of the bar's patrons, silently daring anyone else. It didn't take long before one man at a table near the back disrupted the sudden awkward silence, scrambling to his feet and starting to head for the back door.

"Khansari!" Katrina shouted.

"We want that man," Raquel announced in Norwegian, or at least she thought it was a reasonable enough translation. She repeated it in English. "That man's an international fugitive! We don't want trouble with any of the rest of you!"

Iraj Khansari had gotten halfway down the hallway to the back door when it flew open. His eyes bulged as he realized it had been kicked in by Ward, now raising the Rattler compact rifle and pointing it, right at his center mass.

Ward didn't quite smile, but he couldn't completely hide his satisfaction. "Show me your hands! Show them!" But Khansari froze. "Your call, pal. What's one more dead body?"

But Khansari just turned around and ran the other way, stopping, skidding, and trying to make a sharp turn around the bar, toward the doors to the kitchen. He passed through the large metal double doors...

...and a moment later, crashed back as if he had hit an invisible wall, tumbling to the floor.

Alec stepped through the double doors, holding a large saucepan. Katrina scrambled down with a zip-tie to bind Khansari's hands. Ward smiled, lowered his rifle, and waited. He thought through all the various quips the old Alec would utter at this moment.

*"He couldn't take the heat, so he got out of the kitchen."*

*"You can't skip out on the check like that."*

*"Careful, that drink packs a punch."*

*"This is why he should have ordered takeout."*

But none of those lines arrived. Alec just looked at his teammates, holding one hand on the nine-millimeter Glock 48 in his holster, and nodding, confident that Khansari was no longer a threat to escape or counterattack.

Raquel explained to the crowd that the man was a dangerous fugitive. While the assembled men, women, drunks, and barflies of Flam didn't exactly warmly nod in response to her explanation, no one seemed eager to object to the capture of the man, either. They eyed Ward's compact rifle warily.

Raquel reached into a coat pocket and put a stack of Euros—probably four thousand dollars or so onto the bar—but didn't remove her hand.

"Is there a back room we can book for a private party?"

"Will you hurt him?" the bartender asked, eyes locked on the cash.

"That's up to him," Ward mumbled.

"No," Katrina said firmly. "Just question him. We're going to leave soon."

The bartender nodded and pointed to the hallway behind Ward.

# CHAPTER TWO

ÆGIR BRYGGERI BAR AND BREWERY
FLAM, NORWAY
MONDAY, APRIL 5

"I've seen red devils in the British Army, drank some green devil in France, and rooted against some blue devils from Duke, but you are the first 'White Devil' I've caught," Ward chuckled.

Khansari now had one hand bound to a chair. Katrina had gotten him a glass of water, and even offered him an alcoholic drink from the bar, wondering if it would loosen this tongue. He had declined. Katrina knew Khansari didn't abstain from alcohol; she had checked the table he ran from and found a mostly consumed bottle of beer.

"His *nom de guerre* is the White Demon, not the White Devil," Alec declared. "There's a difference."

Khansari couldn't hide the fact that his ears perked up at this.

"Sure, Iraj here is pretty pale by Iranian standards, so maybe somebody nicknamed him 'White Demon' way back when for his light skin," Alec began. "But in Persian, 'White Demon' translates to 'Div-e Sepid.'"

Alec explained that "Div-e Sepid" was the name of a villain from pre-Islamic Persian mythology. Rostam was a Hercules-like hero, who encountered Div-e Sepid, an unbelievably nefarious sorcerer and conqueror of massive stature who led a bloodthirsty army. If Rostam hadn't slain Div-e Sepid, the White Demon would have gone on to conquer the entire world. Some historians think Div-e Sepid was inspired by some real historical warlord from the north, some lighter-skinned tribe from somewhere past the Caspian Sea.

Khansari raised his eyebrows. "I'm surprised that there's an American who recognizes the reference."

Alec stared back with contempt. "Well, I had a lot of time to catch up on reading during my quarantine."

*There's the Alec I know*, Ward thought.

Raquel reached into her satchel and slammed a photo onto the table before Khansari.

"Gholam Gul," she said. "Founder of the terrorist group Atarsa."

Khansari's expression was sad, but he said nothing. After a few moments, she removed another photo, taken within an abandoned airport terminal in Cyprus.

"He died a terrible death. Multiple skull fractures."

Khansari winced and looked away from the photo. Ward circled around Khansari and leaned in to whisper behind his ear: "My buddy here did that to him." The Iranian looked up in concern at Alec, but Alec just shrugged.

Katrina pulled up a chair and sat directly in front of Khansari.

"We're not looking for a confession," Katrina declared in a tone that was firm, but not harsh. "We already know everything we need to know from tracing the bank records you thought were secret. You wired almost a million dollars to Gholam Gul after he left VEVAK, the Iranian intelligence service."

Khansari chuckled a bit. "They changed the name from VEVAK to VAJA—Vezarat-e Ettela'at Jomhuri-ye Eslami-ye Iran."

"Yes, but you guys called yourself VEVAK when Gul left," Katrina said sharply. "You helped plant the seeds that grew into the terrorist group Atarsa."

Khansari looked at the photo that had Gholam Gul's face intact and shrugged. "This all seems like ancient history now, doesn't it?"

"You think we forget stuff like this?" Ward growled.

Raquel stared hard at Khansari and recited the litany of Atarsa's crimes from memory. The bombing of Café Vernunft in Berlin. The poisoning of CIA Director William Peck. A first wave of stabbing attacks on civilians in Detroit, New York, Beverly Hills, Cleveland, Charlotte. Attempted second wave attacks on Ground Zero in New York, Sidwell Friends school in Washington, Philadelphia, Burlington, Peoria. Successful third wave attacks in restaurants in Columbus, Nashville, Jacksonville, Boston, and Washington again. A series of decoy attacks in Princeton, Buffalo, New York again, and Chicago. And then the Night of Sirens, falsely implicating thousands of Americans in the attacks and setting off violence and unrest throughout the country. It all added up to 438 Americans killed, and more than two thousand injured, all starting about two years ago now.

"No, Iraj Khansari, the United States of America does not forget something like that," Katrina declared.

"That all feels small compared to the virus," Khansari responded with a bitter chuckle. He straightened his posture in the chair and jutted his chin. "If you're going to kill me, then kill me."

"We could," Katrina said evenly. "But I think we've all seen more than enough death in our lifetimes. Surely, you noticed your VEVAK colleagues dying in mysterious accidents after the Atarsa attacks. We did more digging and figured out that the Iranian government wasn't as oblivious to the plans of Gholam Gul and Sarvar Rashin as they claimed. At minimum, you guys knew he was planning attacks, and as soon as Rashin popped up in those threatening videos, you knew this was your old friend and his handiwork."

"Is this what you want to hear?" Khansari asked, his ire rising. "That VEVAK and the Revolutionary Guard knew what Gul was planning all along, all the way up the chain of command to Qasem Soleimani? What difference does it make now?"

"No, we already know Soleimani signed off on Gul's plans to create Atarsa," Ward chuckled. "That's one of the many reasons he turned into a red smear on the side of the road to the Baghdad airport."

"No, that's not what we want to know now," Katrina said, suddenly changing her tone—softer, almost sympathetic. Her demeanor transmuted like quicksilver. "We know you're AWOL from Iranian intelligence. You're just lucky we found you before your old bosses did. What we want to know is why."

Khansari's expression changed.

"This is a very far-off, very tiny place to hide away, Iraj," Katrina said. "You stayed in Iran when the pandemic was at its worst. *Sag sâhebesho nemishnâse.*" That was a Persian phrase; literally it meant, "a dog doesn't recognize its owner," meaning a state of chaos. Khansari looked down upon her words.

She glanced over at Alec. Two years ago, he wouldn't have been able to resist the urge to punctuate her description with "human sacrifice, dogs and cats living together, mass hysteria!" But he remained stone-faced.

It was as if Khansari was a balloon, and Katrina had figured out how to slowly release the air. He seemed to shrink before them, slumping down, taking a deep, slow breath.

"For a while, we thought the virus would get you before we could," Ward jabbed.

Khansari shook his head. "From what you've told me, I suspect you found a way to intercept our communications...but you have not seen the true picture of how the virus tore apart my country."

He looked at each of them.

"You know the official numbers are a lie. My government—"
He paused. It wasn't really his government anymore. "*The* government in Tehran reported deaths before they reported any infections. The number of cases and deaths may be ten times what my government said. We lost thousands of people just from trying fake cures. Drinking pure alcohol. People blinded themselves, made themselves sick. The virus swept through the prisons, guards abandoning their posts. Riots and panic spread faster than the virus itself. They reopened the businesses too early, set off another wave of infections. Families begging in the streets. Every country's economy tumbled, ours collapsed. Police can barely keep order in the streets. Everyone believes it was a conspiracy—mostly blaming the Americans, but others blame the Israelis or Arabs or Chinese."

"If things are so bad, how is the regime staying in power?" Raquel asked.

"Everyone else is hurt worse," Khansari shrugged, shaking his head. "Who's left to seize power and set up a new government? Someone in the Health Ministry blurted out what everyone knew—the information we got from China was a pack of lies. But the day after he told the papers the truth, Revolutionary Guards shut him down. The alliance with Beijing mattered more, at least then. We couldn't even speak honestly about our own people dying." His expression changed to a tight smile, and he chuckled. "There was a joke going around, a great university professor was on his deathbed in the hospital, and one of the top mullahs rushed to be by his side—to inform him that his infection was not so bad and that he did not have government permission to die."

Katrina nodded. "Is that when you ran?"

"NO!" he barked back. "I would never leave my country in its hour of need. And the first green shoots of recovery were sprouting when I decided to leave. It will be the longest of roads, and my country will never be the same. The home I knew is gone forever."

"What made you leave?" Katrina insisted.

"We were still counting our dead, trying to sort out fact from rumor. Some of my colleagues believed this was a punishment from Allah for straying from the faith. Others said this was a sign the Glorious Revolution had born bitter fruit. We had become accustomed to lies, blind loyalty, too obsessed with appearing strong to openly discuss our weaknesses."

"A lot of countries paid the price for that mentality in their leaders," Katrina said, nodding.

Khansari continued. "We thought enduring sanctions was a price worth paying for a nuclear program. But what good is a nuclear weapon when your cities and villages are being conquered by a virus? We would accept any ally against you, the Great Satan. Chinese workers were building our projects in Qom. There are seven hundred Chinese seminarians in Qom's university. The flights of Mahan Air..."

Raquel interrupted. "You mean the state-run airline that the Iran Revolutionary Guard Corps uses to smuggle weapons."

Khansari sighed. "Yes. The airline kept flying to cities in China, long after the scale of the pandemic was clear. We unknowingly invited the virus into our homes. At first my leaders didn't discuss the virus, because it wanted parliamentary elections and festivals to go forward as scheduled, and that only spread the virus further. Our doctors are smart and brave, but they cannot overcome decisions like that. The sick and dying overwhelmed our hospitals, and we had no choice but to start digging mass graves. Everything I had spent my life trying to prevent happened before my eyes. I had to admit, our old way of doing things had failed—we had not protected the people. I knew things had to change."

He looked at Katrina, then Raquel, then Alec, then Ward. Khansari seemed to be trying to decide something.

"A few months ago, I was called into a meeting of the top intelligence officials—I should point out, the top surviving intelligence officials. We knew the meeting was something important. I thought it would be about something about our efforts to recover."

He exhaled slowly.

"But it was about something different. We had been contacted by a German—not from the German government, someone with a German name. He had made our government a secret offer. He wanted an enormous sum, and we were being asked to determine how much …" he paused. "My leaders wanted to know how much money we could gather to pay the German's price."

"The German's price for what?"

Khansari looked at the ceiling.

"My superiors did not want to say. They just wanted to know how quickly we could assemble tens of billions of Euros. The more they refused to say what the money was for, the more those of us—loyal servants of the revolution, loyal servants of the people—wanted to know. I wondered if there would be a mutiny, right there in the conference room. Finally, they admitted what the German had offered them."

A painful silence seemed to stretch on forever.

"The German claimed he could engineer another virus, one that would only infect and kill people with particular genetic markers," Khansari said, wiping a tear.

Katrina couldn't help herself—she leaned back in revulsion at the thought.

"An ethnic bioweapon," Raquel gasped. She knew the concept had been discussed for years, but most scientists believed it required an ability to manipulate the genetics of viruses beyond the capacity of current technology. No one was certain how well a virus designed to kill only certain kinds of people would work, whether it could mutate, whether some members of the targeted group could prove resistant. But everyone who had ever studied the issue came away shuddering at the thought of genocide in a jar, the ability to devastate or even wipe out a single ethnic minority without firing a shot—and leave neighboring ethnic groups untouched.

"Did they get the money?" Ward demanded.

Khansari shook his head. "The German's price was enormous, beyond imagination, even before our currency crashed. He wanted something like nine hundred billion rial."

Raquel did the math in her head. "That's about 20 billion dollars."

"That would have been an enormous sum, even before the virus," Khansari said. "We were teetering on the edge of being a failed state. My country's leaders couldn't afford to pay, and right before I left, I heard they had told the German they could not afford it but wanted to negotiate. Last I heard, he was not willing to reduce his price."

Katrina stared at him. "But that didn't mean they were not interested."

Khansari tearfully nodded.

"It was then I realized it," he exhaled, the despair of a defeated man. "We were guilty. You probably think we got just what we deserved. Our people were innocent, but our nation was not. All our collaborations with every murderer around the globe, all that blood on our hands. And at a time when our people were suffering on a scale we had never imagined, because we had failed to prepare and protect them, my leaders could not change their priorities. They were entranced with the thought of starting another epidemic, as long as it would only hit those we believed were our enemies."

He looked at them despondently. "I spent my life preparing to fight decadent infidel bastards like you, but it wasn't you who came and killed all my people. The virus was our true enemy, but my leaders couldn't see it."

Katrina had come to this tiny village in Norway, knowing that Khansari needed to be caught, and that the CIA needed to know why he had fled his home country. A few at the agency's Iran desk wondered if he could be convinced to defect, although Iranian intelligence had been through such wrenching changes during the outbreak, his knowledge might be outdated already. No doubt many, including Ward, believed Khansari deserved to be executed for his role in helping set up the Atarsa terrorist group.

But Katrina finally understood that nagging sense of apprehension that had been present in her mind since she first heard about Khansari disappearing from Tehran and resurfacing in Norway. VEVAK—now VAJA—rarely had disloyalty in its ranks, and career intelligence officers didn't just walk off the job. She had theorized it was outbreak-driven burnout, now rampant in almost every profession that responded to the virus. But some part of her—the part that Alec used to joke gave her prophetic dreams—was warning that Khansari was his own kind of patriot, and that only something unspeakably awful could get him fleeing his home to another continent.

"That's why you left, and why you can't go back," Katrina said, surprising herself with a tone of compassion. "Your government can't resist the temptation to make a terrible situation even worse."

Khansari gathered himself.

"Iran will survive, but it will never again be as I loved it. The Iran I knew died with all of the virus victims. We lost so many doctors, engineers, artists, wise men, imams, mothers, and fathers. There's this argument about whether we're a 'failed state.' By any measure, our state failed our people. We chose to believe in an illusion until it's too late—and even now, we'll still believe in that illusion that we are strong. We fear the truth more than death."

Like everyone else, Raquel was still grasping the ramifications of what Khansari was saying. But finally she shook herself into a new focus.

"Who is the German?"

"In another life, I would have resisted telling you," Khansari chucked bitterly. "But I fear that if this German can do what he claims, someone will buy what he offers. If not my government, then someone else. The name my superiors used sounded like....*Holland-beach-wear*." He closed his eyes, and tried to remember how the word in the alien tongue sounded. "Hollen... Hollen-besch-wore."

The quartet of Americans looked at each other, trying to jar their memories. A look of inspiration came across Alec's face.

"*Höllenbeschwörer*," Alec declared. "It's German for 'Hell Summoner' or 'Hellraiser.' Someone who brings Hell to earth."

"It's a start," Raquel declared. She checked her watch. "Let's get moving. I don't know how long we can count on those patrons not calling whatever passes for cops around here, and we have a boat to catch."

Katrina got up, walked around to Khansari's chair, and cut the zip-ties. Ward cradled his rifle.

"What are you doing?" Ward flared irritation.

"We're not taking him with us," Katrina said firmly. She and Raquel exchanged a quick look that amounted to an argument, but eventually Raquel nodded.

"Fine, I'll take him out back and put his body in the water," Ward growled. Khansari's eyes bulged. As hopeless and bereft as he felt, he wasn't eager to die.

"We're not killing him," Katrina decreed.

Ward took a step forward. "I'm real sorry he feels like he wasted a couple decades of his life in service to a barbaric regime." His voice dripped with sarcasm. "Sorry, Khan-sorry. And I'm sorry Iran's a few steps away from looking like a Mad Max film.

But he's still the man who financed a terror group that killed a lot of Americans, and putting men like him six feet under is what we do. Even if it's not something you've got the stomach for anymore, I still do."

He turned to Raquel, expecting her to settle the dispute. But Katrina didn't wait.

"This decision is not up for discussion," she vowed.

"You're damn right, it's not," Ward said, almost laughing. "Fish gotta swim, birds gotta fly, and I gotta put down bastards who kill my countrymen."

"No, you don't. Let's get ready to go," Katrina declared.

Alec finally piped up, standing between them. "I hate to see you two fight. Split the difference and maim him?"

"Look at him," Katrina lowered her voice. "His country's been reduced to shambles, he can never go home again, he realizes he spent his life in service to a lie, and he's hiding away in the frozen armpit of the world, drinking to forget. You're itching to kill a man who's already dead inside. Why are you so eager to put him out of his misery?"

Ward raised his eyebrows and looked Khansari over. He hadn't thought about him that way.

"Death would be a relief for him," Katrina declared. Ward nodded and relented.

Ward put a firm hand on Khansari's shoulder and whispered in his ear. "You're going to live to see another day. But if I ever hear that you're anything but miserable, I'll hunt you down and end you."

# CHAPTER THREE

JUST OUTSIDE ÆGIR BRYGGERI BAR AND
BREWERY
FLAM, NORWAY
MONDAY, APRIL 5

Khansari belatedly realized that the Dangerous Clique's process of "releasing" him would not be simple or painless.

Raquel removed a needle and injected a radio frequency identification chip into Khansari, warning him that attempting to remove it would release a tiny cyanide capsule and kill him. The chip had three purposes: it could provide Khansari's location, monitor his heart rate and body temperature, and depending upon how clearly it was transmitting its signal, Dee could attempt to use him as a walking eavesdropping device. The chip had no cyanide capsule, but Raquel had no qualms about allowing Khansari to think there was, so he wouldn't try to remove it.

Before they left him, Katrina grabbed him and held his shoulder, looking into his eyes, uncomfortably close for his tastes.

"Your life isn't over," Katrina declared. "Even if you can't go home, you have a chance to help people. You're a smart man. Figure out some way to help those who need it most."

Khansari stared at her in confusion. But before he could ask why she was so convinced that something good and noble could still be found in a former spy for an autocratic fundamentalist regime—and financier of terrorism—she was gone.

Outside of the bar, it was a brisk hustle through the wind and snow to a small Zodiac boat at the end of the pier. From there, it was a quick, but not pleasant journey over modestly choppy waters to the modest, slightly run-down freighter waiting for them at the mouth of the fjord. At least two parts of the mission had succeeded: they had learned why Khansari left Iran, and the Norwegian government would never know they had been there.

***

The good news was that the World Health Organization had declared SARS-CoV-2, the virus commonly called the coronavirus, contained. The various forms of vaccines had finally reached the public, and several forms of treatment seemed to work if the infection was caught early enough.

But the fallout of the crisis appeared likely to haunt the world throughout the 2020s. The death toll had been the worst of any viral outbreak in decades. Country after country grappled and lost against a kind of enemy that they thought had been left behind with the advent of modern medicine. Governments around the world had instituted quarantines, lockdowns, and social distancing on an unparalleled level, sometimes enforcing them with draconian force and being met with violent resistance. Public surveillance systems and cell phone monitoring, once considered unthinkable for the civil liberties implications, became rapidly adopted in Western countries.

The shutdown in human activity was so widespread that early in the outbreak, seismologists at the Royal Observatory of Belgium said they could hear and track movements in the earth that they could never hear or detect before. The world had literally grown quieter; the sudden drop in all kinds of human activity created a measurable reduction in the vibration on the earth's crust.

New York City residents described an eerie quiet spreading over the city that claimed it never slept—except for the disturbingly frequent sound of ambulance sirens. Morgues and mortuaries ran out of room. The wait for cremations reached a month. A Brooklyn cremation chamber broke down from overuse. A city funeral home tried to cope with the overload by renting refrigerated trailers; their stopgap measure was discovered when a pedestrian reported fluid leaking from one of them.

As the pandemic progressed, some hospitals built glass observation booths for families to safely say goodbye to their loved ones. The process of dying and mourning changed dramatically as well. Some countries required cremation within twelve hours, disrupting the traditional funeral rituals. All the funerals had limited guest lists. Jews could no longer sit shiva. Muslims could no longer gather in person to offer prayers for the dead. Airlines stopped offering international funeral shipments, meaning that whatever a person's last requests, those who died outside their homeland would rest eternally where they died.

Some of those who survived the virus described its effects as hellacious—"scar tissue in the lungs," they called it; "pulmonary fibrosis" was the medical term. Many who recovered described a lingering cough and shortness of breath. The list of reported lasting effects was long, varied, and ominous: blood clots, inflammation of heart muscle, persistent fevers, intermittent or permanent loss of the senses of taste, smell, or both; exhaustion and fatigue syndromes, memory loss, concentration issues, dizziness, and aches and pains.

The medical community's belief was that the virus only killed one-half of one percent of all who caught it. But it left plenty of people not quite what they once were.

But the biggest changes were psychological, and many feared those would last the longest. Historians who studied the 1918 epidemic found that it compared to other major historical events like World War One—people didn't write detailed accounts or memoirs of their experiences during the pandemic. The general sense was that most people didn't want to remember the period from January 1918 to December 1920. No one wanted to remember the stretch from the first cases of "strange pneumonia" in Wuhan, China to the long, slow, painful conclusion, either.

Nearly every person on the planet had experienced something traumatizing, and many had been denied the simple assurance of human touch to heal their pain. When the virus tore through Italy, it made a mockery of Italians' long lifespans, and turned their reassuring, life-building gestures—hugs, kisses, closeness among families, tight-knit communities—into liabilities. The virus brutally punished the Italians, Spaniards and French for their traditional habits of touching others. The Germans and British were spared a bit because of their habitual reserve and distance.

For millions, the scale weighing the costs and benefits of living in the big city tipped too far in one direction, even before the riots and violence gripped American cities as spring turned to summer. Some moved out as fast as they could, others more methodically. Before the outbreak, people had worried that too many jobs and too many people were coalescing in too many big cities. Now cities seemed like the most dangerous place to be, and the exodus from urban areas was accelerating as the year continued. Millions of people and families who had endured quarantine in small apartments realized they never wanted to be stuck indoors for long stretches again. If another pandemic ever broke out, they would make sure they would get through it in a house, with a yard, or even a farm or ranch. Wide-open spaces suddenly looked a lot more appealing.

Some perceived a silver lining to the hurricane clouds that had lashed the world. More young people expressed interest in the healthcare profession, and applications to medical school skyrocketed. The expectation would be that those incoming classes would get their chance soon; month after endless month of treating waves of patients left many doctors with varying degrees of post-traumatic stress syndrome. Psychological and physical burnout wore away at the exhausted medical systems around the world.

The crisis forced almost everyone in the world to become an amateur student of virology and epidemiology. And while this storm had passed, it wasn't just the pessimists who feared some other dangerous contagion was likely to come down the pike someday.

***

"It will be about a day to get back to Amsterdam," the captain said. Raquel did the math in her head. One day of sea travel, another day to clear customs and health inspections for return to the United States, presuming that day's flights between Amsterdam and Dulles hadn't been canceled, another day to get time on the new director's schedule. Three days wasted in the hunt for this Hell Summoner, unless Dee could get something started.

The situation was serious enough that she instructed Dee to send a priority message to the new director.

***

A day and a half later, Raquel and her team stood in a long line at Amsterdam Airport Schiphol. They were no longer required to maintain six feet of distance from those in front of them, but in almost everyone, the habit lingered. If the number of air travelers ever came back to pre-pandemic levels, the lengthy lines would become chaotic. For better or worse, international airports now almost never got busier than midday on a Tuesday in the old days.

Katrina had never liked airport security; she contended that if the success rate for the Transportation Security Administration was deemed good enough in her profession, Gitmo would be empty and terrorist attacks would be as common as traffic jams. She always found it a little ridiculous that after completing a top-secret and lethal mission for the Central Intelligence Agency, she still had to assure a Customs and Border Protection officer that no, she was not bringing in meats, animals, wildlife, cell cultures, snails, or more than $10,000 in currency or monetary instruments. Occasionally she fantasized about opening up her carry-on to reveal a giant supply of soft cheese from France, and boasting to the CBP officer, "this is the Food and Drug Administration's worst raw and unpasteurized nightmare, and I've got the skills to get past you and any backup you can call."

But the US Transportation Security Administration looked positively cheerful and professional compared to the rapidly assembled new Health Security Administrations manning the airports across the world.

Above the heads of the travelers standing in line, a recorded woman's voice repeated a warning in several languages. "Please answer all health security questions fully and completely. Withholding information or hiding symptoms can result in fines, imprisonment, and mandatory quarantine periods."

"I think you hit brain matter, Nurse Ratchet," Ward grumbled as the foot-long swab was removed from his nose. A pair of unsympathetic eyes glared at him from above the surgical mask. The Dutch Health Security official completed her check with all of the warmth and kindness of an old East German Border Guard.

"Hey, if you think our job is tough, imagine shoving swabs up the noses of strangers all day," Katrina said dryly.

\*\*\*

The sudden advent of mandatory health checks for all air travelers—complete with nasal swabs that retained DNA samples—forced the Central Intelligence Agency to take new and somewhat drastic measures to protect its personnel as they traveled the globe.

Before the virus and the new health security measures, Dee had masterminded what she had thought was a creative solution to protect her teammates: a systemic, ongoing corruption of the world's fingerprint databases. If the police in Norway had somehow obtained Katrina's fingerprints from somewhere in the bar, they would not match any listings in any databases either in the United States or internationally. Not only had Dee creatively edited all existing public records of Katrina, she had set up a self-perpetuating computer virus that sought out any request for matches to her fingerprints from anywhere on the Internet. No matter how many times the police checked, Katrina's fingerprints would not match any police records or databases in Mexico, Turkmenistan, or any other country she had worked in. As far as the world knew, Bukhara-Uzbekistan-born American citizen Katrina Leonidivna had completely different fingerprints, no criminal record, and lived a quiet life.

But the growing use of facial recognition technology required Katrina, Alec, Ward, and Raquel to have several full legal identities, with Social Security numbers, tax records, etc., each to go along with the passport they had, with each passport photograph slightly altered—just enough to not align with a perfect match of facial recognition AI programs. The alteration of the photo couldn't be noticed with the naked eye, and so far, not a single customs or border patrol officer had given the passports a second look.

Just weeks earlier, Dee had unveiled another version of the NSA team's custom-made virus, designed to detect records that matched the DNA of any of the team members, and either delete or scramble those files. But the agency's management wasn't convinced this was an effective long-term solution. First, it only worked for any database connected to the Internet and that the virus could find; any institution that kept its DNA records in a system that was functionally sealed off from the outside world would be unaffected. Secondly, for the labs that were connected, eventually they would notice how many files were getting corrupted and start to interpret the corrupted files as confirmation that the DNA belonged to a spy, criminal, or someone else who wanted to blind the authorities.

For CIA personnel, operating overseas on nonofficial cover required a lot of international travelers to blend in with—businessmen, tourists, aid workers. The number of people traveling from country to country through airports plummeted with the outbreak and was a long way from recovery.

Air travel wasn't just impeded by the lingering economic troubles. The increasingly global populist movement calling itself Nationalists Without Borders—Katrina kept pointing out the name was a contradiction—argued that international air travel had been a frivolous luxury of elites, whose "globalist" habits had brought the virus from a city in China most people had never heard of to every corner of the planet. NWB argued that international air travel should be banned and used only when absolutely necessary and found themselves in an odd alliance with climate change activist groups who argued that international flights unnecessarily added to carbon emissions.

Some political parties in North America and Europe catered to NWB, but they had not yet succeeded in banning international air travel anywhere. But they had made international air travel somewhat stigmatized, an exhibition of conspicuous consumption that demonstrated gauche habits. This was far from a universal consensus; celebrities still showcased their getaways in

St. Tropez, Ibiza, Cuba, and Maui. But the virus-driven economic crash pushed the dreams of vacationing in another country out of the reach of millions of people who had previously enjoyed it. The tourism industry was finding the climb out of the pit to be long, slow, and difficult. Travelers never knew when their weeklong trip to some exotic and alluring locale could turn into a mandatory multiweek quarantine. And that was separate from the mandatory nasal swabs at both ends of the trip.

A second health check awaited them at Dulles. Ward habitually asked the Health Security personnel if they wanted to check his prostate as well.

*** 

Once Katrina's nasal passages had tested negative for SARS-CoV-2 and its known mutated variants, she stopped in the airport concession stand. The flight would be long, and she tried to periodically check in to how the rest of the troubled world saw itself. Open-source intelligence could offer insights that the most secret vaults of foreign governments could not.

*The New Yorker* cover declared, "Solitary. Unshared. Private: The Rebirth of Print," with just a hint of self-congratulation.

The cover of *Sports Illustrated* had young female mixed-martial-arts fighter that Katrina didn't recognize. Team sports leagues had struggled to offer something resembling their usual product through so many pandemic-driven suspensions, cancellations, and interruptions. Solitary sports that didn't involve close contact enjoyed a resurgence; golf, tennis, and NASCAR gained in popularity. Interest in MMA grew by leaps and bounds, satiating the public hunger for attractive faces and violence that Hollywood no longer met with action movies.

There was some excitement about the Olympics starting up again, in part because of the rival competitions planned for the summer. The outbreak forced the delay of the Tokyo Summer Games, and then another delay, and then a third delay. After more than a year, the International Olympic Committee voted to hold the next regularly scheduled summer games in Beijing, China. That decision outraged many around the world who believed China had permitted the outbreak either through a lab accident or exacerbated it through multiple weeks of publicly insisting the virus was not contagious. Many suspected the Chinese government had bribed or intimidated the members of the International Olympic Committee. About half the world's countries announced they would boycott the Olympics in Beijing, and Tokyo offered to host a rival competition in its never-used facilities built for 2020. The world's governments started announcing their country's teams would attend either Beijing or Tokyo, with the divide along a predictable authoritarian/democratic split. Some argued the Tokyo competition should be called the "Free Nation Games." With China, Russia, and Iran the top competitors in Beijing, Alec suggested the Tokyo competition be called ATTRACT: "All Those Trustworthy Reported Accurate Coronavirus Testimony."

Katrina knew her agency was on the highest alert for terror attacks designed to disrupt either set of games.

The cover of *Entertainment Weekly* declared "The New Home Theaters Are Actual Theaters." When the pandemic closed down movie theaters around the world, most theater chains declared bankruptcy, and then small groups of wealthy people purchased them for hosting the private parties of those who had already recovered from the virus or tested negative. Private, invitation-only movie theaters had become the new luxury status symbols in America's wealthiest neighborhoods.

Underneath the red border of *Time* magazine was a telephoto lens image of a Mexican man and woman, holding a machete and a gun, standing on a purloined luxury yacht, under the headline of "The New Pirates of the Caribbean." The magazine's cover story explored how the Gulf of Mexico and the Caribbean had become a criminal playground in the aftermath of the pandemic, with all kinds of contraband moving from one place to another and old-fashioned piracy returning to the seas. The magazine reported some cartels had brought in veteran Somalis as "consultants" to their burgeoning piracy operations. Some compared the atmosphere to the time of the "Cocaine Cowboys" who had lived out the real-life version of *Miami Vice* in the region in the 1980s.

Katrina studied the image on the cover, taken by a tourist with a top-of-the-line camera in Cancun. The man and woman had apparently just walked onto a luxury yacht where several wealthy couples were having a party, forced the owner and his wife and guests off, and then sailed the yacht away—but not without leaving the previous owners with a six-pack of beer as consolation. The magazine didn't seem to mind the way the image glamorized their criminal act. The man was handsome, just starting to have a little gray at his temple, and the woman seemed to define "erotic peril," looking voluptuous in her black bikini top and holding her machete. Katrina felt like she had seen them before...

...and then she wondered if the pair could possibly be Juan Comillo, a.ka. "the Jaguar," and Esmerelda, a pair she had tangled with in Mexico City almost two years ago. She made a mental note to check in with the agency's Mexico station. Perhaps the trail to those old foes hadn't gone as cold as she thought.

Katrina glanced at the next magazine with a blue border, one about American politics, started to move on, then went back.

"Our Colder World," the headline declared, and she initially thought it was another screed insisting that because climate change had initially been called "global warming," the whole thing had to be a hoax. But Katrina picked it up and learned the cover essay was about a coldness of another sort. In the United States, since the pandemic started, the divorce rate had risen noticeably and the rate of marriages, births, and adoptions dropped dramatically. Some people still wore masks in public; many retained the mental habit of trying to stay six feet away from everyone. Among America's young people, the habits of the Japanese "otaku"—shut-ins who were obsessed with their online lives and increasingly neglectful of their offline life—had spread widely. The opening anecdote of the essay was about a bicyclist hit by a car in a busy intersection in New York City— and the bystanders' hesitation about running to check on him. Absenteeism at workplaces had jumped, even as more were supposed to be working from home. There were stories of people just disappearing—packing a bag and leaving spouses, children, and elderly parents behind. In the aftermath of a global near-death experience, millions—perhaps billions—were rethinking what they wanted out of life in the time they had left, and stumbling through, looking for answers. And nearly a year of deeply unnatural "social distancing" had left Americans and the rest of the world distrustful, wary, suspicious, and increasingly disconnected from one another.

"It's as if Atarsa won," Katrina murmured to herself. She skipped ahead to the end.

"The world has turned cold," the essayist concluded. "And we're all struggling to figure out how to reignite the flame."

Depressed, Katrina shook her head and put the magazine back, then picked up the distinctively yellow-bordered cover of *National Geographic*. The cover image of that issue was the familiar green globe with red spikes, Public Enemy Number One for a period that hadn't been as long as it felt. The headline was the unspoken question on everyone's mind: "How Soon Will We Face the Next Pandemic?"

\*\*\*

The global sense of trepidation was sparked in large part by a BBC interview with Dr. Allen Pittman, considered one of the best virologists in the United Kingdom, who began his career in the Royal Army Medical Corps and who went on to do ground-breaking research at Porton Down and Public Health England. He had helped coordinate a great deal of the British response to the virus. *Time* magazine ranked he and his team tenth on its list of nominees to be "Newsmaker of the Year."

But five months ago, just as the United Kingdom prepared to lift another round of restrictions driven by the outbreak, Pittman suddenly announced he was retiring from Public Health England. He was only forty-eight. Shortly after he retired, he agreed to a lengthy interview with the BBC, and his comments had—in an ironic phrase he would appreciate—gone viral.

"As terrible as this coronavirus was for the world, we could face another, worse outbreak at any time," Pittman told his interviewer. "We could have a filovirus, which would be even worse. These are Ebola, Marburg, the ones that the public thinks only can be found in the deepest jungles. But they once discovered a new virus in monkeys in a lab just fifteen miles from Washington, DC, creatively called the 'Reston Virus.' One or two minor twists of fate and you would have had a major outbreak of an Ebola strain in the American capital in 1989. Picture people trying to fight a contagious hemorrhagic fever with 1980s-level medical technology in a densely packed city with considerable international air travel. Of course, we could face the same problem in a year, or five years from now. Maybe never, but I wouldn't bet that way."

Pittman's interviewer shifted uncomfortably in her seat and asked him why he was so certain that another virus would be coming to menace the world.

"Right now, all around the world, people are interacting with animals—hunting them, capturing them, raising them, and eating them. We fear malaria from mosquitoes and Lyme disease from ticks, but we are oblivious to the viruses, bacteria, fungi, and parasites that live in all kinds of animals—bats, yes, but livestock, fish, sea mammals, birds. There are millions of different kinds of viruses; if there were a thousand more virologists like myself in every major city in the world, we would never identify and classify them all. Thankfully, the vast majority are harmless to humans, but viruses evolve through mutation to survive. They are driven by the same survival of the fittest as all other life on earth. Once a virus jumps to humans, the viruses that are most contagious and most resistant to antibodies survive and reproduce. A virus is a much more efficient assassin than humanity could ever be."

"Is this happening because of climate change?" the interviewer asked. Sharp-eyed viewers noticed a long blink from Pittman as he resisted rolling his eyes.

"The viruses are not occurring because of climate change, but as humans look for resources in places few people have gone before, it increases the odds they encounter a novel virus, meaning one no human body has seen before and has no built-in defenses to stop," Pittman said with the patience of a teacher trying to explain the Pythagorean theorem to kindergarteners. "Deforestation, expanded human development—all of this is basically an open invitation for more new viruses to enter human bodies. Every day, people go into jungles, forests, deserts, swamps, caves. They kill animals and eat them, collect bat guano for fertilizer, use all sorts of body parts for all kinds of medicines, both folk and real medicine. Wildlife trafficking is the fourth-largest illegal trade in the world. Wet markets like the one in Wuhan are still open all over Asia, animal guts and bacteria spilling into the street. The question is not 'will there be another viral outbreak like this,' but 'when?' and 'how bad?' My long history of fighting with government bureaucracies makes me believe that most of the world's governments and publics will choose to believe that the next outbreak will be far-off and minor. Thus, when it happens again, most of the world will be unprepared. Again."

The blood seemed to be draining from the face of Pittman's interviewer. "Why are you leaving government service, if you think the world's governments are so ill-prepared for what's coming next?"

"Because I spent most of the past two decades trying to sound the alarm, through SARS, and H1N1, and MERS, and Ebola, and Zika, and most of the time people didn't want to hear it," flashing just a bit of anger. "Lawmakers never want to spend the money. Medical stockpiles aren't as popular as jobs programs. Excess hospital capacity looks like a waste right up until the moment you need it. Normalcy bias—the belief that tomorrow will be like today because today is a lot like yesterday—is such an overwhelmingly powerful force that it can effectively paralyze people. The human brain has difficulty processing new information under stress. For all of my frustration with government, this is a problem of human beings, not a problem of particular leaders."

Pittman's interviewer pushed back at his conclusions: she saw it as good journalistic skepticism; he saw it as just another manifestation of normalcy bias.

"Surely, after everything we have been through, we will be better prepared for the next outbreak. All of our innovations, all of our technology, all of what we've learned—"

"Knowledge is only power when it is applied," Pittman replied curtly. "The Great Plague of Athens in 430 B.C. killed a hundred thousand people and began the process of ending the era of Athenian democracy. Thucydides wrote about how people ignored warnings and made the outbreak worse. They clung to whatever explanation reassured them the most, despite the evidence before their eyes. And once it was too late, when people could finally see the scale of the threat they faced—well, as Thucydides wrote, 'for the violence of the calamity was such that men, not knowing where to turn, grew reckless of all law, human and divine … Men who had hitherto concealed what they took pleasure in, now grew bolder.' The greatest democracy of its era collapsed when everyone felt they no longer had much to lose, or a future to plan for. Science cannot produce a vaccine against hedonistic nihilism."

His BBC interviewer could not hide her emotions, rejecting everything Pittman was asserting. But after a moment of staring at Pittman with a *how dare you?* glare, she composed herself, and expunged most of the sarcasm from her tone. "It appears that in addition to being one of the country's top virologists, you're quite a historian as well."

"Benefits of a classical education," Pittman responded with a small, wry smile.


## SENSITIVE BUT UNCLASSIFIED—PAGE FIVE

FROM: RHIANNON STREET
TO: RAQUEL HOLTZ
RE: PSYCHOLOGICAL EVALUATION
SUBJECT: KATRINA LEONIDIVNA

TRANSCRIPT—CONT.—

**LEONIDIVNA:** Like I said, I'm fine. Invigorated, in some ways. Eager, even. But I suspect the reason the seventh floor wants you to talk to me is they think I've lost my previous comfort with using deadly force.

**STREET:** Have you?

**LEONIDIVNA:** Hasn't this world seen enough death for a while? I have no doubt that if I'm in a kill-or-be-killed situation—or if I walk in on some psycho with a gun to my husband's head again—I'm pulling the trigger. But if we do our jobs right, it never comes to that. I want to pursue my work in a way that minimizes the odds that I ever have to do that.

**STREET:** Your team's primary mission over the last twenty years or so has been hunting down terrorists and other threats to Americans. Isn't it extremely likely that sooner or later, you'll find yourself in a situation that requires lethal force?

**LEONIDIVNA:** I think it would be good for this agency to get out of the business of killing people, don't you agree? We're the Central Intelligence Agency, not the Central Assassination Agency. The military was built to kill people. The Pentagon, JSOC, the drone strikes—let them pursue their missions the way they see fit. We were founded to inform American policymakers with what they need to know to make good decisions. We're a civilian agency.

**STREET:** So what do you feel like your mission ought to be?

**LEONIDIVNA:** The whole world has just been through something terrible. A time like this is the right time to focus on fixing what is broken. After World War Two, this country took big steps to help people all around the world. We enacted the Marshall Plan to rebuild Europe and the Bretton Woods agreement to stabilize the international economy, helped found the United Nations, World Bank, International Monetary Fund, Voice of America, and NATO, and formulated the policy of containment and the Truman Doctrine. At home we desegregated the Armed Forces, took the first steps toward the Civil Rights movement, built the Interstate Highway System, created the precursor to NASA, Chuck Yeager broke the sound barrier, discovered nuclear fission, invented the transistor, which was the building block for all future computers. Ten years after the Holocaust ended, Neil Armstrong was a test pilot in the program that turned into NASA. Don't tell me we can't pull ourselves up from the worst of times!

After the worst, we as a country—and with so many like-minded people around the world—looked hard at what could be better, and we made it happen!

**STREET:** That's a remarkably positive attitude. Very few of the people I speak with in here can see the possibility for good right now.

**LEONIDIVNA:** And that's what's driving me crazy. We have a window of opportunity to build a better world than the one that existed before the virus. For once, everyone on earth faced the same enemy. For once, just about everyone was vulnerable—race, creed, color, gay, straight, bi—didn't matter. If you weren't in one of the higher-risk categories, someone who you cared about was. Money couldn't really protect you much. Big city, small town, democracy, dictatorship. Red state or blue state. For once, scientists and doctors in every major country on earth were working toward the same solution. We weren't looking for treatments and a vaccine because we just wanted to save our people—we wanted to find a cure for everyone.

But for some reason, a lot of people are so scarred, so scared—that they just want to curl up and die. And I worry that we're going to miss this chance.

**STREET:** Is that what keeps you up at night?

**LEONIDIVNA:** Metaphorically, but not literally. I think…

I think I want to spend my time between now and retirement playing some role in building that better world. One where everyone feels safe, where everyone feels respected and treated with dignity, where everyone can see the potential of technology and innovation to tackle any problem—climate change, famine, ethnic divisions, rogue states. We should be starting a worldwide effort to shut down the exotic animal trade right now—both for us and the risk of exposure to new viruses.

**STREET:** What is keeping you up at night?

[lengthy pause]

**LEONIDIVNA:** The virus threw the world into a situation where we couldn't shake hands, couldn't speak closely, couldn't hug. God help those who weren't married—not that Alec's mood swings were easy. I'm not surprised the quarantine drove that spike in the divorce rate.

We couldn't be together for funerals. Weddings. Births and brises and christenings. Then we all had to wear masks—we couldn't even see each other smile. We had to keep everyone at a distance. Everyone had to see every other person they encountered as a potential carrier.

If you wanted to kill love, hope, and human connection, that virus was a pretty powerful way to do it. If we hadn't developed the treatments and the antibodies … another year or two of this and maybe the virus would have truly broken us. Already the world seems colder, more wary, distrustful, and paranoid. The only reason we didn't have more angry mobs is because people wanted to avoid each other.

Compassion, empathy, affection, gratitude … the world wasn't exactly filled to the brim with that before the virus hit. And now we've exhausted all our reserves.

What keeps me up at night is the knowledge that some people like the world better this way and want to keep it this way.

END TRANSCRIPT

EVALUATION: By every measure, Katrina remains physically and psychologically capable of handling her duties or work on the team. That said, I think she is likely to explore other opportunities, outside of the CIA. If management wishes to keep her engaged in these activities, they will need to ensure she remains convinced that her actions are helping build that better world she envisions. Katrina knows her work is effective, but she needs to also be reassured that it is meaningful.

My assessment of Katrina is that despite the ordeal of the past two years, she remains the same combination of rarely equaled strengths and vulnerabilities she tries to hide.

My nagging fear is that she's gotten so good at hiding her vulnerabilities, I can't detect them anymore.

## SENSITIVE BUT UNCLASSIFIED—PAGE NINE

FROM: RHIANNON STREET
TO: RAQUEL HOLTZ
RE: PSYCHOLOGICAL EVALUATION
SUBJECT: EDWARD DALE RUTLEDGE

TRANSCRIPT—CONT.—

**RUTLEDGE:** Look, let's just skip ahead to why I'm really here and why you're asking these questions. The seventh floor thinks I killed that Chinese guy and worries I'm a risk out in the field.

**STREET:** By "that Chinese guy," I assume you're referring to Bao Fang Min, shot in the head on Connecticut Avenue.

**RUTLEDGE:** Yeah. That one.

**STREET:** Bao Fang Min, part of the Chinese embassy's diplomatic staff in Washington, secretly an intelligence officer with China's Ministry of State Security, and a figure actively involved in Chinese efforts to spread disinformation that the coronavirus was a US bioweapon.

**RUTLEDGE:** I'm not saying I was sorry to see the little bastard go. I told this to everyone who asked, everyone who would listen. A lot of men could have made that shot.

**STREET:** The killing of Bao Fang Min put every American in China at greater risk.

**RUTLEDGE:** So did the coronavirus. Eating pangolin burger cooked in gutter oil at a wet market puts you at risk, too. Maybe Americans shouldn't be hanging around in a country where the government can grab you in the middle of the night, throw you in some hellhole prison without trial, and use you as a bargaining chip.

**STREET:** Did you kill Bao Fang Min?

**RUTLEDGE:** I would never deliberately take any action that I believed would put innocent Americans at risk.

**STREET:** My, what a carefully worded response.

**RUTLEDGE:** I was on a hunting trip. Alec can vouch for my location. I was nowhere near the Chinese embassy.

**STREET:** Remind me again, what's your longest recorded sniper kill?

**RUTLEDGE:** Probably about twelve hundred yards. In Afghanistan. Nowhere near enough for the record books, but that's about the farthest end of the training range.

**STREET:** Twelve-hundred yards, that's more than half a mile. So you wouldn't really have needed to be most people's definition of "near" the Chinese embassy to kill Bao Fang Min, now would you?

**RUTLEDGE:** You know, it's not like there's a short list of people pissed off at the Chinese government, either then or now. Pro–Falun Gong protesters practically lived out there outside the embassy for years. Then the Hong Kong protesters, the Uyghur protesters, and then the virus protesters. Any one of them could have taken that shot. Bao Fang Min took a dumb risk just walking down the street.

**STREET:** The Diplomatic Security Service report concluded it was a sniper firing from a nearby rooftop.

**RUTLEDGE:** No, the report speculated it was a nearby rooftop. No physical evidence. Shooter must have cleaned his brass afterward.

**STREET:** Lucky for the shooter that there were no reliable witnesses.

**RUTLEDGE:** Well, it was Bao Fang Min's bad fortune that just about all of the witnesses were Falun Gong protesters, Hong Kong protesters, Uyghur protesters, and virus protesters. The problem for the cops wasn't a lack of a confession, the problem was three dozen contradictory confessions, as all of those protesters claimed to have been the one who shot him.

**STREET:** Some would call it the perfect crime.

**RUTLEDGE:** I'm sure the shooter would appreciate hearing that.

**STREET:** Before Bao Fang Min's assassination, you openly expressed great anger about China. The way Beijing handled the virus—

**RUTLEDGE:** Letting it get out of their own lab, yeah.

**STREET:** That's just an unconfirmed rumor.

**RUTLEDGE:** The day people get sick outside the gates of Fort Detrick, people are gonna look hard at USAMRIID. [The United States Army Medical Research Institute of Infectious Diseases at Fort Detrick, Maryland.] Besides, the virus, their lies about it, trying to get off the hook by saying it was an American bioweapon—shouldn't something like that anger everyone?

**STREET:** Your teammates say your mood changed after Bao Fang Min's assassination.

**RUTLEDGE:** Well, the sun sure seemed to shine a little brighter the next day, didn't it?

END TRANSCRIPT

EVALUATION: First, it is extremely likely that Ward killed Bao Fang Min.

Second, it is extremely unlikely that anyone will ever be able to prove it.

Before we started, Ward revealed that he had brought a flask of whiskey and asked if he could take a swig before we started. I agreed. Even if the contents of our conversation were not protected by doctor–patient privilege AND not classified, any testimony obtained from someone under the influence of alcohol is extremely likely to be ruled inadmissible in court.

Ward enjoys being perceived as a simple good old boy from Oklahoma who loves his guns. He is very, very bright; smart enough to know the advantages of being underestimated as just a simple good old boy from Oklahoma.

Most of the "Dangerous Clique" are career CIA, trained as case officers like Katrina, analysts like Alec, or technical operations officers like Dee. Ward was shaped by the Rangers and his experiences in Kosovo and Afghanistan and preparations for Iraq before coming over to the team. He has always been the one most comfortable with using lethal force. On paper, he is more than physically and psychologically capable of continuing his duties on the team.

What should concern agency management is that Ward has now become comfortable freelancing—deciding for himself when someone deserves to die for their transgressions. We know about Bao Fang Min because Ward wanted the world to know that someone could reach a Chinese spy who thought he was untouchable. Presuming Ward killed him, he could have arranged for Bao Fang Min to simply disappear one day. The next time Ward feels like killing someone who deserves it, he may execute his prey in a way where not even we have any suspicions that he did it.

# SENSITIVE BUT UNCLASSIFIED—PAGE NINETEEN

FROM: RHIANNON STREET
TO: RAQUEL HOLTZ
RE: PSYCHOLOGICAL EVALUATION
SUBJECT: ALEC FLANAGAN

TRANSCRIPT—CONT.—

**STREET:** Your teammates told me that over the past two years, they've witnessed a major personality change in you.

**FLANAGAN:** That's probably true. I'm not the same man I was two years ago. Then again, how many people are the same as they were two years ago?

**STREET:** I think they miss you being the one who made the jokes and broke the tension in a bad situation.

**FLANAGAN:** I get it. Dee's our hacker, Katrina's our ninja, Ward shoots people and blows stuff up, and I'm the one who keeps them in the mental state to do what they need to do. But you know, it's not clinical depression if you've got something to be depressed about. We all got a great big reminder of our mortality and the fragility of life—of everything. And no one's really sure if we're out of the woods yet. Shocking if I'm not the funny guy I used to be!

**STREET:** What you're describing is very common among men your age.

**FLANAGAN:** I am not having a midlife crisis! I had a real crisis right around my midlife! You know, assuming that this *is* my actual midlife, and I don't get shot in the head or keel over anytime soon.

**STREET:** It sounds like you're having a harder time coping with the risks that you and the team traditionally encounter.

**FLANAGAN:** You know, we've been doing this for almost 20 years. Katrina and Raquel and I. More good times than bad. None of the bad times were all that bad—we're all still alive, and nobody would have bet that way. Ward and I … we put a lot of bad people out of business. And oftentimes, that meant putting them six feet under. And that never bothered me.

**STREET:** Yes, I remember our conversations.

**FLANAGAN:** And people like you, and Katrina, and Raquel started acting like that when it came to … sending bad guys to Hades, I was starting to get … how's the best way to put it?

**STREET:** Cavalier?

**FLANAGAN:** I was going to say "comfortable."

**STREET:** How about displaying a gleeful disregard for the deliberate taking of human life?

**FLANAGAN:** I think some guy in MI6 accused me of being a "highly functional psychopath." Of course, at the time, I was just thrilled that he called me "highly functional."

Look, when I cracked the skull of Gholam Gul in Cyprus, I didn't feel any guilt. He was a bad guy, killed a lot of innocent people. I would argue with anybody I didn't have anything to atone for, or feel bad about. Katrina worried about this a lot, I didn't. You get involved with terrorism, you've made your choice. What guys like Ward and me do is the natural consequence. I was the goddamned consequence.

**STREET:** So what changed? I notice you brought this up without me asking.

[long pause]

**FLANAGAN:** I believe in Jesus and heaven and all the rest. But I also believe in karma. Do good, and the world will appreciate it and reciprocate it, somehow, maybe not the way you expect. Do bad and the world will bring payback to your door someday.

For a long time, I thought Ward and I were karma. Or we were karma's Amazon delivery guys. If you tried to kill Americans, we were your free overnight shipping of payback. And after we killed Gul and Sarvar Rashin, I was really sure that was true.

**STREET:** And?

**FLANAGAN:** And then the world...broke. Worse than 9/11, worse than the recession. Worse than when Sarina disappeared. It was like, Thanos snapped his fingers or something. Although even he left half the world untouched. The whole idea of karma was...Nothing made sense. And I started to realize maybe I wasn't that righteous and good person that I was convinced I was.

**STREET:** Wait...are you saying you feel like the coronavirus happened because you had become too comfortable with killing?

**FLANAGAN:** Doc, for fifteen years, when somebody was trying to kill people, Katrina and Ward and I dealt with it. The Grand Bazaar. Strauss. Qong Ras Khan. The Brotherhood of Elbis. Hadramout. Atarsa.

And then this...thing comes along, killing people like nothing before, a 9/11 a day, and I can't do a damn thing about it. It's the perfect comeuppance for my arrogance. The perfect hard lesson of how wrong I was for so long.

**STREET:** What exactly do you feel like you should have been able to do about it?

**FLANAGAN:** Well, that's the point, isn't it? You can't punch a virus. You can't blow it up. You can't shoot a virus, although I'm sure Ward tried. I thought I was powerful and then something—God, Fate, the Universe—decided to teach me just how powerless I was. While we were stuck in quarantine, I ended up reading this anthropologist, Ernest Becker. He argued that humanity developed the desire to kill other people—either in war or in murder—because it gives us the illusion that we can control death.

**STREET:** I see.

At age sixteen, one of your best friends went missing and was never found—a situation that must have felt like the equivalent of death. Do you think that you might be particularly driven to seek out a way of feeling like you can control death?

**FLANAGAN:** Maybe. Or maybe it's because my wife is a friggin' modern samurai and she works in counterterrorism. I've lived with a lot of risk for a long while. I'm no Buddhist, I can't practice nonattachment to the things I love and fear losing.

**STREET:** A key part of life, and maturity, is coping with loss and understanding that we can't control everything.

**FLANAGAN:** You know ... Atarsa had this plan. It was going to stir up paranoia, divide everyone, get people to see every stranger they encounter as a potential threat. They wanted to tear up our social fabric, and leave us scared, angry, Balkanized—a nation of suspicious little enclaves, always seeing the worst in each other, and unwilling to take the risk of helping each other. It could have worked. We were an angry and divided nation even before they started killing people and sending their messages. But their plan didn't work—we tracked them down and killed them before they could finish their plan.

And then the virus came along and did a lot of Atarsa's work for them.

END TRANSCRIPT

EVALUATION: By some measures, Alec does not appear to match a diagnosis of post-traumatic stress disorder. He does not describe flashbacks, nightmares, or a noticeable increase in anxiety. His irritability appears to be within preexisting normal parameters, and Katrina does not describe him as behaving uncharacteristically aggressive or having angry outbursts.

However, he absolutely checks the box for "feelings of guilt or shame," he displays negative thoughts about himself and the world, his behavior matches "detachment" in some ways—although the long period of recommended social distancing made measuring his behavior much more difficult—and his behavior and comments do partially align with depression or being emotionally "numb."

The records of his evaluation at the shooting range indicates he's actually improving his performance by some measures.

At this point, I do not see sufficient evidence to declare him physically or psychologically unable to handle his duties with the team. In fact, I think he is using the structure and routine of his work as a form of therapy. I would urge continued monitoring and therapy sessions, and please quickly report anything else about Alec that concerns you. Alec's new demeanor is either a sign that he's reached a new level of maturity about the team's unique duties …

… or he's so tightly wound now that he could suddenly snap without warning.

# CHAPTER FOUR

LIBERTY CROSSING INTELLIGENCE CAMPUS
TYSONS CORNER, VIRGINIA
THURSDAY, APRIL 8

For nearly two decades now, Raquel Holtz had tried to minimize the interaction between her team and the rest of the CIA's structure and hierarchy. Five years ago, the Office of the Director of National Intelligence and the Counterintelligence Center had concluded that at least one and probably two moles were leaking extremely sensitive classified information from the CIA. Because the leaks appeared to be to multiple hostile foreign governments and groups—including, in some theories, Atarsa—one prevalent and fearful theory was that the mole or moles was essentially selling services to the highest bidder.

Despite a hunt for suspects that would have impressed the legendarily paranoid James Jesus Angleton, the mole or moles' identities had never been determined and no one could be certain that the leaks had stopped. Raquel and her team had always preferred to operate with as few people as possible knowing exactly what they were working on, and where, and why—generating the "Dangerous Clique" nickname. As far as anyone could tell, none of their work had been compromised.

Former CIA Director William Peck had barely tolerated the methods of Raquel and her team. But somehow a member of Atarsa—no one had ever figured out who—had gotten close to Peck and poisoned him, triggering a drug-induced mental breakdown during the taping of an interview for *Meet the Press*. In a small miracle, the video of Peck shouting about bugs controlling people never popped up on the Internet. Peck's successor, Richard Mitchell, seemed more appreciative of the team and its methods, after some initial friction. The future of Raquel's Dangerous Clique unit looked as secure as it ever had.

And then the following spring, Mitchell was diagnosed with coronavirus. He died two weeks later.

The acting director took over, and a few months later the president appointed the new long-term replacement, Barbara Stern. On paper, Stern was perfect, a career that included a few years early in her career as a CIA analyst, then a lateral move and rising through the ranks of the State Department, stints at the Council on Foreign Relations, teaching at Harvard University, and serving as a senior staffer on the Senate Select Committee on Intelligence. She signed on to advise the man who went on to win the most recent presidential election, and authored several white papers that examined the state of the world in detail without generating the slightest bit of controversy—or interest for that matter. She was respected on the Hill, in the administration, and in the press, and hadn't made many enemies within the agency.

Stern made a commanding figure and looked younger than her sixty years. She carried herself with a certain regal authoritative presence, the strict, attractive professor who all the college boys signed up for, and then quickly regretted. As a public speaker, she made Ben Stein's economics lessons from *Ferris Bueller's Day Off* look like a Robin Williams routine.

Stern was sufficiently qualified, but as far as anyone could tell, no human being on earth actually *liked* her. At her confirmation hearing, the senators heard a great deal about her cool head in a crisis, which was the polite way of suggesting she was a Vulcan and incapable of expressing emotions. (More than a few who had worked under her had wondered if she was somewhere on the spectrum.) She had an abundance of colleagues who respected her and appeared to have a dearth of actual friends. She was unmarried, no children, no siblings, and two parents who had passed away from the virus. Her lack of a husband prompted some gay rights groups to begin touting her as a groundbreaking selection, the first lesbian to be nominated to be director of the Central Intelligence Agency. Less than a day later, a behind-the-scenes argument revealed no one had actually *asked* her if she was a lesbian, and the press statements were quietly deleted from the websites. To the extent Stern demonstrated desire at all, she was heterosexual. This demonstrated desire consisted of her public comment years earlier that former CIA Director William Colby was more handsome than actor Gregory Peck.

When the image consultants came in and tried to remake Stern for her confirmation hearings, they did what they could, and physically, she gave them a lot of raw material to establish a reassuring, even imposing presence. But the appearance couldn't hide the personality, or lack thereof. Stern had a brilliant analytical mind that couldn't be shut off. Her encyclopedic knowledge of China, Russia, and the Middle East had taken up so much mental real estate that it left room for only a theoretical understanding of interacting with other human beings. She made cold fish seem cuddly.

But the Senate confirmed Stern by a wide margin, and so far, the president was satisfied with her work.

That morning, when Raquel and Katrina were finally called into the seventh-floor conference room of CIA headquarters, they noticed that Stern seemed ... by her standards, almost emotional. She had facial expressions, voice modulations, and everything.

"The claims of Iraj Khansari worry you, and I believe you are right to be worried," Stern said, in what probably was meant to be reassuring but came out the opposite.

But Stern then laid out all her reasons for wariness about Khansari's story. The Central Intelligence Agency spent a lot of resources and time and effort keeping tabs on every biological weapons program around the world—China's, Russia's, North Korea's. All of the CIA desks watching those programs reported they had no indications of missing scientists, no virologists or bioengineers who had nervous breakdowns or addictions or gambling habits or other reasons to start freelancing as bioterror-for-hire.

Compared to nukes or chemicals, bioweapons were easy— one step above making pancakes. The Rajneeshee cult had sickened 751 people in Oregon in 1984 by contaminating salad bars in restaurants in an effort to sway a mayoral election. But Hell Summoner's offer was completely different: ruthlessly lethal but with precision that appeared, up until now, scientifically impossible.

Creating a new virus that would only attack certain people was theoretically possible but difficult, according to assessments by the CIA's medical minds—as well as the CDC, National Institutes of Health, National Academy of Sciences, and other institutions. Each step in the process had been achieved in various lab tests; much of modern gene therapy was based upon developing noncontagious genetically engineered viruses that would encounter a sick person's cells, inject new DNA that had some sort of needed trait like an ability to fight off a particular disease, and then let that virus spread throughout the body. With time, the patient's body would absorb the new DNA and start generating new cells that included the ability to fight off that disease.

"I've asked the US National Center for Medical Intelligence to revise and update their assessments of whether building an 'ethnic bioweapon' is possible, and if so, how much time it would take to assemble and how someone would go about it,"

Stern declared. She looked at Raquel, wondering if that would satisfy her.

It didn't come close. Raquel pointed to the NSA's recently completed report that they had picked up brief references to an "offer" in communications among government officials in Serbia ("Pakao Sazivac"), Myanmar ("Maingalarpar"), and Equatorial Guinea ("Portador de la muerte"). All of those names translated roughly to "Hell Raiser" or "Hell Summoner" or "Death Bringer." But the references were vague and brief, usually amounting to "what do you think of Hell Summoner's offer?" and "don't talk about that on this line."

Stern noted there was a strong possibility someone was trying to con these governments out of fortunes with a fake or mundane virus.

"Cambridge certainly thinks creating an ethnic bioweapon is possible," Raquel answered. "Back in 2019, they warned—"

"Yes, I remember that report concluding they could theoretically be created, but a lot of scary concepts exist in theory," Stern said. "I also remember the Palestinians and the European papers claiming that Israel's Nes Tziyona research facility had built an anti-Arab virus. We never found even a hint that it was real. I'm old enough to remember the claims that the South Africans were going to work on a so-called 'pigmentation weapon.'"

Raquel flipped through her papers. "Yes, and this precise scenario with someone offering to make an ethnic bioweapon already happened a generation ago. South Africa's Truth and Reconciliation Commission uncovered this when they were investigating the Apartheid regime's biological weapons programs."

Raquel held up a paper. "Daan Goosen worked in the South African equivalent of the surgeon general's office. He told the commission that Wouter Basson, the head of the country's biological weapons program—here, let me read it out loud...'This document was delivered, he said, to the military attaché in London, and this document contained a proposition from someone in Europe, and this guy says he's got a product, a bacteria, which has got the possibility of only affecting, making sick and killing pigmented people. That was in 1984. Dr. Basson asked me to research this fully, investigate it literature-wise. Not doing physical work on it, but to study the literature and the possibilities scientifically. Is that a possibility? And I did an extensive literature research and studied the sciences around it and we felt, concluded, and I shared it with him, that it is a definite possibility.' Later in his testimony, Goosen said he never followed the lead."

Katrina looked up in surprise. Clearly, since the moment they had stepped out of Flam, Raquel had obsessively researched the possibility of an ethnic bioweapon.

"That sounds very ominous," Stern said, nodding. "But we have to balance that testimony against the fact that as far as we know, no one ever deployed a bacteria that only targeted pigmented people. No one has ever admitted researching it, no one has ever leaked intelligence about it, no one has ever chatted about it in a way that the NSA could track. If it existed, someone would have talked about it, or tried to sell it to someone else again. It's not like the Apartheid government was too ethical to ever use a weapon like that! The fact that there's no evidence that a morally bankrupt regime like the South Africans ever used it would lead me to suspect that it never existed, and someone was trying to con their military attaché, selling them magic beans."

"If those magic beans are castor beans, they could make ricin," Katrina remarked dryly.

Stern tilted her head, wondering if Katrina was mocking her. "I would also remind you that after Apartheid ended, Wouter Basson was accused of using his knowledge to become one of the country's biggest Ecstasy dealers, so I think we should take his tales of offers to military attachés with a grain of salt."

"The man was nicknamed 'Doctor Death' before Jack Kevorkian," Raquel shot back. "Look, the whole world has just had a front-row seat for how much a virus can devastate any society—democracies, dictatorships, rich, poor. Some scientist out there just realized that his knowledge about viruses is a multibillion-dollar lottery ticket. The Iranians can't afford to buy it, but somebody else out there will. Maybe not even a state actor—just somebody wealthy who's got some group he hates. The clock is ticking here, Madam Director—"

"Holtz, that's enough. You've already convinced me, there's no need for histrionics."

Raquel was stunned and pleasantly surprised. Usually she had to spend a lot more time arguing.

"First, this information does not leave this room until we know more," Stern decreed. "Not the Hill, not the White House, not other agencies beyond Fort Meade and NCMI. If this gets out, it will set off a panic. Second, your team will start the hunt for Hollensch—for Hell Summoner. Nobody ever knows what you're doing anyway, so that will keep it quiet. If we get a name for the person behind Hell Summoner, then we inform stations around the world. Make something up, say they're dealing in dual-use technology, violating National Institutes of Health restrictions on research, whatever—something to justify dragging them in off the street. Meanwhile, hopefully someone will be able to give a definitive answer if this kind of virus really could be made."

Raquel nodded. "And if they can?"

Stern's coldness finally seemed reassuring. "Then we'll destroy the lab with the hottest fire we can find. I'll call in a fuel–air explosive if we have to."

Katrina cleared her throat. "One more point … this doesn't align well with my … belief that we should be minimizing our use of lethal force as an instrument of policy, but someone needs to say it."

She took a deep breath.

"Whoever Hellraiser is, we'll need to erase them and their accomplices from existence," Katrina declared. "Destroy all their research, all records on them, anywhere, as far back as we can find—online, paper, everything. We need the world to believe that creating an ethnic bioweapon was never possible, so that no one will ever be tempted to look again. Because if it is, and it ever gets used, everybody will be looking for their own version. It's a road map for endless biowarfare all the way to human extinction."

Stern visibly recoiled. "I can't imagine it would ever come to that."

Katrina shook her head. "No one could imagine the coronavirus, either."

***

Lars Egner-Baerwald, head of the Germany's Social Democratic Party and Germany's minister of finance, had no idea he would be "proof of concept."

On the first day of the last month of his life, Egner-Baerwald presided over a frustrating party meeting. The German government, like almost all of governments around the world, was struggling to come to terms with another projection of once-unthinkably-low tax revenues and the greatest strains on public assistance programs that anyone could remember. Egner-Baerwald once thought of himself as an inspiring idealist, but the responsibilities of his coalition government now put him at odds with many within his party. Even before the virus, the personal income tax rates in Germany would make most Americans break out in hives. They had passed emergency tax hikes a year ago, but the hard times triggered by the pandemic were passing slower and more painfully than a kidney stone. Egner-Baerwald realized he had spent most of his adult life climbing the greasy pole of politics, only to find that once he reached the top rungs, he had only accumulated the power to choose an option from a vast menu of bad options.

The current chancellor was a Christian Democrat, but some thought Egner-Baerwald had a chance in the next election—or they had, until he had accepted the finance minister position and become the grumpy, grim face of bad times. One newspaper had started nicknaming him "Herr Enttäuschung"—"Mr. Disappointment."

A loyal Social Democrat, Egner-Baerwald had always believed in getting industry to work in cooperation with the initiatives of the national government. A "strong, coordinated social market economy" was how he described it. The elected government would set the goal, taking into account the best interest of everyone in society, and the private sector would be free to work out the best way to reach that goal.

Now the younger rising stars of his party, scarred and shaped by the world's experience with the virus, wanted to go much further.

Egner-Baerwald had spent much of the meeting arguing with Shakira Erikat, the young, bright, telegenic daughter of Palestinian immigrants. A little more than two years ago, after Erikat's first election win, Egner-Baerwald had met with her privately to congratulate her and told her she could be leading the party one day. Apparently, she had interpreted his well-meaning encouragement as a personal invitation to seize control of the party as quickly as possible.

Erikat was frequently described as an example of the "model minority" of Germany; it was true in the sense that she looked like she could have been a supermodel. She claimed to be a faithful Muslim and famously declared that "freedom must include the freedom for individuals to embrace Sharia," but rarely wore a headscarf and had occasionally been seen consuming wine in public. Egner-Baerwald suspected her true faith was ambition. Since the economic troubles spurred by the pandemic, Erikat had been pushing for what she called a "New Resolution" that would effectively wipe away the line separating the public and private sectors. Berlin would assign Germany's industries sweeping new priorities: hire everyone who needed a job, cap the earnings of executives, convert completely to green power. Her slogan for her agenda was "All the People Must Work for All the People'" which Egner-Baerwald believed was catchy but nonsensical.

Erikat contended that the social media monitoring and censorship that had extended to misinformation about the virus and best practices for public health needed to be extended to a wide variety of topics where "the wrong beliefs can be the difference between life and death"—the value of vaccines, climate change, glorification of war or violence, right-wing extremism, anti-immigrant xenophobia, defamation of public officials. She argued that the eventually aborted 2016 prosecution of a comedian for telling jokes that offended Turkey's president, Recep Tayyip Erdogan, was "a needed step to preserve order at home and abroad."

After listening to Erikat's diatribe for five minutes, Egner-Baerwald couldn't endure it any longer. He interrupted her and noted that her recommendations, taken far enough, meant the end of a free society.

Erikat snapped back, something that sounded like, "old idea of a free society died with the first virus victims!" The other party leaders in the room were unsure whether she began the sentence, "*the* old idea of a free society" or "*your* old idea of a free society."

"How can you not see that everything has changed?" she asked. "The liberties of an individual person simply matter less when we as a society are facing menaces on this scale. For more than a year, it was the coronavirus! This year it is strange weather! Next year, it could be ransomware, or EMP terrorism, or artificial intelligence–driven weaponry, or climate change–driven refugee waves! You are like an ostrich with his head in the sand, when the world is screaming at us, as loudly as it can, 'adapt or die!'"

Egner-Baerwald looked around the room and saw most of the party's leaders—including ones he had counted as allies and friends in many years—were nodding. No one cared that Erikat's agenda would generate pushback from many citizens, or that her economic policies would cause multinational corporations to flee the country, or that her foreign policy ideas would alienate the already rickety NATO alliance. She wanted to spend money they didn't have, to try ideas that had never worked, to solve problems that hadn't manifested yet. Egner-Baerwald had become a man of the left in his youth because it meant skepticism of more power in the hands of the state; now Erikat envisioned the most powerful state in Europe since the war.

The meeting adjourned with all major decisions tabled until next time. But Egner-Baerwald departed the room with one major decision completed: Shakira Erikat would have to go, in one way or another. He had been contemplating it on the way to his car when a man with one of his old campaign posters—from his first run to the Bundestag—waved at him with a smile.

Egner-Baerwald waved back and approached. He was still getting used to the fact that he no longer had to remain two meters away from everyone in public, and the man said he had been a longtime fan, thanked him for his leadership during the country's tough times, and asked for an autograph. Egner-Baerwald thanked him in return and looked for a pen. The smiling, bearded man offered one. The finance minister signed the poster with a note of thanks—the two began the process of a handshake, and then both nervously pulled back and let out a little laugh.

"Still getting used to whether that should come back!" Egner-Baerwald admitted.

"You can never be too careful," the fan agreed. Egner-Baerwald returned to his car.

\*\*\*

Hellraiser had asked for a sample of the target's DNA, swabbed from a drinking glass at one meeting. It cost a mere $1,500 to sequence the target's genome. Then he assembled a complete and detailed molecular profile of the target's cells and built a blueprint—gene sequencers, micro-array scanners, mass spectrometers.

From that, Hellraiser perused a virtual library that offered a wide variety of easily genetically modifiable viruses.

It took a week for Egner-Baerwald to feel the first symptoms of chills, fever, and headache. As required by law, he notified his doctor immediately; the coronavirus tests came back negative. But his doctors found Egner-Baerwald's blood pressure was dropping, along with his low platelet, red blood cell, and white blood cell counts. Tests for all of the usual viruses and bacterial infections prevalent in Germany kept coming back negative.

in the days that followed, Egner-Baerwald experienced severe muscle pain and vomiting. The hospital treated him as potentially contagious, but no one in Egner-Baerwald's life reported similar symptoms—not his wife and children, not his mistress, not his staff or coworkers. After five days, Egner-Baerwald's condition took a dramatic turn for the worse—increasingly severe headaches, loss of vision, slurred speech, and seeming hallucinations. Overcome by worsening symptoms, he lapsed into a coma and died a day later.

It would not be until after the autopsy that a diagnosis was reached: Kyasanur forest disease virus, found only in southern

India and only infecting a few hundred people per year through tick bites. No person-to-person transmission had ever been recorded, and this was the wrong time of year for infections over in that country. No doctor's office or hospital in Germany had recorded any similar cases or diagnoses. A thorough examination of Egner-Baerwald's body showed no signs of a tick bite.

What's more, even in India, Kyasanur forest disease virus only killed three to five percent of those infected. A vaccine for the virus existed, but no supply existed in Germany, as the virus had never been recorded in central Europe.

The medical team that treated Egner-Baerwald regretted, with lingering confusion, that none of their usual methods of treating patients with viral infections worked. The medical examiner lamented that Lars Egner-Baerwald, the man who looked like he could well be the next chancellor of Germany, died painfully and suddenly because of his extraordinary bad luck of catching a rare virus that his body was particularly unequipped to fight off.

It was only in his final moments of life that Egner-Baerwald remembered he had accepted the autograph-seeker's pen with his bare hand.

# CHAPTER FIVE

LIBERTY CROSSING INTELLIGENCE CAMPUS
TYSONS CORNER, VIRGINIA
FRIDAY, APRIL 9

"This trail is gonna lead back to Beijing, you know," Ward said.

He stood at Katrina's desk. She looked up at him skeptically.

With Alec much quieter than before the epidemic, everyone else on the team seemed to adjust their personality slightly to make up for the disappearance of his rat-tat-tat banter and jokes. Ward had become something of a playful troublemaker. Katrina knew he respected her—Ward trusted her to watch his back every time they were out in the field.

On paper, they should have seen more eye to eye. Katrina's direction in life changed on March 20, 1995, when as a foreign exchange student in Japan, she was nearly a victim of the Aum Shinrikyo attack on the Tokyo subway system. Ward's direction in life changed barely a month later, a few blocks away from the Alfred P. Murrah Federal Building in Oklahoma City. Both had been deployed to Afghanistan in late 2001; Katrina was the fresh-from-the-Farm CIA recruit who happened to speak Uzbeki like a native at a time when the agency needed those the most; Ward parachuted in with the 75th Rangers to secure an airstrip that would eventually become Camp Rhino and then later, on a separate mission, a raid on a suspected location of Mullah Omar. They both loved Alec and found him exasperating and ridiculous at times. And they were, by a wide margin, the two most lethal members of the Dangerous Clique.

But Ward was a Waco-born, Oklahoma-raised, West-Point-educated, Army-trained former Ranger who relished his good-ol'-boy image, whiskey, extensive firearms collection, and being underestimated for his Midwestern accent and increasingly unruly lumberjack beard. He could fight everywhere but couldn't blend in anywhere and rarely cared to anyway. He was plainspoken, direct, and in his own mind, pragmatic. No matter who was in office, his true president would forever be Charlton Heston.

Katrina was Bukhara-born, Queens-raised, Georgetown-educated, Agency-trained senior case officer who secretly relished her Good Bad–Girl image, fine wine, extensive book collection, and being underestimated as a woman. She could fight anywhere, but increasingly sought to win a conflict without her foe even knowing she had won. She could blend in almost anywhere, but rarely could resist subtly signaling her cosmopolitan sophistication. She was eloquent, intellectual, and in her mind, a born-again idealist. Her model leader was the twelfth-century samurai Tomoe Gozen.

In the end, their conversations and debates and arguments revealed that Ward was primarily driven to protect and conserve that which was good in the world, and Katrina was primarily driven to explore and experiment and build upon the good in the world.

"You think Hell-Summoner is tied to the Chinese government? I see your exercise program has expanded to include jumping to conclusions," Katrina replied. "What, are you itching to pull a Lee Harvey Oswald outside the Chinese embassy again?"

Ward frowned. "Whoever killed that guy outside the embassy must have felt he was doing the right thing, deterring worse actions by the Chinese government by sending a clear signal of the potential consequences. I see it as a warning shot."

"A warning shot that went through his skull," Katrina dryly observed.

"It warned everybody else," Ward grunted.

"Whoever killed that guy must have erroneously believed that a safer and more stable world can built upon a foundation of seemingly random shootings of spies carrying black passports," Katrina warned. She shook her head and dropped the issue.

"Based on recent history, I think either Hell-Summoner is Chinese, or China is Hell-Summoner's most likely client."

Katrina stared back skeptically. "Tell me, Ward, why would China want to buy an ethnic bioweapon from some guy calling himself Hell Summoner?"

"Uyghurs? Tibetans? What if they could figure out some gene that's common in Taiwan but rare in their own population? Or they decide to settle the score with Japan for Nanking? Heck, if we're the biggest obstacle sanding between them and a whole new world order with a *made in China* label on it, why not figure out what gene is most common in the United States?"

Katrina shook her head. "Because the United States isn't just a rainbow, we're the Crayola sixty-four-pack of genetics. Any gene common enough to do serious damage to the US would also be found in the Chinese. Besides, Beijing is trying to climb out of a hole as an international pariah. Why would they go right back to working with virus when they've become the global scapegoat for the pandemic?"

Ward folded his arms and groaned. "Scapegoat? I think the term you're looking for is *culprit*."

Off her skeptical look, Ward unleashed his long-simmering diatribe.

"Oh, okay, Katrina," he sighed, rolling his eyes. "A city with not one but two separate biological research labs, both conducting research on coronaviruses in bats, one of which visiting US scientists declared in 2018 had 'serious shortage of appropriately trained technicians and investigators needed to safely operate this high-containment laboratory,' and that also had all cell phone activity in its high-security wing suddenly stop in October, and that declared in December that 'a large number of new bat and rodent viruses have been discovered and identified' in job listings, just happens to have a new coronavirus that originated in bats pop up near the local seafood market sometime in November or December. Never mind that a virologist nicknamed 'Bat Woman' told *Scientific American* that her first fear was that the virus was one she had researched in her lab. Never mind that several former employees of the Wuhan Institute of Virology just flat-out disappeared around this time. Never mind that the Wuhan Institute of Virology first denied those employees ever existed, and when confronted with evidence they had, simply changed their story to insist they were fine and not missing at all. Never mind that a doctor in Wuhan who went to Harvard Medical School put out a paper saying that his investigation pointed to an accidental release from a lab, before suddenly withdrawing the paper and insisting—with no explanation—that he no longer believed his theory. Never mind that the CDC and World Health Organization could never confirm that bats or pangolins were present at the Huanan Seafood market. Never mind that the Wuhan Center for Disease Control & Prevention is less than a quarter of a mile from that seafood market, and the Wuhan Institute of Virology is nine miles away. If Atlanta had an outbreak of a terrible new virus, people would wonder about CDC headquarters. If Frederick, Maryland, had an outbreak of a terrible new virus, people would wonder about the Army Medical Research Institute of Infectious Diseases at Fort Detrick. Never mind that the Beijing office of the Chinese Center of Disease Control accidentally released SARS in 2004... *twice*. Never mind that a researcher at the Chinese Academy of Engineering made more than a million dollars illegally selling off lab animals before he was caught in 2014. Never mind that even Chinese state-run media reported about 'chronic inadequate management issues' regarding the disposal of biohazardous materials from the country's laboratories. Never mind that apparently it was common for laboratories to dump biohazardous material into the sewer, and never mind that wet market cooks go into those same sewer systems to find 'gutter oil' that they use in cooking!"

Ward started waving his arms in exasperation. "Never mind that the Wuhan and Chinese governments spent three to six weeks insisting the coronavirus couldn't jump from one person to another, and that it all came from people eating undercooked bats or pangolins, even as doctors were catching it from their patients!"

Katrina gave him some gentle applause.

"I salute your research, but none of that suggests Hell Summoner will work with China."

"Well, why the hell are you so skeptical?" Ward asked.

Katrina sighed. She unlocked and opened up her lower desk drawer and pulled out a three-inch stack of folders and printouts. She dropped it on her desk with a loud *thump.*

"On and off for the past two years, I've been digging into China's biological weapons programs," she declared.

"I have learned more than I ever wanted to know about all of these germs and viruses and bacteria and the rest of this crud. I feel confident concluding that the Chinese government's only interest in Hell Summoner would be if he had some technological innovation that they hadn't developed yet," she declared.

Ward looked over the stack of files. "Well, maybe he—"

"My guess, whoever Hell Summoner is, he's not offering China anything they don't already know," Katrina stated.

Ward paused. Katrina started sorting through the files.

"The Japanese killed 270,000 Chinese through biological weapons attacks and biological experimentation during World

War Two, and the Chinese military has never forgotten that," she began. "The People's Liberation Army is utterly, completely convinced that the United States never gave up our biological weapons programs as we promised in 1969. They're also convinced that the Soviet Union did provide biological weapons to its allies in the 1970s, and the 'Yellow Rain' attacks in Vietnam, Laos, and Cambodia really happened—that was supposed to be a toxic fungus, liquefied into a gel and spread by aircraft or helicopters. For what it's worth, the United Nations says it couldn't verify the claims."

Ward let out a skeptical grunt. Katrina opened up another folder.

"China's military insists they no longer have an offensive program, and they go through the motions of compliance with the biological weapons convention, but just about all of their research done on fighting viruses can just as easily be turned around and used to create offensive biological weapons. In 2000, the head of the Soviet bioweapons program wrote a book, saying their spies had found two rare viruses—Ebola and Marburg—not far from the Malan nuclear testing facilities, and concluded China was experimenting with bacteriological weapons in the 1980s. For what it's worth, our side couldn't confirm that. Chinese military publications openly declare that the United States already has weapons that can target particular genetic populations."

"Huh." Ward's brow furrowed as he read the document and translation for himself. He looked up. "We … don't, right? They're not sitting next to the alien Roswell bodies and the Ark of the Covenant at Area 51, right?"

Katrina gave him a disapproving look, scoffing at his gullibility. But what she described next flabbergasted Ward nearly as much if she had confirmed that a giant warehouse at the Nellis Test and Training Range in Nevada indeed stored aliens, Biblical artifacts, Bigfoot, and Elvis.

"A Chinese doctor announced he had done in vitro 'gene editing' of human embryos in 2018," she continued. "Best of intentions, he found couples where a father had HIV but the mother didn't. He fertilized embryos, used a CRISPER—it's a gene-editing technology, apparently you can just mix and match the genes you want—and disabled gene CCR5, which is what allows HIV to enter cells. The problem is, the same gene also protects you from other viruses, like West Nile. Most doctors around the world find this really risky and morally debatable. The doctor did this all in secret, and according to him, three babies—all girls—are healthy."

"Genetically edited babies?"

Ward's mind spun with the possibilities, both positive and negative. His wife, Marie, had endured two difficult pregnancies along the way of raising their six children, and more than once, doctors had speculated that her later pregnancies heightened the risk of birth defects. Year by year, they had endured and encountered broken legs, croup, coxsackie, ear infections, roseola, head lice, pink eye, and God knew what other maladies that stemmed from the children's uncontrollable need to touch things. If you could go in before birth and tweak any genes that made a child more vulnerable ... why not? But once the Communist Chinese government had the power to edit the genes of children ... what would their agenda and worldview spur them to create? A generation of genetically perfect supermen? Splicing in animal DNA? Clones?

Katrina nodded and let out a small laugh. "I told Alec this and he asked if the girls were named 'Khan,' 'Noonien,' and 'Singh.' China threw the doctor in jail for three years—in part because they banned the use of reproductive technologies for those with HIV."

Ward's eyes bulged, and he shook his head. "*That's* what bothered them? Not the mad scientist equivalent of giving teenagers whiskey and the car keys, and hoping for the best?"

Katrina opened up one of the thickest folders in her stack.

"China has no less than thirty-two facilities doing biomedical research that could easily be applied to developing a virus designed to target only particular populations," she said, shuffling through the paper quickly. "The State Research Center for Viro-Biotechnology Engineering in Beijing, the Wuhan Institute of Biological Products, the People's Liberation Army Institute of Disease Control and Prevention, PLA Key Genetic Engineering Laboratory... and those are just the ones we know about. Institute of Microbiology and Epidemiology in Beijing, Beijing Huifenglong Biotechnology Development company, and the Institute of Medical Equipment in Tianjin have all done extensive field tests of aerobiology, studying how different biological materials aerosolize and disperse in wind patterns—far too much testing to simply be preparing to protect their people against an attack."

Ward whistled and examined the documents. China had an extensive network of facilities that looked like they could mass produce a near-unlimited supply of whatever pestilence, plague, or poison they wanted.

"I agree that they are a malevolent and heartless bunch of bastards over there, but they are rational and not suicidal," Katrina declared. "I don't know about you, but I find it rather refreshing after nearly two decades of dealing with jihadists who say, 'my tea is cold, should I put on a suicide vest today?'"

By now the folders covered all of her desk—photos, charts, documents, reports, and translations of articles from Chinese military journals. She spread her arms wide over all of her accumulated evidence. "China's already got gene-editing knowledge and technology, an infrastructure for research and development that rivals ours and the Soviet Union at its height." She leaned forward. "So, you tell me, Ward ... when Beijing has all of that ... what the hell would they need Hell Summoner for?"

# CHAPTER SIX

SOMEWHERE IN CENTRAL GERMANY
SATURDAY, APRIL 10

The man who called himself "Hell Summoner" secretly believed his *nom de guerre* was a little over the top, but he obviously couldn't use his real name and he needed a way to get the attention of the world's most notorious and gleefully amoral regimes. His asking price was roughly twenty billion dollars. If it was ever paid, that sum would put him somewhere between 38th and 41st on the *Forbes* list of the world's richest people.

Before meeting in person, he had his associate—a tough man who could sniff out cops and spies easily—meet them first and verify all of their information.

Once a potential client had passed the test, he began his meetings by noting that he was there to give a biological presentation, not a geopolitical one. He noted that the last two years had demonstrated that almost every penny spent on tanks and planes and traditional military forces had been a waste. Many people around the world hated China but no one had never figured out how to bring life in Shanghai and Beijing to a halt—until one particular virus either escaped from a lab, or was eaten in an undercooked pangolin or bat, or made some other jump into the never-identified Patient Zero. Millions of people around the world hated the United States, but no one—not even al-Qaeda, or ISIS, or Atarsa—had kept Americans in their homes for months.

Cyberwarfare? That was kids playing video games. The fight for low-Earth orbit dominance among the superpowers, including America's ludicrous new "Space Force"? Silly exercises by people who had seen too many *Star Wars* movies. Even traditional terrorism looked small-time, ludicrously ineffective, as pitiful and inconsequential as an angry teenager's tantrum.

Hell Summoner argued that the awesome, world-altering power of the virus had even made nuclear weapons effectively obsolete. He asked the representative of North Korea why on earth a regime would spend billions on a weapons system that required large, expensive permanent structures like launch silos, whose location could be easily determined.

In one quiet meeting with one official from an unsavory regime after another, Hell Summoner's pitch followed:

*SARS-CoV-2 has just proven to be the most devastating weapon on earth—with the important caveat that it could not be controlled; it simply spread from person to person and country to country without regard. And this is what has bedeviled biological weapons developers throughout history. Fate, chance, human behavior, and the winds could always bring your most dangerous weapons right back to your doorstep, sickening and killing your own populations.*

*Until now. The ability to control what a virus did and who it could harm the most had always previously been limited by insufficient technology, skill, resources, and knowledge. For a mere twenty billion dollars, I can give you the power to sicken and slay any foreign population on a massive scale.*

*Before we go any further, do not misunderstand me. I do not believe in the supremacy of any race. Hitler could have assembled and organized a master race of fair-skinned Teutonics, but even if he hadn't been stopped, eventually he would have marched them into a land without shade and watched them die off from* melanoma and skin cancer. Any race can be the "strongest," depending upon what particular challenges it faces.

But your ability to survive a virus, pathogen, or disease often depends upon your genes, and differences in genetics are what define different ethnic groups. Diseases do not care if they are called racist.

People of Eastern European, or "Ashkenazi" Jewish heritage were much more likely to have Tay-Sachs, Bloom syndrome, cystic fibrosis, Gaucher disease, and others. If you are African or African American, you are much more likely to be diagnosed with sickle cell anemia. In 2016, researchers at the University of Montreal's Department of Pediatrics determined that the immune systems of African Americans react more strongly than those of European descent. That looks like an advantage and it is—unless your body's immune system reacts too much and it starts attacking healthy cells and you develop an autoimmune disease like rheumatoid arthritis or lupus or Crohn's disease or multiple sclerosis.

It may surprise you to learn that what I offer—immunity from deadly, weaponizable biological threats—already exists in nature in rare cases. Think of anthrax, perhaps the most notorious biological weapon because of the 2001 mailings to American law-makers and media. It causes a toxic reaction in the bloodstream, but not everyone's blood reacts the same way. In 2012, geneticists at the at Stanford University School of Medicine measured the cellular resistance to a toxin that mimics the effects of anthrax on a wide range of samples: eighty-four Nigerians, sixty-three Americans whose ancestors came from northern and western Europe, forty-four Japanese, and forty-three Han Chinese. Their study concluded, "out of the 234 samples, lymphocytes from three individuals of European ancestry were thousands of times more resistant to killing by an engineered hybrid toxin." This trio was not completely immune to anthrax, but much more likely to sur-vive exposure. And these genes were parents and children. It is an *inherited trait. In other words, some small groups of Europeans are partially immune to anthrax.*

*If you doubt me, everything I describe to you is laid out in the scientific journal* Proceedings of the National Academy of Sciences.

*Another example: In southern Nepal and northern India, there is a region called Terai—grasslands, swamps, and wetlands. It is rampant with mosquitoes. It also home to about nearly two million people known as the Tharu. The Tharu fascinated scientists since the because the Tharu are naturally nearly immune to malaria. The odds of a serious reaction from malaria in a Tharu person are about seven times less than the average person. They survived for centuries in an area where malaria repelled outsiders. Up until the 1950s, only the Tharu people could live in the Terai region.*

*I would note that the World Health Organization showed up and started up a malaria eradication program. And the Tharu found themselves forced off their land by outsiders and Nepalese military. Well-meaning anti-disease programs ended up forcing a population into impoverished servitude. A bioweapon can be a shield, as well as a sword.*

*Genetics are not fair. Short of gene therapy, we cannot alter our genes.*

*A few years ago, a fifteen-year-old girl with cystic fibrosis in London was battling a life-threatening infection. She had successfully received a double lung transplant, and she had been given immunosuppressive drugs to ensure the new lungs could work with her body. But with her immune system down, she contracted* Mycobacterium abscessus. *This is the bacteria that can cause tuberculosis and leprosy—and in this girl, this infection proved indestructible, no matter what antibiotics her doctors tried.*

*The bacteria spread to her lungs, her liver, and all over her skin.*

*The girl was going to die...and doctors turned to microbi-ologists at the University of Pittsburgh who were working on viral engineering. They tried something never tried before: they bioen-gineered their own virus, called a bacteriophage—a virus that can only attack bacteria. This virus was effectively "programmed" to seek and destroy* Mycobacterium abscessus *and leave everything else intact. Engineered correctly, a bacteriophage is the biological equivalent of a sniper—extraordinarily precise at hitting the tar-get, with no collateral damage to anything else.*

*The girl lived. Within nine days, she was able to leave the hos-pital. She is alive and well—and living proof that we can build a virus to kill whatever we want—and not kill anything else.*

*Why do you think the White House staff and stewards gather bedsheets, drinking glasses, and other objects the president of the United States has touched? Why are all of these objects sanitized or destroyed? Because they recognize the potential of someone assassinating the president with a virus engineered to target only his DNA. They would not do it if this was only a far-fetched theory.*

*On July 31, 2009, the US State Department issued secret instructions to its staff to collect biometric information on rank-ing North Korean diplomats, permanent representatives of the United Nations Security Council, the director-general of the World Health Organization, and a variety of other diplomats. Almost no one noticed this particular revelation from the WikiLeaks exposé because a Manhattan real estate mogul didn't tweet about it. Ask yourself why the United States government found it so advanta-geous to possess the DNA of other countries' diplomats.*

*Depending upon the size of your target, an engineered virus is the perfect way to kill or incapacitate someone or a group of people and ensure that it looks like natural causes. Even if medi-cal and law-enforcement authorities did determine a new disease striking a particular figure or group was suspicious, they would* have no way to trace the attack back to you. *This method leaves no fingerprints.*

*Cost is not the factor that it once was. I can generate a whole-exome sequence—essentially mapping out the target's human genome for less than one thousand US dollars. If you want me to target one particular individual, and you don't want any collateral damage, I will need a sample of the target's DNA. If you're a little less choosy about who suffers from the virus besides one particular target, I will only need a sample of DNA from the target population. Family, tribe—ideally, one precise identifying gene of the genetic cluster.*

*Gene sequencers, micro-array scanners, mass spectrometers— I have plenty of this equipment already. You can find it on eBay. Chemicals, lab supplies—laboratory instruments are a ninety billion dollar a year industry before the coronavirus hit; the rapid and widespread increase in medical research around the world probably increased that by thirty percent over the past two years. The equipment I use to do this cannot be tracked or traced. There's just too much of it around the world. You might as well try to track me down by reviewing every purchase of test tubes on six continents.*

*No, what truly will cost you is knowledge, the knowledge of the human genetics and viruses. I have it, and very few people know it as well as I do. I have no criminal record, no profile in the world's intelligence agencies, no reasons for anyone to suspect that I have the ability to produce this. As far as the world knows, I run a small medical research company, one of the thousands, perhaps tens of thousands around the world that sprung up since SARS-CoV-2 arose to menace the world. My staff is less than half a dozen. We have no leaks, no potential turncoats, no weak links for some hostile force to exploit. You heard nothing about me until I contacted you.*

*You could order your illegal biological weapons program managers to work on a project like this, but they would be starting from scratch. Trust me, gentlemen, you do not want to develop contagious deadly biological weapons through trial and error. Of course, if the world ever learned that you were working on developing a weapon like this in your own secret laboratories, the response would probably make the 2003 invasion of Iraq look like a sternly worded letter. I would remind you that in the past, the United States government has pledged to respond to attacks involving nonconventional weapons with its own nonconventional weapons. Please keep in mind their nonconventional weapons sit in silos across the Midwest and tend to leave places uninhabitable for thousands of years.*

*Oh, and did I mention that Israel has never signed nor ratified the Biological Weapons Convention?*

*Instead of the spectacularly risky path of trying to develop an ethnic bioweapon yourself, you could simply name the target, meet my price, and rest assured that someone or some group of someones will soon die of natural viral outbreak and never know you had anything to do with it. At the very least, our conversation should have you thinking seriously about who would want to launch this kind of attack against your own population.*

*This form of attack is not only untraceable, it is unstoppable. We saw the futility of quarantines during this pandemic. One release in one departures lounge in one major international airport, and your customized virus will be on five continents within a day. Asymptomatic carriers will breeze through health security checks in airports and train stations and border crossings. It will probably be a week before the first symptoms, and targets won't be in doctors' offices and hospitals until days after that. By the time any doctor determines that all of the infected share a particular gene, it will have spread far and wide through the target population. Those who are not infected will be forced to self-quarantine indefinitely. We just saw how long it took to develop a vaccine with the entire world mobilizing every possible resource, at absolute top speed, under the threat of SARS-CoV-2. Will the world move as fast when the only potential victims of a virus are Han Chinese, or Bengali Indians, or Bantu Kenyans, or Uyghurs, or Chechens or Rohinga or Ashkenazi Jews?*

*No, no, the world will not run to its battle stations to save one particular tribe. By my estimates, it would take three to five years to develop a vaccine—and by that point, my friends, your targeted population won't have enough people left to do the wave in a sports stadium.*

*Yes, my price is high—some would say exorbitant. But I think the worldwide economic cataclysm from the coronavirus demonstrates the sheer power of what I am offering you. This is the next wave of warfare, and everything that came before is as obsolete as the wooden ships that witnessed the battle between the* Merrimack *and the* Monitor, *ironclad ships during the American Civil War. Our current moment is comparable to the advent of the atomic age in Hiroshima and Nagasaki, or the dawn of the modern age of asymmetric terrorist warfare on 9/11. Someone once said that everyone has a choice of whether to be green or brown—green as that which is growing and adapting to the environment around it, or brown as in the dying, decaying matter that will fuel the growth of everyone else.*

*What will it be, gentlemen? Green, or brown?*

# CHAPTER SEVEN

Despite the green light from Stern, daily life for Katrina and the rest of her team did not change much, as their hunt for Hell Summoner lacked a place to start. CIA personnel watching the Iranian government could corroborate that Iraj Khansari attended the meeting he described, but not the substance of what was discussed. The other figures at the meeting had not let anything slip in their communications, at least as far as the NSA could tell. Stern ruled than an attempt to capture and interrogate the other attendees of the meeting would be way too much risk for too little reward.

About a month after the Dangerous Clique's operation on Cyprus two years earlier, the NSA determined that the few remaining Atarsa sleepers had established contact with each other through a chat room, and sought to avenge the deaths of Gholam Gul and Sarvar Rashin by identifying and killing those who had slain their leaders. The CIA director at the time, Richard Mitchell, felt Katrina and her team ought to know about what he called "menacing chatter."

"I hate that term. Chatter is not menacing," Katrina responded. "Actions are."

Mitchell ignored her and noted that these identified remaining sleepers were angry young men, loners who already dwelt on the fringes of society. In light of the agency's problems with leaks and moles, the director urged Katrina and the rest of her team to "practice situational awareness" and make sure they didn't fall into any predictable routines. He also told Katrina, Ward, Raquel, Dee, and Alec to urge anyone close to them to adopt the same practices, or perhaps even change addresses, ideally without disclosing their role in the CIA operations against Atarsa.

Raquel was incredulous. "You want us to tell our spouses and parents and siblings that they ought to promptly move out of their houses for no particular reason?"

Mitchell shrugged. "Tell them the real estate market is really hot right now."

Alec's parents, Joseph and Aneta Flanagan, had already contemplated moving someplace warmer, now that they were retired. They packed up their house in Westport, Connecticut, a de facto museum of Irish American history, and moved down to Nag's Head, North Carolina. Alec warned his parents they would be evacuating in the face of hurricanes on a regular basis, but they'd had enough of northern winters full of icy sidewalks, snow-shoveling, and ornery home heating systems.

The Flanagans settled in and loved their new coastal living. But shortly after the scale of the threat of the coronavirus became clear, Dare County, North Carolina took the unusual step of closing off its lone access road, US-64. The county consisted of the middle part of the Outer Banks and Roanoke Island, and could metaphorically pull up its drawbridge from the rest of the country. For more than a month, the county barred nonresidents from entering; the police checkpoint on US-64 turned away anyone who didn't have a driver's license with a home address within the county lines. Local officials insisted that because they had no cases, they had a rare opportunity to ensure no county resident would catch it.

This meant an armed line of police barred Alec from visiting his parents, a restriction he found enraging and legally dubious. He bellowed that if the police "want to see my permit to travel wherever the hell I wish, they can look at the one under the bulletproof glass at the National Archives!" Katrina had to dissuade him from driving down and figuring out a way around the quarantine, out of a mix of filial piety and a reflexive desire to defy any government official telling him he couldn't do something he had previously done.

During the pandemic, both of Alec's older brothers, Martin and Michael, caught the virus. Michael compared it to a bad case of the flu and recovered at home within two weeks, but Martin required hospitalization. Now, more than a year later, Martin said that he still felt like his lungs weren't 100 percent—he had stopped jogging and got winded after climbing three flights of stairs. But he was happy to be alive. From outward appearances, the Flanagans survived the pandemic with minimal cost. But Alec knew his time on this earth with his family was limited—either they would go, or he would go, perhaps long before his time, as a result of his work—and the virus had forced his family to spend a long and precious stretch of that finite amount of time apart.

For years, Katrina had urged her parents, Abraham and Ziva Leonidivna, to move out of the borough of Queens in New York City. When Katrina's family had first arrived in the United States, they stayed with another Bukharian Jewish family. (Immigration officials had mis-transcribed his original surname Leonidov, but Abraham, worried that any objection would lead to him being sent back, adopted his new feminine surname as if it had been handed down from God on a stone tablet.)

The Leonidivnas moved to a small apartment, then a slightly larger one, then a small house in Rego Park. Despite Katrina's nudges, but her father insisted that the world had, at most, three hundred thousand Bukharian Jews, and most were in Queens, and, he believed, almost all of them were distant relatives. Abraham and Ziva liked their access to their restaurants with chebureki, the traditional bakeries, the specialty markets with endless varieties of smoked fish. Everywhere else, people thought Bukharian Jews were Russian Jews, Abraham complained. His son-in-law Alec helpfully observed that most Americans couldn't tell the difference between ethnic Russians and Russian Jews, either. The Leonidivnas were not religious but liked having the synagogues nearby for weddings, funerals, and brit milahs.

A couple of years before, the Leonidivnas had finally moved to a spacious house in Forest Hills, once the home of the US Open tennis tournament. As far as Abraham Leonidivna was concerned, he had climbed to the top of American life, a classic immigrant success story, and was ready to enjoy retirement.

But when the sheer scale of the coronavirus's threat to the city became clear, the Leonidivnas finally relented and agreed to move out, finding a small Bukharian Jewish community in Miami Beach, Florida. Katrina sighed that her parents were out of the frying pan and into the fire—now living in the land of alligators, insane drivers, hurricanes, wet-mop-to-the-face-humidity, and the perpetual headline-grabbing "Florida Man," who was always doing something bizarre and insane, like shoplifting live crabs in his pants and then attempting to evade police cruisers in a golf cart. Abraham said he worried his new neighbors might be drug dealers—his entire perception of the city had been shaped by *Miami Vice*—but Alec assured him that in the absolute worst-case scenario, his new neighbors would be Miami Dolphins fans.

But the Leonidivnas realized they didn't like south Florida much and thought about moving back to New York City. They returned to Queens after six months to visit friends in their old neighborhoods...and found the neighborhoods they remembered were already gone. One out of every thirty-nine people in Rego Park caught the virus; one out of every four hundred people died in Forest Hills. Many of the old family restaurants and bakeries closed down, unable to make ends meet on takeout and delivery. Quite a few old friends had moved out of the city like the Leonidivnas. The entire visit proved depressing, learning about which friend of a friend had died, which ones survived but suffered lingering lung issues, which ones had lost their businesses, and which ones had moved. They decided to remain in Florida, for now, wondering whether it would be easier to just move to northern Virginia to live closer to Katrina and Alec.

The Leonidivnas' new home in Miami Beach was just across Biscayne Bay from the home of Dee's father, Ernesto Alves, in Little Havana. Ernesto never caught the virus and managed to keep his restaurant going on delivery and takeout during the lockdown periods. But Dee found her return visit to the neighborhood of her childhood as depressing as the Leonidivnas' return to Queens. The tourism industry in South Florida had collapsed, taking all kinds of small businesses down with it—restaurants, cafes, bars, clubs, ice cream shops, bed and breakfasts, souvenir shops. Marti Park turned into a food distribution center for the needy. One in four Little Havana residents who tested for the coronavirus came back positive. Dee said it felt like something out of Lois Lowry's *The Giver*, as the virus swept through her community and simply wiped out those above a certain age. For once, Domino Park had a lot of empty tables.

Ward's parents had passed on before the virus arrived, and his in-laws self-isolated with the discipline of monks. But when Ward wasn't off on government assignments or hunting trips for deer, wild turkey, or Chinese state security officials, his wife, Marie, found herself attempting to home-school six children all by herself. It sounded like the pitch for a sitcom, but Marie argued she had been involuntarily cast as the protagonist of a dark psychological drama on Netflix.

Like so many parents across the country, the Rutledges muddled through the best they could. Ward was confident his kids would turn out all right; as a father, he believed that if he could instill a willingness to work hard, an appetite for learning and reading, and an ability to think critically in his children, the rest would take care of itself. Marie concurred but had lingering doubts about whether the hastily assembled "distance learning" program put together by their local public school was really much learning at all. Before the cancellation of the school year, the Rutledges insisted their kids limit their screen time and get outside and enjoy fresh air. Now their education turned into an endless series of Zoom meetings. At one point, Marie fumed at the kids that it was time to get off the computer and do something healthy, like watch television. The Rutledge children had one another, for better and worse. Without school, and strong recommendations against play dates, children all across the world had to make do with Zoom chats and phone calls. Marie noted that many criminologists considered solitary confinement to be a form of torture and an inherently psychologically destabilizing form of punishment for convicted criminals. Now the country wanted to isolate all children from all of their non-sibling peers indefinitely.

Raquel's parents moved out of a retirement community in Maryland that was particularly hard hit, and her husband, Vaughn, yanked his mother out of an assisted-living home once the threat of the virus in those facilities became clear. Raquel periodically joked that she found working counterterrorism much less stressful than being under one roof with elderly parents.

Everyone in the Dangerous Clique concurred that once a parent reached age sixty-five or so, they developed the ability to tap into deep reserves of stubbornness that had built up over the decades. Senior citizens would do what they wanted to do, virus be damned. They hadn't lived this long just to spend their golden years stuck indoors, eating delivery food, and trying to figure out the "input" button on the remote control.

And everyone in the Dangerous Clique knew that the world's most stubborn senior citizen might have been Harold Hare, the longtime case officer and retired deputy director of the Central Intelligence Agency, code-named Merlin. Hare authorized Raquel's creation of the Dangerous Clique and became a trusted mentor to her and Katrina. He was a legend in the intelligence community and the kind of man who didn't like retirement, and kibitzed with agency personnel at every opportunity, a fixture in the seventh-floor dining room at lunchtime.

The Hare marriage had always fascinated Raquel. Harold Hare was the kind of man often married to his work, living a life of deep cover, with frequent travel and absences. He was handsome enough and charming; he could be the life of the party with his magic tricks and stories from around the globe. Dolores Larissa Barrett was, in her younger days, gorgeous, an heiress, and something of a Washington, DC socialite. She could have had any man, and she picked Harold—the man living a life of a spy behind his past Air Force service and public identity as a Kremlinologist for the US State Department. She became active on a variety of charity boards and the cocktail party circuit and had collected more than her share of gossip and intelligence every weekend evening, whether or not Harold was in the country. If she had wanted to be, she could have been the successor to Washington' best-connected socialite, Pamela Harriman.

Raquel strongly suspected Dolores, Harold, or both were infertile, and for some never-quite-explained reason, they had never pursued the path of adoption. For much of Harold's adult life, he had lived in a way that would have made it difficult to be a good father, or at least a regularly present one. Perhaps driven by a frustrated appetite for a legacy, Hare proved to be one of the most active mentors in the agency, constantly "adopting" talented newcomers and teaching them what he knew, cultivating and pulling younger staffers up the ladder, inviting them to dinners and barbecues as an extended social circle. The Hares had no biological children, but many "work children." In recent years, Raquel had increasingly looked over Hare like she was a dutiful daughter and he an aging parent.

Raquel went back and reviewed every group Hare had crossed in one way or another during his illustrious career, and came back with a list that featured the KGB, the FSB, the old East German Stasi, the Iranian mullahs, China, North Korea, al-Qaeda and all of its affiliates, the Taliban, Hezbollah, Hamas, the Pakistani ISI, the Abu Nidal organization, Islamic Jihad, the IRA, ETA, the Grey Wolves, Shining Path, the Red Brigades, the Greek Cells of Fire. Somehow, he always came back in one piece, although he could tell plenty of stories of close calls and scrapes and *how I got this scar.*

And then a virus from somewhere over in China killed both Harold and Dolores.

God knows where Harold caught the virus, or whether Dolores caught it first. Neither one was easily dissuaded from disrupting their normal routines. Raquel had feared that Alzheimer's was starting to grip Harold; he was more forgetful, erratic, and increasingly focused upon matters of faith and mysticism and believed that their life's work had been part of a grand struggle of good and evil that humanity did not understand. He believed Katrina had been descended from some sort of warrior tribe of women in Uzbekistan, the "Qyrq Qyz" or "Kirk Kus," perhaps the inspiration for legends of the Amazons.

Dolores died three days after Harold. Their funeral, in accordance with state directives, could have no more than ten people in attendance. The many friends and former colleagues who could not attend joined a "virtual wake" over Zoom that everyone deemed a poor facsimile of the real thing. Raquel intended to hold a real memorial service now that the coronavirus had passed ... but could never quite bring herself to schedule it. That would be the final goodbye—and perhaps if that in-person ceremony hadn't occurred yet, in some way, Raquel felt, Harold Hare wasn't really entirely gone.

From outward appearances, the Dangerous Clique survived the pandemic just fine—no hospitalizations, no lingering illnesses. But all of the team's members got out of bed every morning and went to either Langley, Fort Meade, or Liberty Campus believing they had a unique opportunity to make the world a better, safer place, striking down the next notorious terrorist, terror financier, illicit arms dealer, or other malevolent malcontent early in their careers. And for nearly two decades, they had ... until one day a threat came along that proved them as helpless as anyone else.

*\*\**

But a week after the clique had returned from Norway, and days of reviewing NSA intercepts, Dee sent a series of emoji-laden ALL CAPS texts just before midnight Sunday, insisting everyone get into the office as soon as possible.

"You wanted anything unusual involving potential bioterrorism that was caught by NSA in recent weeks!" Dee began excitedly.

"Hot off the presses, so to speak: A known Russian Foreign Intelligence Service officer, using a form of electronic communication that he thinks is secure—spoiler alert, it isn't—reached out to a small mercenary group, told them to get to Salzburg, Austria, by Wednesday, April 13 for a meeting, and to quote, 'take preparations for the presence of biohazardous materials.'"

Raquel's eyebrows rose as the information brought a stronger kick than her double espresso. "Okay, that gets my attention."

"The Russians want to buy a bioweapon?" Ward asked, raising a skeptical eyebrow. "Isn't this like them going somewhere else to buy borscht and vodka?"

"Russians have been claiming that American scientists have been trying to develop a biological weapon that kills only Russians for years," Katrina said with an amused chuckle. "Back in 2017, Vladimir Putin claimed that the United States was collecting tissue samples from Russians and contended that America had installed biological weapons research facilities in Georgia, Kazakhstan, Azerbaijan, and Ukraine."

"Projection," Alec muttered.

Katrina continued that after coronavirus broke, Russian biologist Igor Nikulin appeared on state-run television, contending the virus had been released in Wuhan to make the world think it was a Chinese bioweapon. He also said it was a population control measure by a secret global government, *and* that the CIA did it.

She noticed Ward's smirk. "The coronavirus wasn't a bioweapon," she declared.

"Well, not an *American* one," Ward chirped.

"Ward has a point, but not the one he thinks he's making," Raquel declared. "The Russians already have well-developed bioweapons programs. We've seen their assassinations with the Novichok nerve agent. In 2019, they had an explosion at the State Research Centre of Virology and Biotechnology in Siberia—this is where they keep their anthrax, Ebola, and smallpox. We're lucky they didn't have another Chernobyl."

"And if they had, they would do everything possible to ensure the world never knew," Katrina noted. "Dee, who's the mercenary team?"

Dee looked down at the printout.

"The Zhelezo Volki—the translator's note says 'Iron Wolves.'"

Katrina and Raquel exchanged a grimacing look that implied, "Oh, not these bastards."

Raquel rose from the conference room table and began the three-step process of unlocking her office door. Once inside, she headed to one of the giant piles of papers, books, folders, and other materials in the corner.

The fallout from Edward Snowden and painfully successful hacks of the Office of Personnel Management and Departments of Justice and Homeland Security left Raquel with a newfound enthusiasm for old-fashioned, noncomputerized methods of storing information. Over time, the corners of her office had more and more paper files, some written on a typewriter whose ribbons were put into the nightly "burn bag." She increasingly preferred her own old-school system to hinder anyone looking through her papers trying to steal secrets. Everyone else called her security system "being disorganized."

"Your filing system is going to give me OCD," Dee marveled.

"You're the reason I'm afraid to keep anything on a computer, hack-of-all-trades!" Raquel shot back. "Ahead of the curve looks like behind the curve when you're about to lap someone. Muhammad Suleiman, the guy who tried to build that nuclear reactor in Syria, used envelopes sealed with wax for all of his sensitive materials—Middle Ages stuff. In another five years, I'll probably be back to using quill pens."

Raquel started tearing through a series of cardboard tubes in the corner.

"Back when it was just you guys off running around exotic foreign capitals, I kept track of the competition in a way that can't be hacked," Raquel declared, just short of smug. "Everybody's got their version of us—either the just-barely-on-the-books or off-the-books team to use for tasks that are never meant to be on the evening news. China has the 'Hulijing,' or 'Nine-Tailed Foxes,' named after a legendary shapeshifting trickster. The Iranians have the 'Simurgh'—it translates to something like 'Blue Phoenix.' North Korea's got the 'Dokkaebi,' the goblins."

Ward shook his head. "Man, we really need a better brand. Whose dumb idea was it to call us the 'Dangerous Clique'?" Alec glared at him.

Raquel finally selected a cardboard tube labeled "Eastern Europe." "And Russia has the Iron Wolves."

Alec perked up. "That doesn't make any sense, wolves aren't made out of iron."

"It sounds better in Russian," Katrina said softly. "The *Zhelezo Volki.*"

Alec tried to repeat the Russian words back to her, and it sounded akin to "the Cello Volkswagen." She shook her head and rolled her eyes at his egregious pronunciation.

Katrina had kept up with the agency's files on the Iron Wolves and rattled off an impromptu briefing. They had started out as a small group of covert operators who cut their teeth under ChVK Vagner, a private paramilitary security firm owned by oligarch Yevgeny Prigozhin, who has close personal ties to Vladimir Putin. She laid out that Russian private contractors had fought alongside government forces in Syria, eastern Ukraine, Sudan, South Sudan, Yemen, Gabon, and Central African Republic. Ukrainian officials called them "the little green men" for their masks and uniforms with no insignias.

"Three Russian journalists died under mysterious circumstances investigating this company," she said matter-of-factly.

"Oh, only three?" Ward chuckled. "What, are they getting soft over there?"

Katrina painted a portrait of Vagner's ruthless efficiency, particularly on the battlefields of Syria and Ukraine. Vagner gave the families of its men relatively generous death benefits, which could be canceled and reclaimed if any member of employee's family leaked information about the group's operations. Vagner gave Putin and his wealthy allies a separate private army whose overseas operations would be largely unnoticed by the Russian public or media.

"Apparently the company's leadership is tied in with some new religious movement—ah, what was their damned name?" Katrina closed her eyes and tried to remember. "The Slavic something—"

Alec's eyes lit up. "Wait, the Slavic Native Faith?" Katrina snapped her fingers and nodded. He let out a long sigh. "Do you know who those guys are?"

"Why am I never surprised when you know about a weird cult?" Raquel asked.

"Ever since Atarsa, it's seemed like a fruitful area to research," Alec quipped. "These are *bad*, bad dudes. The Slavic Native Faith is ethnonationalist paganism. Think of it as a religion that's really compatible with Putinism."

Raquel winced. "Great. More zealots who aren't afraid to die."

"Yeah, certainly sets the stage for fanaticism, but that's not the part that worries me," Alec nodded. "It means they think killing other people is just the natural order of things. A lot of this stuff sounds like it's down the road and around the corner from all the stuff that shaped the Nazis—power of the collective will, the importance of tying your identity to blood and soil, rejection of Christianity as weak and sexually repressed, a belief that one culture and one ethnic group represent the human ideal and are threatened by decadent outside influences..."

"I know that tune. Old Russian habits die hard," Katrina sighed, thinking of her parents' departure from Bukhara.

After the group had shared a collective shudder, Katrina refocused the conversation to what was known specifically about the team called the Iron Wolves. They had always been a small group, a mix of military, intelligence, and skilled civilians who requested permission from Vagner to spin off and become independent contractors. As Vagner grew and became more active, both private sector employers and the Russian government desired a smaller, lighter, more easily mobilized group of operators, acting in civilian identities for targeted assassinations. The CIA's Russia desk believed both Vagner and officials in the Russian government received kickbacks for the group's work for outside clients. The Iron Wolves were suspected in connection to several assassinations all over Europe, but particularly in Ukraine.

***

Had the Soviet Union not grown into one of the great monstrosities of the twentieth century, Katrina's family might have remained in Bukhara. Jews had come to Bukhara sometime around 800 B.C.—allegedly one of the lost tribes, depending upon whose legend you chose to believe. Some old neighbors in New York City had told Katrina she looked like she had "Mongol blood" and might be a descendant of Genghis Khan, who conquered and largely destroyed Bukhara in 1219. The history of the Jews of Bukhara was an alternating current: brief periods of tolerance and prosperity in between long stretches of wide-ranging oppression and humiliation. In the 1700s, Uzbek rulers would ritually slap Jews in the face when they paid their taxes, one more state-sanctioned indignity to reinforce their underclass status. Katrina's father told stories that treatment under the Uzbeks was so harsh, her forefathers perceived the arrival of Tsarist Russia in 1868 as a form of liberation. Within a generation or two, the Tsar's policies proved to be so much worse that her ancestors were rooting for the Bolsheviks.

Her ancestors' bad luck continued, convincing Katrina at a young age that no one should ever count on someone else promising liberation. Liberate yourself, because no one else will.

The Bolsheviks may have been the worst deal for her ancestors. The Red Army arrived in 1920, and Uzbekistan officially joined the Union of Soviet Socialist Republics in 1924. Not too long after that, Stalin concluded that all religions were a menace and the hammer dropped on the Jews fast and hard. Synagogues were closed. This was the beginning, her father used to say, of living "between two scorpions"—fearing anti-Semitic Muslims on one side and anti-Semitic Soviet authorities on the other. In one more dose of bitter historical irony, some Bukharan Jews sought to escape to a safer life in central Europe—heading right into Germany and Austria as the engines of the Holocaust were warming up. Others immigrated to what was then Palestine and would soon be Israel. Katrina's grandfathers were drafted into the Red Army, as was her father. After the Six Day War in 1967, apparently both scorpions were angrier and more eager to sting than ever. Abraham Leonid knew he wanted out and started exploring any and all options of getting out of the Soviet Union.

Had life in Bukhara not been so brutal, she might have remained and become some shopkeeper's wife. Russia was a ghost that had haunted her family—but ironically one that had driven the Leonids fleeing to a better life than they ever would have enjoyed if they had remained. Congress had passed the Jackson–Vanik Amendment that drastically increased the pressure on the Soviet Union to permit Jewish immigration, and her father saw that as a miracle.

Until her teen years, Katrina's appearance and faint accent inevitably brought questions of "where are you from?" and she learned that Americans were wary about Russians, believing Russia to be a country that consisted entirely of onion domes, parades of nuclear missiles, and bearded men in big furry hats doing the squatting Cossack dance. When she met Alec, she concluded his understanding of the country was largely shaped by *Red Dawn* and comedian Yakov Smirnoff. (On an early date,

Alec cited Smirnoff: "Many people are surprised to hear that they have comedians in Russia, but they are there. They are all *dead*, but they are there.")

Katrina knew the modern Potemkin Village that was Russia's façade of normalcy. It was a police state that was completely in bed with organized crime, full of Communist nostalgia and statism but awash in energy industry cash and oligarchs. It was an autocracy, plutocracy, kleptocracy, and arguably kakistocracy— rule of the worst or most unscrupulous—rolled into one. Perhaps most important, Putin's Russia believed that rules were for other countries. Every method of leverage over other countries was worth experimenting with—threats to cut off energy exports or increase prices, cyberwarfare and hacking of sensitive systems, social media messaging, diplomatic pressure, bribery, threats, unofficial deployment of military forces, and when the opportunity arose as in South Ossetia, Abkhazia, or Crimea, outright invasion. When Russia spotted a goal it wanted, it used methods few other countries dared—polonium poisoning for foreign leaders, nerve agents for overseas dissidents, hack and disclose the personal emails of hostile political figures or the recorded phone calls of diplomats. The Russian state had not yet encountered a consequence it feared, and its leadership continually probed to see where the opposition's redlines were.

The FSB had even broken into a US military attaché's house while he was away and killed his dog. The message was clear: we can do whatever we want to you, and no one can stop us.

The Iron Wolves promised more of the same.

# CHAPTER EIGHT

WEDNESDAY, APRIL 15
SALZBURG, AUSTRIA

The Swiss company Crypto AG got its first break with a contract to build code-making machines for US troops during World War II. With the money from that lucrative contract, Crypto AG became arguably the world's preeminent maker of encryption devices, generation after generation, setting the pace of technological innovation in secure communications. The company's clients grew and grew until they included the governments of more than 120 countries included some particularly secretive ones like the Vatican, India, Pakistan, Libya, and Iran.

Crypto AG was also a secret subsidiary of the Central Intelligence Agency, who had access to every communicated message on any device ever manufactured by the company.

The US National Security Agency also gained access to everything Crypto AG made starting in 1970, and that was just one part of their bag of tricks. The NSA had "zero-day exploits" in software, that the manufacturers themselves didn't know about; sometimes the NSA would learn about exploitable weaknesses in software from criminal hackers and then use those loopholes themselves rather than warn the software manufacturers. US Cyber Command shut down the notorious Russian Internet Research Agency "troll farm" in Saint Petersburg on Election Day for the US midterm elections in 2018.

Starting in 2014, the Dutch spy agency—the General Intelligence and Security Service—managed to get secret access to the infamous Russian hacking group "Cozy Bear," widely believed to be affiliated with and compensated by Russian intelligence. The Dutch hacked not only the Russians' computers, but also the surveillance cameras inside their workspace, according to former US officials. They not only could monitor the Cozy Bear hackers' efforts to break into American systems, but they could see their faces.

Dee had told enough of these stories to condition her teammates to learn "if it is typed, it can be hacked." And that when the NSA really wanted to break a firewall, they can do so—it was simply a matter of resources and time. And so when the entire National Security Agency tried to figure out when and where the Iron Wolves mercenary team would be meeting with someone—a meeting that could involve exposure to biohazardous materials—it took just six hours to determine the meeting was for noon on Wednesday in the courtyard of Salzburg Fortress.

***

On a sheer rocky hilltop, four hundred feet above the city and presiding over it like an ancient master, was one of Europe's mightiest castles, never stormed and never conquered: *Festung Hohensalzburg* literally translated to "High Salzburg Fortress."

The courtyard was a public place; even with the worldwide collapse of the tourism industry, Salzburg Fortress would have locals exploring its halls and towers and parapets and striking views of the mountains and valleys of eastern Austria.

To the extent Americans knew anything about Salzburg, they remembered it as the setting and scenery for the classic film *The Sound of Music*. But the only children that ran through Mirabel Gardens singing "do re me" were from the families of deranged American tourists in the old days. They arrived expecting to find cheerful singing nuns, naval captains who needed to learn to love again, and Nazis with unexpected car trouble.

Modern visitors were often surprised to learn that the names and ages of the children were changed, three children were deleted from the story, and that "Edelweiss" was not a traditional Austrian folk song but was written by Rodgers and Hammerstein in 1959. Those who consulted a map would ask how landlocked Austria had a navy and learn that the real-life Georg von Trapp had been a World War I submarine captain in the navy of the Austro-Hungarian Empire, which controlled the port city Trieste (now part of Italy) and the Slovenian and Croatian coasts. Tourists would also learn that escaping Nazi-dominated Austria by hiking to Switzerland is not an option, as the border is roughly two hundred miles away. In fact, locals chuckled at the film's closing scene, as the family is depicted hiking in the direction toward Germany and the Kehlsteinhaus, known to Americans and the British as Hitler's "Eagle's Nest."

Salzburg was picturesque with a spectacularly preserved city center, twenty-seven churches, and one of the world's great art festivals—befitting the birthplace of Mozart. But it was home to roughly 150,000 people over twenty-five square miles, not counting tens of thousands of tourists who were in the city at any given time. The most recent census counted a bit more than one thousand Russian expats in the city and it was a popular place with Russian tourists; the Iron Wolves would blend in and likely had multiple FSB agents on the ground to call for assistance if needed.

\*\*\*

Wilhelm Ballett hadn't liked this idea from the start.

The Russians were unlikely to pay Hell Summoner's exorbitant fee. The Russians had suffered from the virus as much as anyone else—not even their gargantuan propaganda efforts could hide this. Like the Iranians, they were unlikely to be willing to pay twenty billion dollars, or ten billion dollars. Maybe they could be convinced to buy some virus designed to target Chechens—assuming they hadn't bioengineered one of their own already—but the Chechen genetic stock was surprisingly diverse. But knowing the Russians, they would place the order, steal the virus once it was concluded, and dump the decapitated bodies of Hell Summoner and his team in a river somewhere.

But Hell Summoner's negotiations with the best prospect had slowed, and he wanted to see if the Russians were serious.

Ballett saw the redhead.

And the others watching her. They weren't cops. He knew cops; not so long ago, he had been one. Bundespolizei, specializing in biological chemical weapons. These others looked military from their gait and body posture. There was at least one giant Russian, who had to be the muscle; his sloped forehead suggested his ancestors had skipped a few steps during the evolutionary process. Some bearded older man was pretending to read his phone, but kept watching the redhead, and not in the lustful, old man way. This meeting might as well have a flashing neon sign saying THIS IS A TRAP above it.

Ballett was going to have no part of this. He acted like he was bored by the old castle and headed for the exit.

*** 

Zoya Zakrevskaya could tell something had gone wrong. Hell Summoner—or whoever would be meeting on his behalf—was late, and the word from the Serbians was that the man was punctual, professional, and direct. First five minutes, then ten, then fifteen.

Even worse, Zoya was certain that others were watching her. A couple over on one side and the red-bearded hillbilly in sunglasses on the other side. She had seen a man leave a few moments ago—was that Hell Summoner? He had seemed to be sneaking glances at her. If it was, she needed to find him, and get him away from this other team watching her.

Zoya spoke into her microphone.

***

The giant Russian, Dimitri Guryanov, moved from one side of the courtyard to another, positioning himself between the red-bearded American and the exit. Dimitri smiled at him. The American smiled back at Dimitri. They simultaneously moved their hands to their jackets, putting their fingers on the triggers of their concealed weapons.

Meanwhile, the older Russian, Sergei Markov, approached the couple of the tall American man and the Eurasian woman and in surprisingly good English asked for directions.

"I don't speak Russian," Alec grunted, eyeing the hard-featured man, who seemed to be carved from stone.

"I'm speaking English," Sergei responded.

"Then I don't speak English," Alec shot back.

Katrina spotted Zoya moving for the exit at a far-too-fast-for-casual pace and stepped away from Alec and Sergei. Sergei reached for her arm; Alec reached into his jacket pocket and pointed his pistol at the Russian.

Katrina pulled her arm away from Sergei's grip. Zoya looked back, saw Katrina, and broke into a sprint. Katrina kicked it into her top gear, and the chase was on.

***

Katrina tore through the courtyard and hallway, and past the marionette museum whose aging displays reminded her too much of her encounter on the horrific Island of the Dolls in Mexico City a few years earlier. She had to descend two flights of narrow and uneven stone stairs against the flow of a few tourists, and nearly lost her balance and stumbled off the last step. She tried to make up speed as she saw a flash of red disappearing into the tram—and nearly knocked over a pair of French tourists, skidding to a stop before the closed tram doors. The French tourists yelled at Katrina, and this caused Zoya to turn around, inside the tram, wondering what the commotion was about. A striking Eurasian woman, breathing heavily from running, was glowering at her in frustration.

Through the glass, Zoya's wide blue eyes stared at Katrina with trepidation. Colored contacts, Katrina suspected, like her suspiciously too-vibrant red hair.

Katrina thought about trying to somehow jump the walls and slide down the tram tracks, but she concluded she would probably break a bone trying to make the jump. There was nothing to do but wait for the ascending tram to arrive, disembark its load of tourists, and take that one down, and hope she could still spot Zoya in the crowds. At least the trams had huge windows, making it easy to watch for that redhead emerging from the small station building halfway down the hill.

***

Alec smiled in satisfaction at the Russian, until he realized that Sergei's other hand was also in the pocket of his overcoat ... and the overcoat had a similar bulge from the point of a concealed pistol.

"We are at a ... what is the term? Mexican standoff?" Sergei declared with a grim chuckle.

Alec shook his head in disapproval. "I'm just appalled at your culturally insensitive language."

He tried to glance over Sergei's shoulder. "Ward, a little help here would be nice."

Ward was looking up at his own considerable Russian foe. "Buddy, I've got the Muscovite Andre the Giant in my way, and he looks about ready to eat me."

Alec and Sergei stared at each other, a bit like gunfighters in a showdown in the Old West. Neither one wanted to fire—that would bring attention, and cops, and probably botch the whole operation. But neither one could let the other one escape.

Finally, they heard Dee's voice in their earwigs. "Don't worry, fellas, I've got this."

Ward stared at Dimitri. Alec stared at Sergei. For about a minute, nothing happened.

"Dee, today would be nice," Alec said to the air.

"Attention, Iron Wolves," Dee's voice rang in the earwigs of Dimitri and Sergei. "You have far too much faith in your boys at Spetssvyaz." That was Moscow's equivalent of the NSA, in charge of all of the secure communications of the Russian government. "I've hacked your communications, and you should know that we have a team of snipers with you in their crosshairs. You're going to show us your hands, and then you're going to let the men in front of you walk out the front door."

"This is a bluff," Sergei declared, nervously looking around at the roofs above him. "If your snipers were here, I would have laser sights upon my chest."

Dee laughed. "Who do you think we are, JSOC? We stopped using laser sights years ago! This is the CIA, Boris. We use combination ultraviolet-infrared sights now. You guys won't develop that for another five years. You can't see them. I would order a demonstration, but... well, you wouldn't be around to appreciate what you saw, if you catch my drift."

Sergei looked around again, then stared at Alec. His American foe seemed to be smiling far too confidently.

Sergei muttered something in frustration, and Dimitri removed his hand from his pocket. Ward smiled with satisfaction, and then Sergei did the same.

"Wise choice," Dee declared. Alec gave Sergei a little salute as he stepped past him.

"Dosvedanya," Alec chuckled.

\*\*\*

"Nice bluff," Alec said, as they scrambled past the marionette museum.

"Yeah, I'd get far away from them as soon as you can," Dee said, watching from the drone high above. "They're going to figure out there are no snipers pretty quick. Katrina is at the bottom of the hill, approaching something labeled on the map 'Stiftsbackerei St. Peter'—I guess it's some kind of very holy bakery."

Much to Alec and Ward's frustration, Katrina had already descended in the other tram and so they sprinted downhill the long way. This meant running on heavily sloped switchback paths, paved with gray square stones, just wide enough for one vehicle. They skidded, slipped, stumbled, and tumbled all the way down to a cemetery and catacombs of Saint Peter's monastery.

They heard Katrina shouting something in Russian—and it sounded like an order to stop.

Ward and Alec tore through the cemetery passing a row of large crypts, owned by local wealthy families and protected behind elegant wrought iron gates.

Alec suddenly recognized where he was. "Hey, this is where the Von Trapps hid—"

They followed the shouts, leading to an alley behind a building that was the oldest bakery in Salzburg. Back in the twelfth century, a grain mill had stood on this site, with the mill grinding the grain into flour powered by the building's surprisingly large waterwheel, about fifteen feet in diameter. The waterwheel still turned, although the source of the water wasn't visible. It was here that Katrina had seemingly cornered Zoya.

"Stop!" Katrina shouted, breathing heavily, her pistol raised. To Ward's ears, it sounded like, "*Ya ne khochu prichinyat' tebe bol', no ya opredelenno sposoben prichinit' tebe bol!*"

"What did she say?" Ward asked.

For once, Alec understood. "'I don't want to hurt you, but that doesn't mean I'm not capable of hurting you.'"

Zoya looked intimidated but didn't raise her arms or offer any other sign of surrender. She breathed heavily... and with each passing moment, grew more confident that Katrina did not want to shoot her.

Finally, after calculating that Katrina was not likely to shoot, the Russian spy tore off her jacket, threw the brown leather satchel over her shoulder like a sling, climbed the fence, and dropped down the six feet, approaching the pool of water churning underneath the rotating waterwheel.

"Don't!" Alec and Katrina cried simultaneously.

She took a deep breath, crossed her arms across her chest and crossed her legs, and disappeared into the dark water.

"Now I know how Tommy Lee Jones felt in *The Fugitive*," Alec murmured.

Katrina swore, then started tearing off her jacket. She dove in after Zoya. Alec saw her black hair momentarily suspended around her like the branches of a tree before she disappeared into the depths.

"Katrina! Wait! Wait!" He nearly doubled over with gut pain from running. "Is this what it feels like when I do something without discussing it with her?"

Ward, a half-second behind, ran to the fence, drew his Beretta, and tried to see under the waterwheel. "I can't see a damn thing down there."

Alec looked around and found a sign that said WASSERRAD. "Dee, where does this water go?"

All he heard through his earpiece was her long whistle as she marveled at some new information. He stared at Ward with incredulity. "That can't be good."

Dee took a deep breath herself. "There's an underground canal that runs from Salzburg fortress down to the city, called the Almkanal. It doesn't come out to the surface until…Universitätsplatz, University Square."

Alec looked around the tiny courtyard housing the waterwheel and tried to remember which arched doorway he and Ward had entered. "Where the hell is that?" Ward got out his phone and tried to find himself on the map.

"It's just past the old church," she directed.

Alec threw up his arms in frustration. "Dee, I'm in Europe. Every building in every direction is an old church!"

"Back the way you came, down Festungstrasse, into the square, make a left. The canal bubbles up to a small fountain in University Square, about a thousand feet to the northeast of the waterwheel."

Alec stopped, and for a moment, wondered if he should run back to the waterwheel.

"Wait, did you just—a thousand feet? Dee, nobody can hold their breath for that long! They're both going to drown down there!"

"They're in the process of draining it for cleaning in two weeks—there's likely a bunch of air pockets all along the way," she said. "Katrina will be fine. Probably."

***

Katrina was certain this was one of the worst decisions of her life.

The only good news was that the water was clean. There was almost no light, just the occasional glimmer of illumination from above, what must have been a storm drain or overflow outlet. Frigid cold bit at her fingers and toes. Her clothing suddenly felt heavy, and she remembered why people usually swam in bathing suits.

The tunnels were narrow, rarely more than three feet wide, and she couldn't tell the depth, but she guessed eight to nine feet. The top of the underground tunnel seemed to be curved in occasional spots, but mostly straight and flat. The current was surprisingly strong, and it carried her quickly, but occasionally she would slam into a slab of marble sticking out from the wall.

Swimming underwater, occasionally she saw or felt some smaller branch tunnel going off, usually too small for a human to fit through. There was no sign of Zoya—Katrina wondered if she would bump into her oxygen-deprived body at some point. She was swimming blindly, hoping the current was taking her closer to some point where the tunnel ceiling rose enough to hide a pocket of air. But to the extent she could get any sense of level, it seemed to be sloping downhill.

Most people could hold their breath for thirty seconds before gasping. Women's lung capacity was about four liters; men had about six. Harry Houdini amazed audiences by holding his breath for three to four minutes; the modern world record holder had held his breath for twenty-two minutes. The difficulty for most people underwater wasn't the lack of oxygen, but the buildup of carbon dioxide in the blood. Katrina was fairly certain she could do two minutes, probably three, and maybe even four. But the exertion of swimming was making it more difficult. She reached up to the top of the canal tunnel and felt for air ... but her fingers just felt wet and scraped against the top. She realized the friction from her hand was slowing her down.

She felt the pressure in her ears building, her lungs burning, failing to resist the urge to exhale the air in her mouth through little bubbles. She marveled that she had somehow not encountered

Zoya yet. She relaxed, trying to save energy and let the current carry her, but then hit another large stone sticking out from the wall, slamming her shoulder against it. Pain shot up and down her neck, arm, and back, and she involuntarily released more of the air in her mouth. She kicked with her legs, trying to get her head and mouth to the top of the tunnel—desperately hoping some air pocket would be around the next bend.

The good news is she did find one—the bad news is that gasping in the musty air in the barely inch-high air pocket got water in her mouth and nose. She got a gust of delicious oxygen but then immediately coughed, and lost control of the body, as the current swept her farther. She tried to swim back to the air pocket, but the current was too strong, and her muscles were straining.

***

Alec and Ward tore through the narrow streets, momentarily relieved that the post-virus economic woes meant Salzburg had a fraction of the tourists it would normally have and that they didn't have to fight their way through crowds.

"It's back toward the river, then a left," Alec said, constantly checking the map on his phone, the street names, and trying to figure out what separated a "square" from just a larger-than-normal space between old buildings.

"There's the church she was talking about!" Ward said, pointing.

"No, that's the Franciscan Church! We just passed Margaret's Chapel, the cathedral is over there, just past this one is the Collegiate Church, and University Square's just beyond that!"

Ward's head spun back and forth, trying to figure out which old baroque church was which. "God, you Catholics were the Starbucks of the Middle Ages!"

Alec suddenly paused at a storm drain. "Honey, we're coming to get you!" he shouted down.

\*\*\*

Katrina couldn't hear anything under the water beyond rushing sounds and the increasingly deafening sound of her heartbeat in her ears. Each heartbeat was using that little bit of oxygen left in her, each pump trying to cope with more carbon dioxide than her body was designed to handle.

But she saw something lighter up ahead, and that persuaded her that she could get out of here. Light could only come from the surface in this ancient canal system, she told herself, and if the surface was visible, air had to be one final push away. This was worth spending her last bit of reserve energy, whatever strength her tired legs and burning thighs could muster, kicking, kicking, trying to get higher—

*Gasp!* Somewhere before the light, her head surfaced above the water, discovering a sizable pocket of air in a small round chamber along the underground tunnel's path. She inhaled, coughed, and breathed deeply for a full minute. She looked at the roof of this little room within the tunnel—she saw four streaks, finger-width apart, digging through the moisture, algae, and moss on the chamber ceiling. Zoya had surfaced in this room as well, moments earlier, Katrina realized. The Russian agent was probably still alive. Beneath her, around her feet, she could feel the strong current, and there was a faint light form the direction of downstream. She took several deeper breaths, then dove under again.

She saved her strength and let the current carry her farther, discovering that the canal emptied into a larger underwater chamber, and a pump was forcing the water up into a tube. Light poured down into the water in a circle like a spotlight. A grate had been removed, and water flowed down. Beyond the roar of the rushing water, she heard a weird discordant sound, almost like off-key singing, and she wondered if a choir was performing in the square above her.

She pushed herself up the diagonal tunnel, against the current, by bracing first both arms and then both legs against the sides of the waterway; spider-climbing was what her instructors had called it. The water flowed over her but not overwhelmingly. She climbed up into a small fountain, and she opened her mouth and deeply inhaled fresh air as she emerged to the surface again. But she instantly knew something was terribly wrong—the noise that had been growing louder was not singing.

It was screaming.

She sloshed around in the small, teardrop-shaped fountain, about a foot below the stone of the university square. An iron fence with diagonal slats surrounded it; Euro coins slipped beneath her feet and fingers. A small circular spraying fountain was at the wider end of the teardrop, a large marble slab stood beside her, and at the point of the teardrop, where she emerged, the water disappeared back into the fountain's pumping system. She wiped the water from her eyes, shook the water from her ears, and tried to figure out what was going on with the screams.

She peeked over the precipice. The fountain was on the west end of a narrow square, filed with a slew of farmers' market stalls. But whatever the square had usually been, today it was chaos, as vendors, customers, passersby and tourists had all scattered upon seeing... four men with handguns pointed at each other.

A trail of water led from the fountain toward that direction, where a soaking wet Zoya was crouched down, her leather satchel hanging and dragging below her. She seemed to be trying to make it toward her Russian teammates, Sergei and Dimitri.

Behind her, Alec and Ward, their own guns raised. The farmer's market crowd had dispersed in screams at the sight of the men's guns.

Katrina reached into her pocket and pulled out her Beretta, inspecting it closely. Modern well-built firearms were designed and engineered to fire normally when wet, even underwater, but she needed to be sure.

***

Moments earlier, Ward and Alec had sprinted into the square, spotting Zoya, who had been standing like a mermaid in the fountain, to the amazement of the locals who immediately started taking pictures of the busty redhead in the wet black top. The two men had gotten halfway across the square, intent upon grabbing her, when Alec barked a frantic warning: "Russians! Russians!"

Upon seeing them, Dimitri and Sergei drew their Udav pistols but did not fire. The market vendors and customers screamed and fled, as Alec and Ward drew their own Berettas.

"You have no snipers," Sergei declared. "If they existed, they would have shot me. Now I tell you, goodbye for good." He leveled his weapon at Alec's head.

And then he felt a shot whiz past his head. He turned and saw Katrina rising from the fountain, her own Beretta having fired the shot. In Alec's eyes, it was as thrilling as Ursula Andress coming out of the water in *Dr. No*.

Within a few moments, the tense standoff calmed. The sound of approaching sirens prompted both the Americans and Russians to holster and hide their weapons and find a quiet corner to ask questions first and hopefully avoid more shooting later.

"Our orders were to find the Summoner of Hell and capture him," Sergei declared. "He didn't show. I suspect he spotted your clumsy surveillance and aborted the meeting."

Katrina stared at him with withering suspicion. "Your way of protecting the world, huh? Grab the guy, and keep his virus-engineering knowledge for yourselves?"

"I am certain your mission is the same," Sergei replied. "A weapon this dangerous and terrible cannot be allowed to fall into the hands of the one government in the world that used atomic weapons in war. The world will be endangered until this virus is in safely in the responsible, peaceable, benevolent hands of Vladimir Putin."

Alec scoffed. "Crimea, Georgia, the Baltics, and Ukraine could not be reached for comment."

Katrina shook her head in exasperation. "In a better world, you and I would be working together. You would think the way both our countries suffered from the virus would have taught us a hard lesson about the need to cooperate in response to threat like this. But it's your move, comrade. Some of my colleagues always expect the worst of you. This is your chance to prove them wrong."

For a moment, Sergei stared at her, chewing something over. "Your idealism is as beautiful as you are. And that would indeed be a better world. But we live in this world, where our experience with the American idea of partnership always turns into subservience. Hard power, soft power—in the end it all comes down to power, and this method of building a virus—if it truly exists—is power. And any power that is not in the hands of my government is a power that can be used against it."

The Americans and Russians parted ways, now knowing that they faced even more pressure to find Hell Summoner as quickly as possible. Each team now faced the threat of the other.

# CHAPTER NINE

SALZBURG HAUPTBAHNHOF TRAIN STATION
NEAR THE GERMANY–AUSTRIA BORDER
THURSDAY, APRIL 16

The work of tracking Hell Summoner started with a review of drone, satellite, and hackable closed-circuit cameras near Salzburg Fortress. Dee and a small team at NSA reviewed all of the available footage, seeing who was in that spot at that time and who looked like they might have been there to meet Zoya. The good news was that the entire time Zoya was in the courtyard, only about two or three dozen people milled around the space, and a couple of them were families with small children. The children could be ruled out, but Raquel noted that because they knew nothing about Hell Summoner's true identity, she couldn't rule out that he would bring children to help his cover.

From there, Dee had to isolate the available facial imagery and see if it matched anything interesting in the extensive databases used by the NSA and CIA. For Americans, photos taken by their state departments of motor vehicles could be shared with the FBI, the Department of Homeland Security, and Immigrations and Customs Enforcement. In addition, US government agencies contracted with Clearview AI to use their groundbreaking facial recognition technology that the company boasted could match any photo to more than three billion images from Facebook, YouTube, Venmo, and millions of other websites.

A few years earlier, Google had begun developing similar technology but scrapped the program, fearing it could have Orwellian applications. Other companies charged in where Google feared to tread. When Dee showed off the new technology to the rest of the team, a shudder went through them, knowing that foreign intelligence services were likely developing their own versions. The world's cities teemed with surveillance cameras, and not even Dee's experimental self-replicating viruses that tried to corrupt any data files that matched their personal criteria would work on this scale. In the years to come, the Chinese Ministry of State Security, Russian FSB, and GRU and other hostile forces were likely to start building up detailed and accurate files on their travels.

Katrina observed that the ability to take a picture of someone, and instantly connect that person's face to all public records and social media accounts was basically a gift-wrapped present to every obsessive creep around the world.

"Darn kids today," Alec grumbled. "Back when I was younger, stalking you took effort and dedication and actual legwork!"

Clearview AI made sorting through the figures in the crowd relatively easy, and one figure quickly stood out: a tall man with classic German features of high cheekbones and a strong chin and a bit of stubble. He subtly looked around while seeming to tour the courtyard, appeared to notice the Russians, and then walked away. Once the team knew where to look, his gait seemed just a little too tense and his pace a little too quick for the circumstances.

But it was the man's identity that suggested a jackpot: Wilhelm Ballett had recently retired from service with the German federal police in Berlin, and his specialty was coordinating responses to chemical and biological weapon threats.

With that information, Dee found it relatively easy to track his movements through his cell phone—his train ride from

Salzburg to Berlin, his home, his favorite coffee shop. The following morning, he traveled just outside the German capital, then turned his cell phone off. As far as Dee could determine, the phone was completely off, with the battery removed.

But Ballet turned off his phone just outside the access bridge to Spandau Citadel.

Spandau Citadel was fortress outside of Berlin, one of the best-preserved Renaissance military structures of Europe. The site had a history going back a thousand years; one section uncovered medieval Jewish gravestones believed to have been stolen from a nearby Jewish cemetery and used as building materials. Surrounded by a moat, it opened up as a museum and historical site in 1989, hosting exhibitions, festivals, concerts, weddings, and corporate events. But the coronavirus pandemic forced a temporary closure that turned into a permanent one. After the pandemic ended, the German government faced a seemingly endless economic downturn and budget crisis. Berlin couldn't justify paying the costs of subsidizing the museums, when doctors and hospitals loudly complained they hadn't been fully reimbursed for Herculean services rendered during the crisis.

Within half an hour of determining that Ballet's trail ended at Spandau, Dee informed the team of a change to the plan. "Stern wants eyes inside that Citadel. She's already got me booked on the next flight out to meet you, in case they've got computers on site. I can't wait for the nasal probes."

"Make sure Stern doesn't tell the Germans about any of this," Raquel declared. "If we've got two moles we haven't caught, how do we know the Germans don't have a mole in their ranks?"

*** 

The train from Salzburg to Berlin had slightly more modest health checks—temperature and saliva swabs, but no deep nasal probes. Those with elevated temperatures were required to board the last two train cars at the rear. No clickety-clack of the rails; Rail Europe ran smoothly and quietly, if not as inexpensively as it used to run. The quartet had half a train car to themselves.

Alec sighed. "Berlin, again. We always end up going back to Berlin. All the trouble in the world seems to come from there. I guess *Counterpart* was a documentary."

Raquel looked thoughtful.

"Some guy I know developed a theory that early human trade routes and settlements were shaped by forces anchored in physical locations, but that couldn't be measured by any physical means yet. Any spot along a river could be fine for a permanent settlement, but certain spots inspired and generated human creativity and ingenuity. But these might just be self-perpetuating cycles—beautiful art and architecture in Rome inspires more artists and architects to congregate there, creating more beautiful art and architecture each generation. Berlin's complicated history means it just attracts more spies, more spy hunters, more radicals…"

"More nut jobs, more trouble," Ward grumbled. "What's this guy looking for at Spandau Citadel?"

The foursome reviewed open-source information about the site on their phones. As their train neared its destination, Alec chuckled in response to something he found.

"Hell Summoner is a student of history," Alec declared.

Off his friends' confused looks, Alec explained that early in the reign of the Nazis, a young chemist named Gerhard Schrader had been assigned to develop new insecticides, to help the Reich strengthen its domestic food production.

Schrader started trying to combine phosphorus and cyanide. In an early effort, he poisoned himself so badly, he spent three weeks recovering in the hospital. But he kept working on diluted versions, and shortly before Christmas in 1936, he made a breakthrough, presenting it to Nazi officials at Spandau Citadel: Preparation 9/91—lethal against insects but also capable of killing a man in twenty minutes. Schrader had stumbled onto a poison more powerful than mustard gas. They named it "tabun," inspired by the German word for *taboo*; their research had officially crossed the line from legitimate pesticide research to chemical weapons research banned by the Treaty of Versailles. Within a few years, Schrader built upon his research from tabun and believed he had an even more powerful nerve agent—one that could kill a man with just a few drops. He and other scientists—Schrader, Otto Ambros, Gerhard Ritter, and Hans-Jürgen von der Linde— realized they had created one of the most effective poisons to ever taint the earth, and named it after an acronym of their initials—S for Schrader, A for Ambros, R for Ritter, and IN from der Linde.

Today the poison was known as "sarin."

"Spandau Citadel was the birthplace of sarin gas," Alec declared grimly. "Ironically, while the Nazis invented it, they never used it. So did the Soviets, the British, and us. Saddam Hussein used it against the Kurds, Assad used it in Syria—"

"Aum Shinrikyo used it on the Tokyo Subway," Katrina declared, her eyes suggesting she was mentally somewhere far away at that moment.

They grew quiet once the train pulled into the station.

The quartet picked up their conversation after renting three rooms and gathering at the back table of the hotel restaurant. The lingering dearth of business travelers left the hotel operating with a skeleton crew.

"When our Russian friends closed in on Berlin, the Nazis used the citadel as part of their defense," Alec added.

Ward chuckled. "You're telling me we're actually going to raid an old Nazi castle? Castle Wolfenstein?"

Raquel nodded and sighed at Ward's gruff giddiness. "Yes. We are literally hunting down a man in the high castle."

"Nazis!" Alec exclaimed, a bit of his old theatrical personality returning. "I hate these guys."

"Everybody hates those guys," Katrina declared, not getting the reference. "Ward, how do you want to play this?"

Ward examined satellite photos of Spandau Citadel on his tablet and saw a great selection for a secure operating base. Occupying an island in the river Havel, the citadel was a giant square with tall bastions and diamond-shaped peninsulas at each corner.

There was only one bridge across the moat, meaning only one way inside and out. The corner to the left of the access bridge was the Julius Turm tower, 113 feet high, a perfect sniper's nest. But Ward concluded an intruder could swim across, and then climb the fairly high walls, or get over by climbing one of the trees outside of the wall that reached above it on the west side.

"Nighttime," Ward declared. "Stealthy."

***

Dee arrived the next day, and she brought four Black Hornet Nano surveillance drones, four-inch-long mini-helicopters that looked like a slightly bulky dragonfly from a distance. Within a few hours, the allegedly closed citadel was getting regular visits from alternating pairs of small drones whose hum was designed to simulate the sound of dragonflies.

The drone footage showed the footprints of four people in the compound. Heavy tarps covered what must have been a variety of vehicles, one that was large enough to be the cab of a tractor trailer. It was impossible to determine whether the vehicles were new arrivals or left behind when the citadel complex closed. The tire tracks did not seem fresh. The person who set up the tarps had ensured they covered the license plates as well.

No one appeared to be active during the day; if anyone was inside, they were perhaps in the fortress's labyrinthine underground cellars and tunnels.

The main gate was locked from the inside with a drop-bar—a heavy piece of wood—that appeared to be a recent addition—probably not a part of the site's security when it was a tourist attraction. Ward concluded it would take considerable force to break the wood and smash the doors open; even a car at high speed probably wouldn't be enough.

Dee determined the citadel remained connected to the city's power grid but was not connected to the outside phone lines or Internet. She did not see cell phones pinging off of nearby towers. Wilhelm Ballett seemed to have dropped off the face of the earth. His phone remained off, he wasn't at his apartment, and he didn't seem to be anywhere else, either.

That afternoon, Director Stern updated the team's orders: if they determined that Hell Summoner and/or any potential viruses or biohazardous material were on the scene, they were not to engage. She had asked the Secretary of Defense to put US Special Operations Command Europe in Stuttgart on standby to raid and contain a potential bioweapon laboratory. The German Chancellor would only be called and notified of the operation after it had begun.

Katrina and Ward formulated the plan. After nightfall, they would swim across, climb the tree, and hop over the wall. Alec and Raquel would cover the front gate. Dee would operate from a rented van parked across the street and watch them with the drones. Once they were atop the trees, Dee would interrupt the power, hopefully resetting any electronic security measures that Ballett and the others had set up inside the walls. After Ward had established an overwatch position, Katrina would open the front gate, and the quartet would inspect the facility for signs of Hell Summoner or any virus production.

They would indeed call SOCOM—eventually. Ward joked he would appreciate their help mopping up after he eliminated the threat.

At nightfall, the Spandau Citadel did not, as Ward hoped, remind him of Castle Wolfenstein. Unlike a gothic Nazi mountain fortress, the citadel's walls stood red brick and white stone, broad and flat, and the front entrance looked more like a distinguished English manor house than a set for an Indiana Jones movie. The wind was mild, and the water in the moat offered a still mirror. In normal times, before the pandemic, decorative lighting illuminated the outer walls. Now the citadel just stood as a quiet, massive tomb, sitting at the intersections of the Havel and Spree rivers.

The clouds intermittently interrupted the moonlight, giving the intruders a near-ideal environment of pervasive darkness. Shortly after ten in the evening, Katrina and Ward slipped into the water with a gentle splash. They swam fast and climbed fast, ending up on the northwestern projecting corner of the fortification known as "Bastion Kronprinz." They found a smooth ramp that led down toward the courtyard, approaching a building labeled BERLINER ARTENSCHUTZ TEAM BAT.

In a van across from the citadel complex entrance on Am Juliusturm street, Dee tensely listened to the Katrina's breathing when one of her drones, currently hovering inside the courtyard, suddenly shook violently and crashed to the ground. The last images, from an awkward angle looking up from the ground, was Wilhelm Ballett's face—and then the bottom of his foot.

The second drone suddenly stopped sending a signal as well. Dee shouted into her microphone that whoever was inside knew they were coming.

And then she heard the loud, high-pitched jamming squeal in her ear.

***

Katrina, Ward, Alec, and Raquel all heard the painful screech and yanked the nubs of their earpieces out. Everything had gone south fast.

Inside the walls, Katrina and Ward heard movement and noise up ahead, closer to the gate. Ward swore that he didn't want to engage until he could get back to a higher point, either the outer wall ramparts or the second floor of a building, providing protective cover for everyone else.

"Anybody could be in any of these buildings," he pointed. "If we go farther into that courtyard, we might as well hold up bull's-eye targets and let them see how sharp their aim really is."

By the gate, they heard someone shouting in some language that wasn't distinct, and then the sound of a vehicle's engine starting.

"No time," Katrina concluded. She pointed at the Berliner Artenschutz building.

"Clear that building, make sure no one's waiting to pop me from there as I move through the courtyard," she ordered. "I'll watch the other side and try to make sure whoever's driving doesn't get Alec and Raquel. Don't argue, just do it!"

Ward didn't like the plan, but he promptly ran to the alcove of the Artenschutz building and kicked in the door.

***

Outside the walls, Raquel and Alec seethed in frustration. The doors were far too thick and sturdy to kick down or shoot down. Hell Summoner, or Wilhelm Ballett—for all they knew, they could be the same man—knew they were coming. Alec wondered if he could shoot through the divide between the wooden doors enough times to break through the drop-bar.

It didn't matter—within a few seconds, he heard scrambling noises and a heavy *thump* indicating someone had lifted the heavy drop-bar. Someone was coming out.

"Get behind me!" he whispered to Raquel. It was one part protective instinct, one part a desire for a free-fire zone in front of him.

Alec stepped back about two yards, squared his feet, and raised his Glock, ready to offer an excessive barrage at whoever came through the door.

And then a black tractor truck with purple-tinted windows smashed through the doors, gaining a full head of steam and nearly knocking the twelve-foot wooden doors off their hinges.

***

*Motormaster*, Alec thought, as he flew through the air, flying off the bridge, toward the moat as the giant tractor barreled down upon the spot where he stood a moment ago. "Motormaster" was the name of the evil tractor-trailer truck on the old *Transformers* cartoon series. He was like Optimus Prime, but a bad guy, and he always wanted to destroy his foes by running them down and smashing them in a head-on collision.

The monstrous machine that crashed through the entrance doors was not a giant robot in disguise—at least as far as Alec could tell—and that was just about all of the good news at the moment. The giant truck—a Kenworth K100 with sleeper—came within about a half second of slamming into Alec and pulverizing him into its grille like a masher pressing into a potato. Alec landed with an ungraceful splash and hit the stony bottom of the moat—not quite hard enough for a concussion or broken bones, but hard enough to leave bruises. He surfaced, gasped for air, and fumed as the tractor disappeared toward the city. Maybe someone would be able to track them on satellite. He suddenly realized that Raquel had been behind him ... and he wondered if the truck had hit her.

Then he saw her peering down from the bridge.

"I tried to shoot out the tires," she groaned. "I felt like Bambi trying to stop Godzilla." She helped him up the stairs adjacent to the citadel's outer wall—and then they heard a lone gunshot from inside—followed a moment later by three more shots.

***

The tractor truck had pulled away, but apparently someone on Team Hell Summoner had stayed behind. Katrina spotted a man—Ballett, she suspected—pulling back a second tarp and revealing a pair of motorcycles.

Katrina fired a warning shot over Ballett's head. Instead of surrendering, Ballett raised his gun and fired in the general direction of the muzzle flash he had glimpsed. The German scrambled back to the doorway, toward a building labeled "Zitadellen Wirtschaft." That building was adjacent to the stony tower in the southwest corner that Ward had wanted to use as a sniper's overwatch position.

Katrina scrambled over to the wall of the Berliner Artenschutz, then scanned the windows and parapets. Was Ballett alone? Where was Ward?

***

Once inside the Berliner Artenschutz, Ward was certain he could hear noises from the floor below him. The building was dark, and he flipped on night vision goggles. He found a stairwell and swiftly descended them.

The cellar appeared to be a series of surprisingly cool, slightly damp vault-like chambers; Ward wondered if he was stumbling into some ancient torture room. The sound behind the large door ahead of him—squealing? Scratching? Someone panicking or scrambling?—suggested lots of rapid movement. Ward wondered if Hell Summoner or someone on his team was trying to pack up a laboratory, secure some virus sample, or destroy evidence. Ward held his Glock with his right hand, reached for the door with his left, and tried to prepare himself for whatever could be on the other side.

Ward opened it, and for the first time he could remember in a long time, he let out a panicked yelp.

It was not a laboratory, as far as he could tell. This particular portion of Spandau Citadel, the cave-like Artenschutz, was a small zoo dedicated to species preservation, nicknamed the Fledermauskeller—"bat cellar." In addition to its status as a historic fortress, Spandau Citadel was also home to one of Europe's largest collections … of bats.

And all of them seemed to be flying at Ward at once.

# CHAPTER TEN

*B*ats.

Before the pandemic, Ward had thought bats were pretty cool—after all, they had inspired Bob Kane and Bill Finger to create Batman. But after learning more than he ever wanted to know about horseshoe bats in Yunnan Province, and the consumption of bats and pangolins in the wet markets all around Asia, and the Huanan Seafood Market, Ward now understood why most people, going back generations, found bats creepy and scary.

Humanity did not fear bats, and snakes, and scorpions and spiders and all the creepy-crawlies out of mere logic, reason, or careful study of venom and fangs and claws. At some point, some human being had to look at a lobster, what looked like a giant sea insect with long antennae, and said, "that looks delicious." No, the fear of the creepy crawlies came from deep within our brainstem, an echo of our ancestors' cries of warning, shaped by painful personal experience. Those experiences had become so horrific and painful that our minds instantly perceived a subconscious flashing sign screaming DANGER anytime we heard leathery wings flapping or smooth scales slithering in moonlight, or any beast baring fangs, or just something with too many legs crawling up our leg.

The recent pandemic retaught humanity that the natural world was constantly trying to kill it. The coronavirus had stopped the world and locked humanity in its homes for long stretches, and everyone now knew that somewhere out there, there was another virus just waiting for the right opportunity to jump into the next Patient Zero. SARS, MERS, Ebola, Zika—they were just the warm-up acts. Scott Gottlieb, a former US Food and Drug Administration commissioner, concluded that if SARS-CoV-2 had hit in 1918, and could only have been fought with the medicine of that era, it "likely it would have been far more deadly than the Spanish flu... far more fearsome." That pandemic in 1918 killed 50 million people. Almost everyone who had been intubated in the most recent pandemic would have died then.

But all around the world, as people adjusted to the quieter, more cautious, post-pandemic "new normal," they realized the world of viruses could throw another sucker punch at any time.

Bats shed viruses like the cloud of dust around Pig-Pen in the *Peanuts* cartoons. Their blood, urine, and guano could all carry viruses, and God help you if they scratched you. Touching a bat in the wild was Russian Roulette—at minimum a lengthy string of shots for rabies. You just hoped the bat you touched didn't carry a microscopic organism that could cut through a human immune system the way Lamar Jackson cut through opposing defenders. For all anyone knew, any given bat could be carrying the Andromeda Strain, Captain Trips, or the Techno-Organic Virus.

All of this was racing through Ward's mind as he stared in horror at the giant wall of diseased flapping wings coming at him—giant flying globs of infection. He ducked down into a ball, covered his head, and prayed.

\*\*\*

Wilhelm Ballett had wanted to double back through the Berliner Artenschutz, but he opened the door to that building and realized that all of the bats in the cellar had somehow managed to escape through an open door, flown up the stairs, and now flapped and fluttered around the entire building. He retreated back into the Zitadellen Wirtschaft restaurant and heard more gunfire, four shots. He realized his only escape route was up the Juliusturm tower. With assailants blocking the entrance gate and bats fluttering around, he figured his best shot at escape was jumping off the top of the tower and landing in the moat.

\*\*\*

"We should have left the van blocking the access road!" Raquel fumed as she and Alec cautiously advanced into the citadel.

"If we had done that, right now Dee would be a hood ornament," Alec quipped. He saw the pair of BMW S 1000 motorcycles that Wilhelm had just uncovered and methodically fired four rounds, putting one in each tire. The two bikes toppled to the ground.

"What are you doing?" she whispered.

"Nobody *else* is driving away from me tonight," Alec answered. He saw a familiar feminine figure across the courtyard. "Katrina!" He tried to shout and whisper at the same time, ending up with a volume that didn't work well for either purpose. "Katrina!"

Katrina emerged from the darkness, illuminated by the moonlight, glaring at him in disapproval. "If you keep yelling like that, someone will shoot you!"

From the entrance to Juliusturm tower, they heard someone trip and start swearing. They scrambled over and saw the feet of someone – Ballett, they suspected – disappearing up the circular stairs.

Alec, Katrina, and Raquel tried to stealthily take positions around the doorway leading to the tower's stairwell.

Alec realized someone was missing. "Where's Ward?"

Katrina looked around in concern. "He was supposed to be clearing—"

Ward suddenly shot around the corner. His speed and intensity could accurately be compared to a bat out of hell, because he himself believed he had just run into a whole bunch of bats out of hell. Ward skidded to a stop in the gravel and started heaving gulps of air; his three friends stared in ominous trepidation, wondering what force on earth could send Ward fleeing.

"Ward, you're the toughest guy I know," Alec murmured with a sinking feeling. "Anything that's got you running is probably going to make me pee myself."

Ward gasped for breath. "It … was …"

Suddenly a significant portion of the colony of bats emerged from the doorway behind Ward. Roughly ten thousand bats called the citadel home each year. When it was open for tourists, guides gave torchlit tours, with plexiglass separating visitors from the species—and their guano. The guides assured visitors that the bats were vegetarian, harmless, and "throughout history been the unfortunate victims of irrational fears of evil and disease." Of course, in light of recent events, the fears of a dread disease from bats didn't seem quite so irrational.

The quartet hit the ground and covered their heads.

"It's enough to make me yearn for the good old days of Snake Island," Katrina grimaced.

After a few minutes, the colony of bats dispersed into the German night. Katrina, Ward, Alec, and Raquel checked themselves for scratches, and sighed with relief upon finding none.

They regrouped and felt even more relief upon seeing Dee in the doorway to the courtyard.

She informed the team that Hell Summoner and whoever was in here had spotted her drones and apparently had prearranged some sort of top-of-the-line signals-jamming equipment on-site—a setup she was determined to see for herself. Dee added she had seen the black truck sweep around the corner and take off to parts unknown; the truck did not have a license plate.

"Don't waste a moment blaming yourself," Katrina instructed. "You're the best. I want you and Raquel to quickly and thoroughly go through here, to see if there's any sign of them working on the virus. Alec, Ward, and I will take care of Ballett up in the tower." The trio looked up.

"The rest of his team got away. That guy's totally going to jump for the moat," Alec predicted.

"Does that guy look like Greg Louganis to you?" Ward scoffed. "That's a hundred feet high and he's got to jump ... what, forty to sixty feet to hit the water, in a moat that's not that deep? If he tries that and misses, they'll be cleaning him up with a spatula."

"Unless that moat is 20 feet deep, we'll be cleaning him up with a spatula anyway, from the stone at the bottom," Katrina observed.

The team split into two groups.

Ward and Katrina methodically cleared the stairway, landing by landing, with Alec right behind them. When the trio arrived at the top of the tower, Wilhelm stood up against a parapet, holding a gun ... pointed under his chin.

"It's better if we can take him alive," Katrina whispered.

"I figure that's why he's posing like Kurt Cobain," Ward growled, keeping his gun leveled at Wilhelm. Sure, his target seemed suicidal at the moment, but Ward knew it could be a ruse and Wilhelm could turn his gun against them without warning.

"Why don't you put that gun down?" Katrina asked softly.

Wilhelm nodded and lowered it from his neck ... but he still held it at his side.

"Whatever you've done ... we can fix the problem, if you help us," Katrina said gently. "We don't want to hurt you. Right, guys?"

Alec and Ward lowered their guns by about a millimeter and offered an unconvincing "mm-hmm" assent.

"Are you Hell Summoner?" Katrina asked.

Wilhelm stared back and shook his head negative.

"He's a genius," Wilhelm declared. "He's ten steps ahead of everyone. He's going to change the world. You probably think he's mad, but I wouldn't have joined him if I didn't believe in him. His vision ..." Ballett shook his head. "Trust me, I was a cop. You'll never ...." His voice just drifted off.

Katrina exhaled slowly. This was confirmation; the trail was hot. But Ward found himself growing uneasy. Alec broke his stance, lowering his gun and wiping the cold sweat that seemed to be breaking out all over him.

"Damn you, you had to make this real, didn't you?" Alec fumed at Ballett. "I wanted this to be a con. I wanted this to be somebody trying to scam the world's worst regimes out of a fortune. Because if you guys really are cooking up Global Pandemic 2: Electric Boogaloo—"

The team heard Dee's voice in their ears. "Comms are back. Raquel and I found their jamming equipment and shut it off. Top-of-the-line stuff, I'd bet it was pilfered from NATO somewhere. And we found a small lab. Don't worry, there's nothing that looks like virus samples. But the whole place smells like bleach. That could be to kill viruses, or just trying to kill off any DNA evidence."

Raquel chimed in. "We can bring in a team to check out this place, but I think they took everything. But there's a whiteboard with something written ...'Haplogroup J-M267.'"

Katrina locked her eyes on Ballett. "What is 'Haplopgroup J-M267?'"

Ballett winced. Apparently, he hadn't wanted them to find that.

"Did somebody place an order for a virus?" Katrina demanded.

Wilhelm Ballett didn't say anything, and tried to maintain his glare, but both Katrina and Alec noticed a slight tightening around the corner of his mouth. He was trying to not smile—a gesture that Katrina and Alec interpreted as confirmation.

"What gene were they looking for?" she demanded.

Alec took steps closer to the German, apparently no longer concerned with the gun in Wilhelm's hand at his side. "What does that mean? Who has those genes?"

Wilhelm didn't answer, but Dee did.

"One second," Dee said, looking up the gene. "Oh, fu—this is bad. That branch of DNA is most commonly found in North Africa, Turks, Arabs, Iranians, Syrians, and quite a few Mizrahi Jews."

Ward let out a long, deep breath. "Goddamn. If Hell Summoner can really cook this up, he could kill millions of people."

Katrina and Alec looked at each other.

*** 

Inside the lab, Raquel felt like she wanted to vomit. "Mizrahi? Is that Sephardic or Ashkenazi?"

"One second, one second, I'm looking," Dee said, scanning through the document on her phone as fast as she could. "Mizrahi Jews are ones who trace their ancestry to the Middle East and North Africa…including…oh, God. Katrina, I'm so sorry. That includes Bukhari Jews."

Raquel felt a split second of relief that any virus targeting Haplogroup J-M267 wouldn't kill her. But it would kill Katrina.

\*\*\*

For a brief moment, Alec could see the vulnerability in Katrina's eyes, but she quickly recomposed herself. She wouldn't give Wilhelm or anyone else the satisfaction. His wife just shook her head and sighed. "Just one more person trying to kill me. They can take a number and get in line."

Wilhelm chuckled.

Alec suddenly started walking straight at Wilhelm, now completely ignoring that Wilhelm still had a gun in his hand. Ward's stance stiffened, Wilhelm's head square in his sights. "Wilhelm, you move that gun, I end you," he warned.

Alec fumed and pointed his gun right at Wilhelm's head. "Who's Hell Summoner? Where do we find him? Where did he go?" Wilhelm was momentarily surprised, but then just smiled. He started to laugh.

"Oh, you think this is funny?" Alec exclaimed incredulously, his eye twitching, a vein in his neck now visibly pulsing. "I'm more tied up in knots than Bettie Page right now, and my trigger finger is itching like I just spent the night feeling up a poison oak, so if you don't start spitting out answers, my next joke will slay you."

"I am not easily intimidated," Wilhelm laughed and shrugged. "Do you really think people who study and work with dangerous viruses are afraid of dying?" He kept giggling. "I've been expecting to die for more than two years now! Do you really think the thought of getting shot in the head scares me?" He laughed so hard he had to wipe tears. "I just had a gun under my own chin!"

Alec realized the absurdity of his threat, and started giggling, too.

Katrina stared at her husband in concern. "Alec?"

"I'm not afraid of pain, I'm not afraid of death," Wilhelm continued between laughs. "There is nothing you can do to me! And without the ability to threaten me … you have no idea what to do with me now!"

Now Alec was laughing really hard.

"Honey, he's right!" Alec giggled. He shrugged and holstered his gun.

"I can think of some things to do with him," Ward growled. He and Katrina exchanged a glance. Either Alec was trying to con Wilhelm in some way, or he was really starting to lose his marbles.

Katrina looked at her husband with deepening concern. "Alec, are you feeling okay?"

Alec kept giggling. "All this time, all of my feelings of guilt—I was worried that the world had been broken because I had killed too many people …"

He suddenly knocked the gun from Wilhelm's hand ot the ground and grabbed the German by the collar and belt. Wilhelm stopped laughing and looked at Alec with concern.

"Alec?" Katrina realized what Alec was about to do.

Alec's eyes grew wide. "Clearly, the world is broken because I didn't kill enough!"

With that, Alec hurled Wilhelm over the tower's parapet. Katrina had just enough time to start the "Nnn" part of "no."

Wilhelm screamed the whole way down—about two seconds until a *thud* ended his high-pitched cry. Ward looked over the side, eyes bulging.

"I suppose there's a small chance he might have survived," Ward murmured.

"That's okay, that felt really good, I might throw him over a few more times," Alec said with surprise and a smile.

"What did you just do?" Katrina gasped. "You shouldn't—"

And with that, Alec flipped out in a way his wife and best friend hadn't seen in twenty years. "What, I shouldn't kill him like that? Or WHAT? What, someone will try to make a virus to KILL YOU? I tried being a—" Alec made air quotes like a maniacal Chris Farley character—"'good person.' For almost two years, I managed to not kill anyone in this job! Look at how karma decided to respond to my newfound 'respect for human life'! *A virus specifically designed to kill you and people like you!* Katrina, love of my life, THIS is the worst-case scenario! Just what do I have left to fear? Just what else are the evildoers of this world going to throw at me that's gonna be worse than this? Aliens? A giant flaming eyeball in the sky with a cursed ring? A Sharknado? This is it, my love! This is the anti–Old Milwaukee commercial—it doesn't get any worse than this! Maniacs recklessly creating something I cannot see that could sneak into your body and take you away from me is my…worst…nightmare. Period! Full stop! This is the *Titanic*! This is Pearl Harbor! This is the 2008 Detroit Lions!"

Alec waved his arms madly and his eyes bulged. "The safeties are off! The guardrails are gone! A world where people are willing to try something as twisted and sadistic and psychotic as this is not going to get anything sane from me in return!"

Katrina stared, speechless, as Alec appeared to be having a full-scale meltdown. But Ward was smiling.

"There's the old Alec I missed," he said, beaming. "Welcome back, old buddy!"

"Oh, you and I are going to be very busy in the coming days!" Alec said, pointing, with manic enthusiasm. "Get in touch with your inner Rambo, my friend, because you and I are going to cut through everybody standing between us and Hell Summoner! By the time we're done, the Terminator's gonna think we're heartless, Charles Bronson's gonna think we were too merciless, John Wick's gonna think we were a little rough, and Martin Riggs is gonna think we're psychologically unstable! By the time we find Hell Summoner, Chuck Norris is going to tell tales about how badass *we* are!"

***

Raquel and Dee heard Alec's unhinged rant through their secure communications, and exchanged a confused glance down below in the makeshift laboratory.

Raquel stared up in disbelief. "I think Alec finally snapped."

Dee shrugged and tried to find the bright side. "At least he's making jokes again!"

# CHAPTER ELEVEN

OUTSIDE SPANDAU CITADEL
SPANDAU, GERMANY
DAWN, SATURDAY, APRIL 18

SOCOM stood down. The CIA would notify the German Federal Police about a potential biological weapons lab operating in Spandau Citadel, and were asked to help track a black truck that had emerged from the fortress in the middle of the night. A half a day later, the Bundespolizei found the truck in an empty lot, and determined the cab interior had been thoroughly doused the with bleach. No DNA evidence would be recovered. Satellite footage suggested three people emerged from the truck, went into a nearby parking garage, and then must have left in one of the dozens of vehicles that departed that morning—far too many to track separately. Whoever Hell Summoner was, he was exceptionally careful, and knew all the tricks that intelligence agencies used when searching for someone like him.

Back at the hotel, Alec's manic episode ended, and once his adrenaline gave out, he collapsed facedown into the bed. After Raquel had thoroughly updated Langley on a secure line, the rest of the team examined what they knew.

Hell Summoner was indeed a real virologist with considerable expertise, and he and his team had been researching viruses, possibly using the bats at Spandau Citadel. They had been researching Haplogroup J-M267, suggesting they had begun looking into how to engineer a virus that target North Africans, Turks, Arabs, Iranians, Syrians, and Mizrahi Jews.

"We can probably cross the Iranians, Turks, Arab world regimes off the list of potential clients," Raquel said. "No matter how nutty those regimes are, they're not going to spend a fortune for a virus that would kill off large numbers of their own populations. The Israelis can be ruthless, but they wouldn't touch this with a ten-foot pole. Our encounter with the Iron Wolves makes me think that the Russians aren't the customers, either. The Russian government could probably make its own virus—hell, they may have already."

"The most likely suspect to me is someone who wants to wipe out most of the Muslim world, and maybe a bunch of Jews, too," Katrina said, shaking her head with dread. "Probably a white supremacist."

Raquel looked down at her phone. "Yes ... but the world's got, what, almost two billion Muslims? Large swaths of the world's Muslims don't fit in the categories of people who have this gene. All the Indonesians and Malaysians and Bangladeshis. Doesn't sound like Pakistanis or Indians have those genes, either. Now ... the world has what, fourteen million Jews? Four or five million of those are Mizrahi? This seems like a very precise gene to target. Whether someone hates Muslims or Jews, they could have picked other genes more common in those particular populations."

"What if the imprecision is the point?" Ward asked, rubbing his chin through his beard. "What if somebody wants to start Armageddon in the Middle East, and he thinks the best way to light the fuse is a terrible virus sweeping through Israel, Turkey, and the Arab world?"

Raquel looked at him. "Dammit, Ward, every time I think I've grasped how bad this is, you find some way to make it worse."

"One other scenario we shouldn't rule out," Katrina said, raising her finger. "Way back with Atarsa, they killed my old source Rat by blowing up a café. It was an assassination, made to look like terrorism. No authority even started to look at their real motivation because they had been so conditioned to see bombings in public places as targeting society at large, not directed at particular individuals. What if whoever's behind this has a specific target—say, the Mossad, or the Jordanian royal family, or some other group—and their way of hitting that target is to wipe out whole societies?" Raquel and Ward chewed that over.

Alec stirred from the bed.

"Follow the money," he moaned. "Who's got a spare twenty billion around? Or assuming Hell Summoner could be talked into a lower price—even a billion?"

\*\*\*

Once word of the targeted gene got back to Director Stern, Langley and Fort Meade combined their efforts to retrace the steps of Wilhelm Ballett. If Ballett spoke the truth before Alec tossed him off the top of the tower, he wasn't Hell Summoner, but he was Hell Summoner's representative for in-person meetings and negotiations with clients. He had walked away from the Russians, but probably had met with the client who ordered up a virus targeting Haplogroup J-M267. The client had to be extremely wealthy, have animosity against Jews, or Arabs, or Iranians, or Turks, or all of the above, and would likely have some sort of criminal or underworld connection.

Within twenty-four hours, the CIA and NSA had tracked Ballett's travels and appearances on surveillance footage in public places to confirm four in-person meetings in four countries, adding that they could not rule out other meetings. But Dee argued that from the four meetings the agencies had uncovered, they only had three realistic suspects.

"The fourth one was an elderly Malaysian bank founder who periodically accused Jews of controlling the world financial markets, but I crossed him off the list."

Ward scrunched up his face. "Why'd you cut that guy slack?"

Dee shook her head. "He keeled over from complications of his coronavirus infection two weeks after meeting Ballett."

Ward nodded. "Okay, I guess that counts as an alibi."

***

Chronologically, Ballett's first meeting was with the dead Malaysian bank founder. His second meeting was with Renaldo Espino, an Argentinian media mogul. The third meeting was with Stanislav "Stanko" Radic, a representative of Bezbednosno-Informativna Agencija, the Serbian Intelligence Agency. Upon hearing that name, Raquel reacted with surprise and irritation, but refused to elaborate other than a terse, "I know his reputation, he's the scum of the earth."

The fourth meeting was with Vincent van der Groot, a Dutch billionaire, whose current location had not yet been determined. The NSA noted that their initial look at the financial records of the three men didn't indicate anything that looked like an effort to send a massive amount of money, though.

The group quickly agreed that van der Groot and Espino made strong suspects. The Dutchman's disappearance particularly intrigued Raquel and Katrina, but all four concluded Espino presented a unique combination of wealth, public expression of hatred toward particular ethnic groups, and an appetite for risk that approached the status of a mental disorder.

Renaldo Alberto Pablo Espino inherited a small media empire in Argentina from his father, a bright, hard-charging cigar-chomping gargantuan narcissist workaholic. The younger Espino turned his father's small chain of newspapers into a larger multinational one, expanding into radio and television stations, magazines, advertising agencies, billboards, and eventually real estate.

He relished and embellished his notorious reputation, telling stories of blasphemous trysts in the backs of churches, drunken tirades and fights at parties, and a wide circle of friends that reportedly included drug kingpins, underworld crime lords, madams, pimps, and all manner of unsavory types. Former Italian prime minister Silvio Berlusconi thought Espino was a fun guy but *molto in una volta*—"a lot all at once." A common joke among Argentina's wealthy was that Espino's obsessive promiscuity had left him with so many sexually transmitted diseases, some of them didn't even have names yet.

Espino had married a trio of supermodels, and none of the marriages had lasted more than two years and no one had detected even the slightest attempt at monogamy; a widespread rumor was that at his last wedding, he had a threesome with two of the bridesmaids. The rumor was considered plausible because the original source of it had been Espino. The billionaire had no legitimate children and, it was rumored, a phalanx of illegitimate ones, all carefully hidden away and silenced with confidential payments. At any given moment, Espino was suing a half-dozen enemies and being sued by twice as many. In a world where money and connections could tilt the scales of justice, Espino won far more frequently than he lost.

Espino liked to brag he had inspired the Dos Equis advertising campaign featuring the nameless "Most Interesting Man in the World," but the company insisted he had nothing to do with it. The beer company's denials became increasingly emphatic over the years, in part because Espino progressively embraced and touted obscure conspiracy theories he found on the internet. In recent years, Espino had used television interviews and newspaper columns to assert:

- America's military arsenal had an insurmountable edge because of technological advances spurred by the captured Roswell UFO held at Area 51.
- Networks of wealthy and powerful Satanists were at work in many countries, pulling the strings and practicing human sacrifice.
- The terrorist group Atarsa was a cult led by a group of Iranians who had been possessed or influenced by a demon like Legion from the Bible, who manifested on this plane of reality as either disembodied voices or a visions of a giant insect or insect swarm.
- A giant secret US government research facility is hidden underneath Denver International Airport.
- Jenny McCarthy was a medical visionary and the world would someday realize the indisputable immunology wisdom of the 1994 Playmate of the Year.
- Secret scientific experiments with time travel at the Large Hadron Collider near Geneva had altered reality and disrupted the timestream, making time move faster and slower at different times, creating the perception that time is passing more quickly as we age.
- The Central Intelligence Agency had been using a small team of operatives to assassinate terrorists and other suspected threats with minimal oversight for almost 20 years.

Ironically, Espino believed Jeffrey Epstein killed himself.

But for the past two years, Espino had been more increasingly focused on the theory that the world's economics were controlled by either Israel or Jews, and that Jews were the secret beneficiaries of most of the world's worst problems. He met with notorious anti-Semites, attended conferences of Holocaust skeptics, and lately had been touting his theory that the coronavirus pandemic had been part of an Israeli plot to depopulate the world.

Espino had been making powerful enemies for years and traveled with security measures fit for a head of state. He had fully expected kidnapping and ransom attempts, or someone enraged by his antics trying to kill him. Puerto Rico was more secure than most other places in the Caribbean or Central America, but he knew that someday someone might decide to come after him in one of his favorite homes.

Dee found one more reason to put Renaldo Espino atop the list.

Several years ago, Espino purchased a luxurious estate on the north end of Punta Santiago, a small coastal community on the southeastern coast of Puerto Rico. He had named his compound in Punto Santiago "Finca de la Imponente Virilidad"—"Estate of the Towering Manhood." But everyone else just called it "the Espino Estate."

What made this particular property stand out was that the beach was right across from a small island called Coya Santiago, colloquially known as "Isla de los Monos." No human beings lived on Coya Santiago, but the island was home to about two thousand rhesus macaque monkeys. They were not native; some off-kilter biologists had hundreds of them imported from India in 1938 and intended to study them in a controlled but natural habitat. The island's Primate Research Center had, until recently, ranked among the world's best. But the island hosted few visitors. The island's monkeys naturally carried Herpes B; left untreated, Herpes B could cause severe brain damage or death. Infections could be triggered by bites or scratches, or in the case of one particularly unlucky researcher, urine in the eye. That case was fatal.

For decades, the researchers studied the monkeys with minimal infections or fatalities. But several calamities hit Puerto Rico in rapid succession: Hurricane Maria, a long, slow economic recovery from the hurricane's devastation and the collapse of tourism, and then the pandemic. As funding dwindled, research trips to study the monkeys grew farther and farther between.

Recently local and national authorities determined the island's population of monkeys was declining from not-so-natural causes. Unidentified teams of men had sailed to the island, trapped them in baited cages, and smuggled them off to parts unknown. The belief in Puerto Rican law enforcement circles was that someone wanted research animals—or, the more paranoid cops theorized, someone wanted to weaponize Herpes B. One popular theory was that Renaldo Espino either knew who was behind it or was smuggling the animals himself, as the disappearances started shortly after he had purchased his estate.

And, Dee suggested, a supply of disease-carrying monkeys might be of interest to someone who wanted to develop a bioweapon.

"Isla de los Monos?" Alec asked aloud. "Island of the Hands?"

Dee shook her head. "Manos is 'hands' in Spanish. 'Isla de los Monos' translates to 'Monkey Island.'"

Alec threw down the file and flipped out again, unleashing a hurricane of profanity so scorching and blasphemous, Howard Stern would have told him to wash his mouth out with soap.

"Lions and tigers and bears, oh my!" Alec fumed. "First hunting after Atarsa got us stuck on Snake Island! Now Hell Summoner's got us going to Monkey Island! Please tell me there's no Honey Badger Island!"

# CHAPTER TWELVE

BALNEARIO PUNTA SANTIAGO
PUERTO RICO
WEDNESDAY, APRIL 22

Puerto Rico is a territory of the United States and has its own branch office of the Federal Bureau of Investigation. While the Dangerous Clique enjoyed a long tradition of minimal oversight, even they couldn't charge in, guns blazing, on American soil without a warrant or law enforcement partner. This meant the team's favorite—and really only—liaison with the Federal Bureau of Investigation, Elaine Kopek, would need to be present. With Elaine joining them, their work legally became part of the ongoing efforts of the FBI Joint Terrorism Task Force. When all was said and done, Elaine would submit paperwork that would offer a carefully-calibrated account of the team's actions that somewhat aligned with reality but was designed to bore any inspector general.

The coronavirus left its mark on this corner of the globe as well. At one point, Mexico overtook the United States in daily reported deaths; like in many other countries, the citizens and public health experts believed the real death toll was much higher than the official numbers—perhaps two or three times higher. When hospitals in northern Mexico were near capacity, desperate infected Mexican citizens crossed the border looking for help in the United States. Mexican health officials noted that the virus almost certainly had spread into the country from their northern neighbor, and lamented that they would have been well served by some sort of impenetrable security barrier that would have ensured no American could enter the country without going through appropriate health checks and testing, and mandatory quarantines if necessary. One Mexican politician asked the health officials whether the impenetrable security barrier they envisioned would be "big and beautiful."

The Mexican people's faith in the government wasn't high before the pandemic and the combination of bad judgment, inconsistent competence, and unconvincing spin only worsened the public's cynicism. In some corners of Central America, the cartels and local governments temporarily put aside their long-standing battles to pool resources against the virus, and in some cities, gangs helped enforce quarantines.

The collapse of the cruise industry and most tourism crushed the economies of the Caribbean nations. Crime and corruption exploded, and some claimed that shipping and tour boat companies had become pirates, robbing any other ships they came across. Government budget cuts meant the small local navies and coast guards mostly stayed in port. As Katrina had noticed in the *Time* magazine cover story, those with will and weapons like the Jaguar and Esmerelda could effectively take anything they wanted.

In Puerto Rico, the safety net that had barely held during the earthquake started to tear and fray during the pandemic. The poverty rate had already been 40 percent and then strict quarantine policies mitigated the spread of the virus, but also hit the legal economy with the destructive power of a wrecking ball. The unemployment benefit system was overwhelmed and distributed meager checks at a glacial pace. A virus breakout among workers in public school cafeterias and several food warehouses disrupted food supplies.

In the desperate circumstances, the island's illegal economy flourished at night—everything from medicine to meat to illicit drugs to nubile-bodied nocturnal companions to military-grade weapons could be obtained for a price. Cops who had always been clean started accepting money to look the other way. People had to make a living, and most honest professions had been effectively banned by the quarantine restrictions. Those who had money could arrive and set up personal fiefdoms protected by private security and live like decadent kings. The island started to develop a reputation as a wealthy man's limitless and lawless paradise. Perhaps an environment like this was catnip for a man like Renaldo Espino.

He purchased and fixed up a large compound just north of the edge of Punta Santiago, across from the north end of Balneario Punta Santiago, the public beach. The compound's lone publicly acknowledged entrance was a long driveway off Calle Dr. Vidal. After examining satellite photos, Ward characterized it as "your basic drug kingpin compound. I'll bet some developer built it on spec." Upon arriving in Puerto Rico, Ward said he would make a shopping trip while the rest of the team made surveillance runs around the roads to the compound.

***

Ward gleefully pulled back a tarp from the back of his rented truck, revealing a small arsenal. "Enforcement against arms smuggling's taken a hit since the quarantine. It was like Wal-Mart for small arms."

Alec whistled. "Please tell me these were the blue light special."

"Whoa, whoa, whoa!" Elaine interrupted upon seeing Ward's newly obtained near-armory. "I don't like the way this is heading. I know you guys are used to napalming jaywalkers overseas, but we are going to bring in Espino by the Bureau's rulebook."

Ward looked like his mom had called him inside to do homework, but Alec just rolled his eyes. His manic attitude from Berlin appeared to be more than a passing mood shift.

"Elaine, dear friend," Alec began. "I know you've got this law-and-order hyper-rational Agent Scully thing going on, and most of the time I love it. But the whole reason we're going after Espino is the suspicion that he's cooking up a bioweapon. This is not like seizing a pile of heroin. Did you read the reports from the Pentagon's Defense Threat Reduction Agency?"

He held up a thick stack of papers.

"Here's the short version: You can get killed by this crap *just by hoping that it doesn't kill you*. If I had my druthers, we would take off and nuke the site from orbit—it's the only way to be sure. So even aside from my general principle that I'm not going to strain myself ensuring the civil rights of human toe fungus like Espino are protected—really, I'm not even going to wiggle a pinky finger—I'm already meeting you halfway by not just hitting the estate with a thermobaric bomb and letting you sift through the charred wreckage for evidence afterward."

Elaine frowned. "That's big of you."

"He's a giver," Ward quipped.

Elaine looked heavenward, sighed, and put her hands on her hips. "How do *you* want to handle this, Alec?"

"The longer this raid goes on, the higher the risk that either Espino deliberately releases his organic artisan black-beans-and-ricin or it accidentally gets released and we're left praying none of us catch exploding eyeballs or something," Alec explained, unrolling the map developed from satellite photos. "Espino's a controversial billionaire with all kinds of corrupt deals. We knock on his door with a warrant, this guy disappears, and they destroy the evidence. This raid needs to go from zero to Ragnarok within ten seconds. Shock and awesome. By the time these guys realize they're under attack, we need to be so far up their ass that we can diagnose their prostate. We need to be all over them the way I wanted to be all over Katrina on our first date—"

"Okay, thank you, Alec!" Elaine cut him off. "Ward, you've done enough demolition to have your own HGTV show. What do you think?"

"We tried the light and stealthy touch in Berlin, and got caught with our pants down," he grumbled. "We would have been better off hammering the main egress point and turning the walls designed to keep us out as a barrier keeping our target in."

Ward ran his finger over various points on the map as Katrina approached.

"High walls on all sides, only one way in or out for vehicles. Probably other ways in and out, I'm guessing underground tunnels, connecting a safe room to someplace in the jungle outside the walls. But that's a slower way out, buys us time. Wall has barbed wire and separate wire with electrical currents running through it. Lot of security for just some rich dude's hangout. Really large Spanish Colonial house, four servants' cottages, and then this separate long building, no windows. Big pool, multiple hot tubs. Guy has a Dan Bilzerian lifestyle."

Katrina looked up. "Who's he?"

"The kind of man who couldn't handle you, honey," Alec chirped. "I'll bet this guy Espino's got so many STDs, the coronavirus took one look at him and said, 'you know, that place doesn't look healthy, I'm just gonna wait for the next one.'"

***

The first signal that something was amiss at the Espino Estate was when the property's power went out, and moments later, the on-site backup generator experienced a failure that the manufacturer guaranteed could not happen. A complete system failure on that scale would have required something on par with the National Security Agency choosing to hack into the generator's network and operating software and overwriting detailed and specific elaborate lines of code with the verse of Dr. Seuss.

With both the localized power grid and backup generator down, the estate's alarms and security cameras stopped working. Even more unusual, the local cellular towers stopped working at the same time, and the walkie-talkies of the guards only received static. It was almost as if a US government surveillance drone overhead was jamming all of their usable frequencies.

Even more strange, the nearest police station—the Distrito Naguabo station—found all of its communications equipment malfunctioning as well. Whenever anyone at that station or the rest of Punto Santiago picked up a landline phone, instead of a dial tone, the person heard a recorded message that declared an operation of the Federal Bureau of Investigation was underway near Route 3 and that everyone should avoid the area. The Puerto Rican police force swore about the FBI's arrogance and "Orwellian tactics" but were in no position to mobilize.

All of these mysterious system failures developed in a matter of seconds … right about the time that Alec and Katrina were approaching the rear wall of the compound.

*** 

"You said there was a door here!" Katrina frantically whispered. "I looked at the map and the drone footage, I told you there was no door here!"

"I said a door would be here, because we are going to *make* one!" Alec said cheerfully, removing a series of small canisters from his satchel.

"Alec, we do not have time—"

"Step one—paste in the shape of a doorway!" Alec narrated. "Step two: Aluminum powder from Etch-a-Sketches. I told you that stop at the flea market was necessary! Step three: Rust from iron wool. Who watched enough episodes of *Mister Wizard's World* to know what that combination makes?"

Katrina glared at him impatiently. Alec just smiled and lit a match.

"This is the formula for thermite, which burns at a couple thousand degrees, almost as hot as you, sweetheart," and he flicked the match. "Which, oh, by the way, might come in handy if we need to destroy some biological weapon inside."

Katrina raised her eyebrow. "But is it safe?"

It was nearly the last mistake Alec ever made, as moments later, the paste and materials started to burn white hot, scorching up and down the shape of the doorway, spraying molten thermite, eating through the concrete like it was balsa wood. Katrina had already backed away considerably, and Alec fell backward, crawling back even farther as flaming bits of melted, virtually liquefied concrete fell near his feet.

"Oh, Jesus, that nearly killed me!" Alec exclaimed. "I thought that I was going to look so cool! I was supposed to look like I was walking away from an explosion in slow motion!"

"Almost as hot as you, sweetheart," Katrina declared sarcastically with a satisfied smile.

But as the last bit of the thermite burned out, the pair gazed upon a perfect person-sized hole in the concrete wall.

"Innovative, but louder than we needed," Katrina concluded. She stepped through the doorway, and Alec was impressed at how she wasn't the least bit worried about brushing against the ember-like heat from the surrounding burned concrete, still glowing in some spots.

"If he's already in some tunnel, this has been a giant waste of time," she murmured.

"Nah, a guy like Espino's not running from his own house," Alec said, examining the contents of the shed. The long shed had two sets of double doors—one on the north side, one on the south. "He's going to hunker down and let the hired help check it out."

They checked their phones; Dee had ensured that the drone overhead was outfitted with thermal vision cameras, giving them a vividly colorful display of four men rushing toward the back of the compound, approaching the shed. Katrina glared at Alec; they had heard his homemade thermite burning through the back wall.

The four men were already splitting into pairs. Katrina signaled with her hand for Alec to head toward the north door and indicated she would cover the south.

"Fine, fine, I've got a three-point plan to deal with my guys!" Alec whispered back.

"A little less conversation, a little more action!" she whispered. She raised one of her two silenced handguns. She realized that once again, she was putting herself in a position to kill—but the bodyguards approaching had no intention of taking prisoners. The she holstered her gun. She put on her night-vision goggles and looked up. She checked her microphone.

"Ward, Raquel ... *now.*"

\*\*\*

The front gate of the Espino Estate was heavily fortified with stone walls, two giant heavy wooden doors that resembled a medieval drawbridge, and no less than four men at the nearby guard shack at any time. The moment the power went out, the quartet doubled as more of Espino's bodyguards and security men prepared for an emergency.

Inside the main villa, Espino and his men headed toward his "safe room" by the light of flashlights and smartphones.

But within a minute, they knew whoever was coming for Espino had to be the most fearsome enemy he had ever made. Because they kept hearing explosions at the front gate.

\*\*\*

The true prize of Ward's black-market weapons shopping had been a South African–made Milkor multiple grenade launcher—basically a giant revolver that required two hands to operate like a rifle and that fired as many as six 40-millimeter grenades up to four hundred yards at eighty-two yards per second. It was far more firepower than anyone could possibly need, outside of a war.

With each explosion, Espino's men found it harder to imagine who was attacking them. A routine kidnapping attempt might have been able to obtain one grenade. Two meant the attackers were surprisingly well prepared. Three suggested this was a major, well-organized effort, perhaps by a top-tier drug cartel. Six, in rapid succession, suggested that the attacker intended to start World War Three. The compound's metaphorical "drawbridge" had suddenly been shredded to burning wood and a pile of splinters. The front gate guards retreated, and the rest of the compound's security team was frozen in place. Espino had hired good men and paid them well. But six explosions, roughly thirty seconds apart, metaphorically also blew up the security team's existing OODA loop—Observe, Orient, Decide, Act. The new plan was a SCREW loop: Scream, Confuse, REtreat, and Wait.

The only guards who were still charging forward were the quartet responding to the reports of some flash or something burning by the landscaping shed in the rear of the compound.

\*\*\*

When the south door of the long maintenance shed opened, the first bodyguard blasted several shots around chest level into the shed. After a few moments, he cautiously entered, followed by another.

They entered, trying to see in the darkness. Then the first guard felt a sudden sharp stinging pain in his shoulder, spreading throughout his body in an instant, and tumbled to the ground with a yelp, followed by the second man. As they tumbled down and the guns clattered on the floor, dropped by their hands that felt like they had been covered by joy buzzers, they saw their assailant, hanging upside down from a rafter by her legs, holding a pair of tasers that had just jabbed their shoulders.

"Tus heridas no son mortals, pero puedo cambiar eso," Katrina declared over their groans. *Your wounds are not fatal, but I can change that.* "Estamos aquí por Espino, quédate abajo, hiciste un trabajo honorable." *We are here for Espino. Stay down, you did an honorable job.*

The two men seemed to groan in assent.

Meanwhile, several rounds pierced the north door—apparently the attacker was shooting through a padlock—and a moment later, the door burst open. The first gunman entered, pointing his handgun at the left corner, and scanning toward the right—

—when his head emerged past the door, a three-pronged garden hand rake pierced his face—hitting an eye, the side of his nose, and a cheek.

"Three points!" Alec shouted.

With his other hand, Alec shot through the door, toward the spot where the drone footage indicated the second attacker was standing. The man tried to dive, but it was too late—he was hit.

With a quick movement, Alec put two shots into the heads of each attacker.

"I know the job market is bad, but for God's sake, do not take work as a bodyguard to a bioweapon-making human snot-rocket!" Alec bellowed at the man with the rake, still stuck in his eye and cheek. "Every single alien hench-being working under Thanos knew the risks of taking that job!"

He turned his attention to the other door, where Katrina had climbed down and kicked away the guns from the two men she wounded. They groaned and twitched, still feeling their muscles spasm from the taser.

Alec approached and whistled. "*Shawking*, positively *shawking*," he said, trying to sound like Sean Connery in *Goldfinger*.

She rolled her eyes. "I think I liked you better before your nervous breakdown. Let's just find Espino."

***

Espino's guards heard both the explosions at the front and the gunfire from the back, and a sizeable contingent of them decided to respond to the sound of the shots.

"Okay, you cockroaches! You want to play rough? Say hello to my lil friend!" Alec shouted, drawing both his Glocks and unleashing a recklessly bold barrage of fire. "Technically she's my wife as well as my friend, and she's taller when she's wearing heels, but—"

"Alec, there are eight of them! Let's go!" She fired a few shots and then tore off toward the nearest building. The guards kept coming around the corner of the main house like clowns out of a car at the circus, and quickly realized Katrina had been right to look for cover.

He followed her as she ran into the long and strange separate facility that Ward had pointed out on the map. When he entered, she was at the top of a staircase.

"You lead them down there, I'll take care of the ones that chase me and rescue you!"

Alec stared up at her, indignant at her presumption that he would need rescuing. Before he could argue, he heard them coming and agreed to lead them into the downstairs hallway.

It was a bad move. The first steel frame door in the hallway was locked, as was the second, as was the third. Only the fourth one finally opened when he yanked on it as hard as he could. The room inside was dark. Just as the goons entered the building, Alec snuck in—and hoped Katrina would be all right upstairs. He closed the door behind him and turned the deadbolt.

Then he heard inhuman cries and commotion in the darkness in front of him.

He finally lit the room with the flashlight on his cell phone.

The room was stacked, from floor to ceiling, with metal cages the size of pet crates. In fact, some *were* pet crates. Inside every one of the seventy or so cages was at least one rhesus macaque monkey. Some had two. Except at the end of the hall, where two of the cages had tumbled off the top of the stack, and a quartet of little monkeys were trying to squeeze through the bars—one had managed to get a third of the way out.

Alec stared in horror. Espino was involved with animal smuggling. And he had a room full of monkeys, all likely infected with herpes B, who could infect you with the disease just by peeing on you. One scratch, bite, or contact with shedded viruses could lead to a fever, headaches, brain damage, and death. Maybe the antiviral medications could save you, maybe not. And stressed monkeys shedded viruses even more than normal. Alec pulled his shirt over his nose and mouth.

He then recoiled as he felt rounds hitting the steel frame of the door. The commotion seemed to be sending the monkeys into a frenzy. Alec felt a tug on his pant leg and realized a tiny arm from a monkey had reached through and tried to grab him.

He frantically scrambled away from that cage. "Take your stinkin' paws off me, you damned dirty ape!"

He instinctively aimed his gun at the little monkey who had reached out at him. "Bedtime for Bonzo!"

But he couldn't pull the trigger. The monkey looked as terrified as he was.

For a moment, Alec wondered if he should uncage the monkeys—keeping in mind that he would make it extremely likely they would be shedding viruses like mad—and then unleashing them upon the guards. Eh, no, Alec realized; that was a surefire way to get a lot of bullets and monkey blood flying around.

But he realized he couldn't do it even if it might work and save his life. The monkeys were simply reacting to their environment. "A monkey's just a monkey. It's just instinct. doesn't even know it has a disease."

He desperately tried to think of a new plan... and then he realized that for all the shouting he was hearing on the other side of the door, the gunfire had stopped.

And then his foes... just knocked on the door.

"Nosotros rendición," they shouted. It sounded like Espino's goons were offering him a chance to surrender. Alec thought for a moment. They could be lying or trying to trick him. But the longer he stayed in the monkey cage room, he more he risked contracting a potentially deadly virus.

He yelled. "All right, I'm coming out. Don't shoot." He thought for another moment. "Por favor." As if good manners might save him.

But he opened the door and found... four guards stood before him, their weapons on the ground, their hands in the air beside their head. He stared at them in confusion. He belatedly realized "nosotros rendicion" meant "we surrender," not, "we want you to surrender." But why?

Then he heard the guards' walkie-talkies, repeating a message in a woman's voice in both English and Spanish.

*"This is the US Federal Bureau of Investigation. We are raiding Renaldo Espino because he is financing the creation of a second coronavirus like SARS-CoV-2. We know his security team and staff did not know that the collected monkeys were being used for bioweapons research. Drop your weapons and come out with your hands up. You will not be harmed or face any criminal charges."*

***

Espino's chief bodyguard unlocked the door to the safe room adjacent to the master bedroom. When the door opened, Espino screamed a furious tirade about their betrayal.

"How could you believe these lies?" he shouted angrily at his men—or more accurately, men who had, until a few minutes earlier, been "his." "I would never work on another coronavirus! You know these policemen, they make things up and drag you into court over nothing!" Apparently, Espino's bodyguards had seen enough while in his service to conclude that his moral character was *not* so sterling and upstanding that he would be above attempting to develop another Covid-like virus and trigger another pandemic.

Ward was eager to slug him, but Katrina decided it would be easier to let him wear himself out by shouting and raging. Renaldo Espino pledged vengeance upon all the federal agents, that he would sue all of them, that he would sue the FBI and entire American government, and that the court would award him the American presidency as compensation. He pledged that his media empire would blacken the names of those who dared handcuff him and detain him. He pledged that he would come back with new men, loyal men, who would hunt down and capture them and throw them into the deepest, darkest prison— then he changed his mind and said he would use rockets to blast them into space. Finally, after about twenty minutes of raging and fuming and screaming, he slumped down.

After a few moments of silence, Katrina walked over to Ward. "Gently," she instructed. Alec looked at her with irritation.

Ward strode across the room, grabbed Espino by the neck, lifted him up by it, and carried him several feet, throwing him hard against the wall and pinning him. Espino gasped and yelped and whimpered and wheezed.

"I said *gently*," Katrina said disapprovingly.

"I think he's got some bumps and bruises coming his way, honey," Alec interjected. "This guy locked up Curious George."

"That *was* my idea of gentle," Ward declared, glaring at Espino's terrified eyes. He released his grip from Espino's neck. "Now you give straight answers to the ladies' questions, or I will gut you like a fish and keep you awake the whole time."

That got Espino's attention.

"Those monkeys you're collecting from the island," Katrina began. "Are they for a man who operates under the code name 'Hell Summoner'?"

"No, no," Espino insisted. "I'm a businessman. I learned about the island, and there are a lot of, let's say, unsavory science efforts going on around the world. But Hell Summoner? No. No, no, no. I sell some here, some there, but never to anyone named 'Hell Summoner'—"

"See, funny thing you're doing there, H. Ross *Peron*," Alec interrupted. "You keep saying 'no,' but your head is moving up and down in a nodding motion. Our brains are wired to connect our verbal statements to our nonverbal indicators—we nod for yes, we shake our head for no. You're nodding because you mean yes, because your denial is a lie—"

Espino looked at Alec in horror. "No! I am shaking my head up and down for emphasis! It's different in my culture, you ignorant American!" He groaned. "I can't believe this! I'm being framed, set up," He rubbed his eye with the palms of his hands. "You fools are imagining things—"

"Now you're hiding your eyes!" Alec said. "First rule of lying, avoid eye contact."

Katrina suppressed the urge to roll her eyes again. Alec's methods to attempt to detect lies through nonverbal tics were not deemed accurate or reliable by the CIA's interrogators.

Katrina confronted him. "We know you met with Wilhelm Ballett. Tell us about Hell Summoner."

Espino's rage caught fire again. He shouted he could tell that they were Jews or working for the Jews, and that they had always been trying to keep good, hardworking, decent billionaire media moguls like himself down. He called Katrina and Raquel whores and bitches, and only the hardest glare Katrina could muster kept Alec's gun holstered. He swore at them, promised to do terrible things to them, to kill them and defile their bodies, to leave what was left of them hanging in the public square. For twenty minutes, he raged in self-pity about how he had built an empire and been repaid in betrayals and disrespect.

Katrina looked over Espino and fought the urge to succumb to contempt. She had done her research on him. He turned his small fortune into a large one by purchasing newspapers, magazines, radio stations, and websites, and turned them into salacious tabloids, full of gossip, innuendo, images of scantily-clad women—circulation went up, but their mental "nutritional value" went down. One of his television channels had specialized in hiring news anchors who had previously been adult entertainers. The coverage of a particular event, legislation, or scandal depended entirely upon Espino's previous relationship with those involved. Perhaps the politics of Argentina was always going to be messy, with angry protests, scandals, allegations of corruption, populist waves, and dirty backroom dealing. But Renaldo Espino was a one-man forest fire, burning through his society's intellectual, social, and moral capital. He wasn't as full-spectrum malevolent as, say, Vladimir Putin. But in his selfishness, narcissism, and eager embrace and promotion of nonsense conspiracy theories and hateful scapegoating did his own form of damage to his country and the world.

Katrina turned away from the others and swallowed hard. She understood why Ward wanted to throw him around by his neck again, and why Alec was already contemplating something ruthless. But punishing Espino meant nothing if Hell Summoner set off a nightmarish new era of perpetual biological warfare. Many people believed they would do whatever it took to achieve their goals but hesitated when push came to shove. Katrina intended to prove she meant it.

Certain Espino's tantrum had ended, she sat in front of him. He features softened so much, Alec did a double take.

"There is still time to change your story," Katrina told Espino. "I don't mean your testimony; I mean the story that everyone else tells about Renaldo Espino. You can be the man who saved the world from a threat instead of enabling it."

"People already love me!" he insisted.

"No, Renaldo. You just told us, and we know you were telling the truth. They envy your wealth and suck up to you. They are always trying to wheedle favors out of you. They see you as a resource to be exploited—not as a flesh-and-blood man of potential greatness. We all just saw how quickly your men—who you had paid well all those years—abandoned you, with no loyalty at all. They don't love you, even though you deserve it."

He nodded. Espino's demeanor had changed almost entirely. He slumped down.

"I try so hard to be a good person, but no one ever appreciates me," he whined.

"This is your chance to change how everyone sees you," Katrina said, putting a hand on his knee—a gesture that was more maternal than sexual. "You can be the one who illuminates the path to Hell Summoner, bringing him to justice and sparing the world a second calamity. No one thought you could do this— least of all yourself. But you can be the one who changed the course of history. Forget your wealth, your empire, your women, the scandals—this would be your legacy. This is what everyone would still be talking about, long after you and I are gone. The world will remember Renaldo Espino... the hero."

He nodded, inhaled, and puffed up his chest.

"I know the man you're looking for," Espino declared. "His representative came to me, probably two months ago. Maybe ten weeks now. He called himself 'Invocador del infierno.'"

"Oh, it sounds way better in Spanish," Alec exclaimed. He turned to Katrina. "*Buenos noches, la senora bonita. Me llamo 'Invocator del Infierno.' Hagamos arder nuestra cama con pasion.*" She tried to suppress a smile and failed.

"Tell us about him," Raquel commanded.

"I offered to sell him monkeys, but he wasn't interested. He said he had everything he needed already." Katrina and Raquel exchanged an unnerved glance upon hearing that detail. "He's a businessman. He wanted twenty billion. I told him I don't have anywhere near that kind of cash, liquid. And I really don't."

"You never met Hell Summoner yourself?" Ward barked. Espino shook his head.

"How did he contact you? How did you contact him?"

"He called my personal secretary from a burner phone."

"How did you leave the meeting?"

"I didn't have the money, but I had heard of some... other people who might."

Ward removed a hunting knife from his belt. "Who?"

"A few years ago, I met a group of..." He looked at Ward's knife. "They were mostly wealthy Europeans. They, like me, shared a frustration with the way Jews run the world."

Katrina and Elaine exchanged an exasperated look.

Ward gently poked at Espino with the knife. "Who's this group?"

"Powerful people in business and politics. I only went to one of their parties in Paris—I think Le Pen was there. I found them bores, and apparently, they weren't impressed with me. Every conversation at that party was a history lesson—Israel this, American Jewish lobby that, reparations for Palestinians, blah blah blah. Anyway, the man who brought me to their party died from the coronavirus."

Katrina and Raquel nodded, but Alec and Ward exchanged a skeptical look. "Who else?"

Espino looked up, trying to remember. "Some... Belgian? Or Dutch? He was very wealthy. Root. van Root, or something." The team exchanged another look of recognition, as Espino's guess sounded an awful lot like Vincent van der Groot. Ballett's meeting partners all appeared to run in the same circles.

"This group," Katrina said, staring at Espino firmly. "What it's called? What's their name?"

Espino got a faraway look in his eyes. "Formally? Nothing. It wasn't a strict organization; it was a bunch of wealthy partygoers. But they did have a nickname for themselves. I thought it was funny, because it sounded Hebrew or something..."

Ward poked him with the knife again. "Well?"

Espino recoiled from the poke. "Ow! All right! All right! They called themselves 'the Shedim.'" Katrina, Ward, and Alec didn't recognize the word at all, but Raquel's eyes widened, as if the name held some meaning for her.

Katrina rose to her feet.

"You've done something good with your life, Renaldo Espino, but your previous crimes must carry consequences."

She pulled Raquel aside. "What do you think, try to use him to find Hell Summoner or these Shedim?"

Raquel gave her a skeptical look. "Hell Summoner's already got his order and he's cooking up the new virus. Assuming we can force Espino to make the call, do you think Hell Summoner answers the phone? What does he need this fat toad for anymore?"

Katrina thought for a moment. "Espino reaches out, trying to warn him that Americans are after him and Dee traces the call—"

Raquel shook her head. "Burner phones, remember?"

Katrina reluctantly agreed that Espino was unlikely to provide a trail back to Hell Summoner at this point. "We need to stick him someplace where he can't have any second thoughts and put out some signal to Hell Summoner that we're after him— or let anyone in the public know someone's cooking up an ethnic bioweapon."

"Send him to Gitmo?" Elaine suggested.

"Don't worry!" Alec jumped up. "Ward, wrap him up for delivery. I've got a way to keep him very quiet." He wiggled his fingers and attempted to sound scary. "As quiet as a grave!"

"Don't kill him," Katrina told her husband.

"A permanent vegetative state technically counts as alive!"

\*\*\*

Ward held the blindfolded Espino in the hallway.

From the kitchen, Alec had brought ten one-gallon jugs of water.

"The only reason I'm not killing you is my wife's demand," Alec declared. "You've got ten gallons here; I'd recommend you conserve it. You're going to be in here for a long while. In the dark, alone, with no food, with no one coming to rescue you, all your wealth and power meaning nothing ... You're going to have a long time to think about all the ways you've hurt people over the years, Espino. You're probably going to wish we killed you."

Alec opened the steel-framed door.

"Oh, no," Espino recoiled from realization. "That smell!"

Ward and Alec had brought the mogul to the threshold of the monkey cage room.

"We're going to leave you with some company," Alec said cheerfully.

And then Espino heard the angry cries of about a hundred monkeys.

"Oh, try not to catch any viruses from those animals you poached," Alec chuckled gleefully. "I'm not going to kill you, Espino ... but I can't guarantee that the monkeys won't."

\*\*\*

The men threw him onto the floor of the room, and Espino heard the door slam shut. He removed his blindfold, but he could barely see anything. The monkeys around him continued to howl, and the sound waves reverberated in the suddenly claustrophobic, windowless, dark room. He nearly tripped over one of the water jugs trying to get back to the door and pounded upon it. He swore all kinds of curses and pledges of revenge. Then he smelled something new, breaking through the powerful odor of the monkeys and their uncleaned cages.

"What is that?" Espino cried. "What is burning?"

"It's nothing, Espino," one of the Americans shouted from the other side of the door. "We're just using a little bit of home-made napalm to fuse this steel-frame door shut."

# CHAPTER THIRTEEN

LIBERTY CROSSING INTELLIGENCE CAMPUS
TYSONS CORNER, VIRGINIA
FRIDAY, APRIL 24

The team now knew that Renaldo Espino was not Hell Summoner's client, but his mention of a secret organization calling itself "Shedim," and Vincent van der Groot's role in it, stirred their intrigue. But by the time the team had returned to Liberty Campus in northern Virginia, Director Barbara Stern and the rest of the seventh floor had already decided the Serbian intelligence operative, Stanislav "Stanko" Radic, represented the next most promising lead.

Stern's decision left Raquel cringing and shaking her head, oddly reticent to refocus the investigation on the Serbians. As the phone call continued, Stern grew unusually adamant and Raquel grew unusually resistant before ultimately relenting to Stern's authority.

Katrina watched Raquel on the phone and wondered what was going on. Katrina had come around to the idea that "Stanko" and the Serbian government made an unnervingly plausible suspect. Serbia had plenty of hardline nationalists who remembered and supported the efforts at "ethnic cleansing" in the 1990s. The country had been sliding back toward authoritarianism even before the coronavirus pandemic. Hooligans romanticized the imprisoned military commander Ratko Mladić, convicted of genocide and war crimes and imprisoned in the Hague. Denial of Serbian atrocities during the war was growing more mainstream. Serb's ethno-nationalists were no fans of Turks, Arabs, or North Africans, who had increasingly come through the country as refugees. The irony was that compared to some other parties of Europe, modern Serbs were not notoriously anti-Semitic—in part because the Holocaust wiped out the Jews of Yugoslavia so thoroughly, the hateful had few Jews around to target with their prejudice.

Right at the end of the call, a comment from Stern suggested that what really had Langley's leadership enthralled is that two decades ago, just as the Balkan wars had settled down, Stanko was "one of theirs"—in the sense that he had periodically traded information for money with a CIA case officer. But the quality of his information had deteriorated over time, and the sense was that Stanko was providing thinner and more dated intelligence and asking for more and more money. The CIA case officer determined Stanko wasn't worth it and after delivering an ultimatum, cut off the relationship.

When Langley transferred the old Stanko files to the Dangerous Clique's office at Liberty Campus, everything became much clearer to Katrina, Alec, Ward, and Dee when they read the name of the case officer from twenty years ago.

*Raquel Holtz.*

"I hated the guy the whole time," Raquel sighed. "I don't know exactly what he did during the Balkan wars, but I know it was bad. For a while his greed made him useful, and his need for the money outweighed his fanaticism. But I could just barely stand sitting across the table from that loathsome pig. This job requires us to work with some of the worst of humanity. Making handshake deals with blood-drenched hands made me hell-bent on getting into management."

"You were in Belgrade in 2000?" Ward exclaimed upon reading the file. "I was with the 75th Rangers in Kosovo. We were practically neighbors!"

She shook her head. "If you had met Stanko, you probably would have shot him."

The newer pages in Stanko's file stated that he had risen in the ranks of Serbian intelligence, and increasingly embraced fanatical Serbian nationalism and all kinds of conspiracy theories—mostly involving the Kosovars, the Croats, most Muslim countries, NATO, and either the Mossad, Jews in general, or any one of a number of mysterious international groups or factions.

Katrina groaned at she looked over the most recent transcript and translation of the Serbian's phone conversation. "Ugh. Every kind of nutty paranoid conspiracy, about the Elders of Zion, and 'Judeo-Bolshevism,' and the Rothschilds, and the Bilderbergers—"

"The Bilder-what now?" Ward asked.

"Bilderbergers," Alec declared confidently. "It's a chain of stuffed animal stores in the mall. You take your kid, and the kid selects how they want their stuffed burger plush toy to look, and dress it up, and—"

Raquel sighed as she read the tasking off her secure e-mail system. Stern wanted her to reach out to Stanko and attempt to set up a meeting. Raquel suspected Stanko hated her as much as she hated him, after she declared the CIA no longer found him a useful asset and wouldn't be handing over stacks of cash anymore.

"There is no way this bastard is going to just meet for coffee," she sighed. "How the hell am I supposed to get him to agree to reestablish contact?"

Katrina thought for a moment. "When all else fails, try honesty," she suggested. "Tell him the virus did a number on our existing sources of information in the region and we're looking to reconnect with old sources, offering a fresh start. Tell him we have a need that he might be able to meet, and that we're willing to pay a high price. Even the hardliners get greedy when Uncle Sam gets out his checkbook."

Raquel thought about it for a moment, and with the assistance of the NSA, placed an untraceable call to a number that Stanko thought only a select handful of associates had.

Stanko was surprised by the call, but to Raquel's shock, not hostile at all. Calling Raquel by the name he knew her by back then—"Rochelle"—he seemed surprisingly cheery and eager to meet after hearing her offer.

"We will meet at the tower in Nis," he declared. "You know the one. One of my favorite places."

She said she did, but Katrina could tell from the look on Raquel's face that whatever the tower in Nis was, her friend dreaded it.

Raquel looked unnerved when she ended the call and shook her head. "This guy's trickier than the devil, and a straight-up psycho. At one meeting, he told me this old Serbian folk tale about a monster called the 'bauk,' a bear-like creature that hid in dark and abandoned places and preyed on anyone who traveled alone. He said that the sound of a bauk approaching was like fingernails scraping against wood—and Katrina, he had this gleam in his eye as he told that story. He was friggin' *gleeful*. It was like hearing a fairy tale from Charles Manson." Katrina could tell that Raquel was shaken by the memory of that conversation.

"If I have to meet this guy, I want Seal Team Six standing around me and holding him at gunpoint."

Katrina started to think through whether something akin to that could be arranged.

***

The "tower in Nis" was actually a small yellow chapel, next to a park in the third-largest city in Serbia.

The Ottoman Empire conquered Serbia and ruled it for centuries, and several times the local Christian Serbs tried to overthrow their Muslim conquerors, with little success. In 1809, the local Serbs lost the Battle of Čegar, but not before inflicting considerable casualties upon the opposition. The outraged Ottoman commander of the city, Hurshid Pasha, sought a spectacularly cruel demonstration of brutality to break the spirit of the insurgency. His soldiers beheaded the bodies of the Serbian soldiers killed at Čegar, skinned the heads, filled the skin with straw, and sent the heads to the sultan in Constantinople.

As if that wasn't bad enough, Hurshid Pasha decreed the remaining skulls would be used to build a tower in the center of the nearest city. Stanko's "tower in Nis" was more commonly called "the Skull Tower," once featuring fourteen rows of seventeen skulls on each of the tower's four sides. When Hurshid Pasha ran out of skulls, leaving the tower's display asymmetrical, he ordered the execution of another thirty Serbian captives—952 skulls in all.

The Tower of Skulls indeed intimidated the Serbian populace at first, but over time the horrific demonstration of malice spurred more support for the insurgency. The Serbs retook the city of Nis by 1878, and the Serbs built a chapel around the tower, turning it into a monument and a grisly reminder of the sacrifice of previous generations of Serbs to overthrow foreign invaders. Fewer than a hundred skulls remained in the tower, but many Serbs still made a pilgrimage to the site—until it was closed during the pandemic, and only intermittently open since.

On this day, Stanislav "Stanko" Radic arranged for it to be open only to himself, his associate, and his expected guests. It was indeed one of his favorite places in the whole country— akin to Pearl Harbor for Americans, the fields near the river Somme for the British and the French, and Stalingrad for the Russians. To Stanko, the grisly horror of the skulls staring out at visitors was the point. This was the ugly truth; this was the history that most people preferred to pretend hadn't happened. What smug, naïve Westerners called "Balkanization" was simply human nature. My tribe against your tribe, forever. The winner got power, wealth, and the women of the vanquished tribe; the losers got enslaved, tortured, or killed. ISIS understood that. The Russians and Chinese appeared to understand that. Stanko suspected most of the Western world would not understand that until it was too late for them.

He could tell that Rochelle, his American handler from all those years ago, did not and could not understand this at all— raised on an insipid, naive, and particularly American vision of harmony, a delusion fed by old footage of Martin Luther King Jr. and *Reading Rainbow* and *Star Trek* and Benetton ads. Her worldview had no room for the reality of human history—endless cycles of conquerors building towers out of the skulls of the conquered.

Stanko chuckled to himself at the thought of Rochelle realizing just how wrong she was today, once she arrived. Stanko's associates vigilantly watched all the roads to and from the Skull Tower. His men watched all the airports, border crossings, and train stations. And his favorite old friends were ready to give her a welcome she could never foresee.

But so far, no one had reported seeing her, and Stanko started to wonder if she bailed on the meeting. His associate in the chapel, Bojana Lasic, glared at him impatiently. He replied with a disapproving grunt.

Two years earlier, he had eagerly recruited Bojana from the lower ranks of Serbian intelligence as his protégé and bedmate, and he had found her living up and down to every man's warnings about beautiful women. She had skills, charm, and the looks to quicken the pulse of a castrated monk, but as an intelligence officer, she proved hot-tempered, reckless, and unpredictable. The past two years proved to Stanko that Bojana was unteachable; she would not or could not overcome her impulsive, combative instincts. Stanko realized he had accepted relief of sexual frustration in exchange for an increase in his workplace frustration.

The walkie-talkie on Stanko's belt came to life and squawked. The leader of Stanko's favorite group of old friends, speaking with a strong northern Slavic accent, reported with uncharacteristic surprise and concern that the sound he heard getting louder was a helicopter preparing to land in the open space adjacent to the chapel. Apparently having his men watch the roads and streets had been a waste of time.

***

The helicopter was a modified MH-60 Black Hawk, the kind used by the US Navy SEALS when they raided the bin Laden compound. Katrina had asked two of the Dangerous Clique's former members to temporarily return to service for the Serbian mission. Thomas Wells, who seemed to be able to fly anything, stepped away from his instruction duties at Naval Air Station Pensacola, and Alejandro Serrano de la Verde, who boasted he could fly or drive anything better than anyone else, temporarily stepped away from his private security consulting job in Dallas.

This particular helicopter had been nicknamed "the Cassowary," after the large flightless ostrich-like beast that was one of the two birds known to have killed human beings. Like its namesake, the helicopter was ugly, dangerous to foes, and fast, at a top speed of 183 miles per hour. Unlike its namesake species, this Cassowary could fly, although not terribly high, weighed down by infrared jammers and various other equipment that kept it virtually invisible to radar and air defense systems. From the US military base at Camp Bondsteel in Kosovo, the Cassowary zoomed across the Serbian border and was hovering next to the chapel of the Skull Tower within twenty minutes.

"Besides anybody this guy has watching the place, the local cops and militia are going to wonder what the hell an unmarked American-built helicopter is doing in their city real soon," Wells shouted over the sound of the rotors. "Whatever you're gonna say to this guy, talk fast!"

Alejandro chuckled. "I thought fast talking is what Alec is best at!"

Alec shook his head as Katrina slid the Black Hawk's door. He shouted back, "I'm giving you one star on Uber!"

Four figures hopped out of the Cassowary, wearing nonstandard gray camouflage uniforms, body armor, helmets, protective goggles, and Kevlar vests. Alec and Ward carried Rattler rifles; Katrina and Raquel carried the slightly lighter and less bulky Heckler and Koch MP7 submachine guns, as well as personal sidearms. Ward flanked Raquel on one side, Alec watched for foes on the other, and Katrina charged ahead, rifle ready.

The Cassowary helicopter had risen to just above the roof of the chapel and started to circle, and Alejandro had slid back to man an M134 minigun out the port side door. Any hostile Serbian approaching the chapel would encounter extremely heavy resistance.

\*\*\*

Inside the chapel, Stanko and Bojana froze at the sight of three submachine guns pointed at them, as Ward continued to watch behind them. Stanko spat a colorful tapestry of Serbian curses that involved copulating, goats, mothers, and various private parts, then gestured for Bojana to holster her weapon.

Raquel studied Stanko's shocked face and contemplated how he had changed in two decades. He carried on the tradition of overweight yet intimidating tough guys in the tradition of James Gandolfini or Bob Hoskins. His hairline was receding, and somewhere along the line he picked up a scar next to his left eye. After a moment, Stanko composed himself and reclaimed his old swagger.

"Rochelle," he squinted in mock disappointment. "Is this any way to greet an old friend?"

Raquel stared back. "I just didn't want you to add my skull to this tower. How the rest of this meeting goes is up to you." She noticed Bojana reaching for one of the two holstered handguns at her side again. "We're off to a bad start, Stanko. Your side piece is reaching for a side piece."

Bojana slowly unholstered her revolver. She kept it pointed down—not at her foes, but still in her hand. Ward whistled in recognition.

"Glad to see you're buying American," he said to her, with an unexpected sense of cheer. "Ruger GP 100 revolver, three-inch barrel, .357 Magnum ammunition. I tell ya, you do not want to get hit with one of those!" Then Ward suddenly dropped his smile. "Holster it or we end you."

Stanko gave Bojana a disapproving look and gestured to her to put the gun back in the holster. She did, but she kept her hand on it. The two sides stared each other down as the helicopter continued to drone above the building.

"Last month you met with a man named Wilhelm Ballett," Raquel declared. "He was working on behalf of someone calling himself Hell Summoner, promising to create a bioweapon to target particular genes. Are you his client?"

Stanko laughed.

"I did not think you were looking to rebuild your old network of sources," he chuckled. "You cannot trick a trickster, and you cannot hunt a predator. You forget, Rochelle, I am the bauk. I lurk in the darkness and strike viciously at those who are unprepared. You reaching out to me, so soon after my meeting with Ballett? You are clumsy. Transparent. You and your cabal think you're so clever. But I know all about your alliance to destroy Serbia. You work with the Muslims, and the Jews, and NATO and Iran and Assad!"

"Yes, because if there's any two groups who love to team up and work together, it's Muslims and Jews!" Alec exclaimed sarcastically. "NATO and Iran? You do realize that no one you mentioned gets along, right?"

Stanko sneered. "Of course, you conspirators would deny the conspiracy! The evidence is everywhere! Plane crashes, so-called accidental deaths, the way the virus spread—"

Alec's temper exploded.

"Oh, *my god*!" he cried in exasperation, cutting Stanko off. "What is it with you damned conspiracy theorists? None of this is how the world works! What do you think, the world's governments are just brimming with competence and effective secrecy? Have you ever dealt with any government bureaucracy? It's like Orwell's Big Brother being administered by Department of Motor Vehicles clerks! No one is competent enough to pull off the vast, complicated secret global operations you imagine!"

Stanko shook his head. "There is a website that reveals—"

Alec cut him off. "The reality is much scarier—nobody's secretly running anything. There is no man behind the curtain surreptitiously pulling the strings. I think you choose to believe in all this crap because you find it *reassuring*! Because if you can find the conspirators and the Cigarette Smoking Man, then presto! You can end all your problems. Guess what, pal, the world is much worse than that! Some lunatic in a cave and nineteen guys with box cutters really can destroy the World Trade Center! The Property Brothers and HGTV can get so many people flipping houses that they create a real estate bubble and crash the world economy! Somebody eating bat soup halfway around the world can set off a global pandemic! The world is full of things that don't make sense like random tragedies and incompetent leaders and *Firefly* getting canceled. The good news that I have for you is that there is no big, bad, vast evil conspiracy. The bad news that I have for you is that there is no big, bad, vast evil conspiracy. This is just the way life is."

Stanko stared back defiantly.

"That's exactly what they want you to believe," the Serbian replied confidently.

Tom's voice echoed in their earpieces, shouting above the engines of the Cassowary above, concerned but not panicked: "Hey, I'm enjoying this *Mythbusters* episode as much as the next guy, but I've got suspected hostiles getting closer on multiple fronts. Whatever you're going to do, do it now."

Katrina aimed her rifle at Stanko's crotch.

"Answer the question," Katrina declared. "Did you pay Hell Summoner?"

The lines around Stanko's eyes, including his scar tissue, betrayed the fact that he took Katrina's implied threat seriously.

"He was a pain in the ass," Stanko declared. "He wouldn't budge off his price, even when my government offered several hundred million dollars. He still wanted twenty billion."

The team studied Stanko carefully, trying to determine if he was lying.

"You're not the first to ask me about him," Stanko added, as a smile spread across his face.

From behind opposite sides of the cube-like skull tower, three familiar faces, clad all in black, stepped out of the shadows:

Sergei Markov, Dimitri Guryanov, and Zoya Zakrevskaya—three members of the Iron Wolves Russian mercenary team— and the were all pointing Udav pistols.

\*\*\*

"Privet, Amerikantsy," Markov declared with a wicked grin. "Wasn't it kind of Stanko to arrange our reunion?" The Russian team leader hid his concern well—the American team wasn't expected to arrive by helicopter, heavily armed and heavily armored. But the rest of the team of Iron Wolves were converging on their location, as well as additional squads from Serbian intelligence. Hopefully the Americans would realize that escaping the Skull Tower would be a bloody, messy fight and agree to surrender quietly.

Katrina, Raquel, Alec, and Ward all muttered various profanities. Katrina concluded Stanko was as devious as Raquel had feared, and the Iron Wolves as tenacious as their reputation suggested.

Katrina also concluded that if the Iron Wolves were here, Stanko was probably telling them the truth. If he was Hell Summoner's client, he would have had some idea where he was now or a way to contact him, and Stanko would not have withheld that information from the Iron Wolves. If the Serbs were the client, the Russians mercenaries would be somewhere else, hunting down Hell Summoner so his knowledge could be used for Moscow's purposes.

*Now all we have to do is get out of here alive*, Katrina thought.

Markov chuckled again and said he hoped to show the Americans the hospitality of Lubyanka Square. Lubyanka was the headquarters building of the Russian intelligence service, the FSB, northeast of Red Square. The massive, palatial, yellow-brick baroque building never took off the old hammer and sickle ironwork from when it housed the KGB. The underground prison was perhaps the deepest, darkest, and most horrific torture chamber of the Stalin era.

The tense standoff continued silently for about thirty seconds—and then suddenly Bojana drew both her guns, and Stanko had just started to shout "no" when the chapel seemed to explode with everyone seeming to fire simultaneously. The Iron Wolves had wanted to take the Americans alive, and Bojana's sudden move set off a gunfight that neither the Russians nor Americans nor Stanko had wanted to start. With cramped conditions and poor lighting, the inside of the shrine around the Skull Tower was a tactically awful spot for a gunfight. And for the government agents who survived, the diplomatic fallout of a gunfight in a Serbian national shrine would be considerable.

Katrina and Ward unleashed their rifles and drove the Russians back behind the corners of the tower—each Russians had gotten off one or two shots while trying to scramble for cover but missed the Americans. Raquel leaped and managed to press her MP-7 right against the gut of Stanko. Borjana focused her fire at Alec, as he tried to use the cluster of stone and human skulls as cover. Her wild, crazed, furious barrage blew out jawbones and cheek bones and eye sockets and chunks of stone masonry down on Alec's head.

BLAM BLAM BLAM BLAM BLAM BLAM

Alec shouted across the room to Ward. "You're absolutely sure she's firing Ruger Redhawks, right?"

Ward, trying to concentrate on any sign of movement on the far side of the giant square of skulls, found Alec's question bizarre, and almost insulting. "YES!"

"Great!"

Borjana unleashed another reckless and not terribly well-aimed barrage, raining more stones, dust, and bone fragments down upon Alec's head.

BLAM BLAM BLAM BLAM BLAM BLAM

At the twelfth shot, Alec popped up from his crouch like a jack-in-the-box, and fired about a third of the Rattler's thirty-round magazine in her direction. A moment later, Borjana's body slumped to the floor, bloody and lifeless.

"This is why you count shots!" Alec loudly announced to anyone who is listening. "Six-shooter revolvers look great, but take longer to reload!"

The Dangerous Clique realized that gunfire was coming from outdoors, too—including the extremely loud, rapid-fire sound of an M134 minigun kicking into high gear above them.

"We're taking fire," Wells reported. "I'm going to try to land where we dropped you off—get your butts back there now!"

"Copy that," Katrina confirmed. "Let's go!"

Raquel kept her rifle pointed at Stanko's belly. "No sudden moves, Iron Wolves, I've got your man!" she shouted. "We're all walking out of here in one piece, or Stanko here will—"

Dimitri and Zoya emerged from behind separate corners of the Skull Tower. When Ward and Katrina returned fire, Markov popped out low from behind the massive Dimitri—and put a single round right into the top of Stanko's forehead.

Raquel recoiled from Stanko's bloody head and the frozen look of horror upon the intact parts of his face. Either Markov had aimed for her and missed, or the Iron Wolves didn't really care about Stanko.

Markov and the other Russians ducked back behind the tower, and Katrina saw their chance. She, Ward, and Alec laid alternating bursts of cover fire until they were through the doorway and out of the chapel. They exited into a dust storm, as the Cassowary was now landing, so close to the building that Katrina feared the rotor blades would scrape the wall.

Alejandro fired the M134 minigun furiously at a group of assailants farther up the block.

"Meter's running!" he shouted after a burst, as the quartet climbed into the chopper.

Within seconds, all four were back on board the helicopter, and Tom took the Cassowary straight up, so suddenly and quickly that everyone felt their stomachs sink further into their guts. Everyone braced themselves as the "elevator" stopped rising and then suddenly tossed them backward as the "car" accelerated madly.

"That was a lot of fun, let's never do it again," Alec groaned.

"We're not out of this yet!" Tom yelled back at him. "Let's hope the Serbian Air Force is feeling sluggish today!"

Katrina glanced out the window and saw muzzle flashes from the Serbians below—thankfully, the UH-60 Black Hawk had been built to be about as durable as possible in these situations—built to handle anything less than a 23 millimeter projectile, ballistically hardened flight controls, redundant electric and hydraulic systems, crash-resistant and self-sealing fuel systems, and energy-absorbing crew seats and landing gear. It was as close as she and the team could get to a flying tank. But even these heavily armored birds could crash or get shot down—all it took was one stinger, air defense system, or Serbian military jet to get lucky and the story of the Dangerous Clique would come to a fiery and sudden end.

Alejandro scrambled back to the other cockpit seat. The Cassowary continued to accelerate, leaving Nis behind it. Alejandro listened carefully and relayed that NATO air bases and surveillance planes characterized the three major Serbian air bases as "hornet's nests" at that moment—seemingly every military combat helicopter and jet unit was mobilizing, although it was too early to tell if any would be able to intercept them.

"Tell me this thing has a Romulan cloaking device," Alec groaned.

"Not quite, but next best thing," Tom shouted. This version of the Black Hawk had hard edges like an F117, rivetless skin, a shrouded tail rotor, special infrared-absorbing paint, and special coatings on the windshield. "All we've got to do is stay unseen for twenty minutes—"

A light on the instrument panel started flashing and beeping ominously, and a moment later, an anti-aircraft missile emerged from somewhere behind them and flew past them, leaving a thin stream of smoke in its wake. The missile slowly sunk and then landed, with an explosion, in some woods atop a hill.

"They saw us!" Alejandro shouted. "Remember, the Serbs were the first country to shoot down a stealth fighter!"

"They're firing and just hoping to get lucky," Tom grimaced. "Maybe we should have cut east to Bulgaria—NATO airspace and might have saved us a few minutes—"

"You guys can get us out of here, that's why I asked for you," Katrina shouted from behind them. "We'll be fine back here, just do whatever you have to do! You're the best of the best!" She knew *Top Gun* had inspired Tom to become a pilot.

Tom winced and nodded. "Yeah, yeah, need for speed, kick tires, light fires! Ladies and gentlemen, please return your tray tables to the upright and locked position."

The Cassowary suddenly dove, hitting an altitude so low that Katrina thought she heard the uppermost branches of the tree-tops being sheared underneath the speeding helicopter.

"Great! Now when we crash, it will be a shorter trip!" Ward shouted from the back.

Tom ignored him. The higher the helicopter flew, the more time it would be in the line of sight of any Serbian forces on the ground, hoping to hit it with a missile.

By flying at the absolute minimum altitude—well beyond the recommendations of any sane military flight instructor—Tom hoped he would make it nearly impossible for the Serbs to get that lucky shot. After a few moments, Tom realized his instructors might have objected for a good reason—the hilly terrain ahead featured taller trees and power lines and the occasional church steeple, increasing the odds of collision. Tom inclined slightly, then started worrying about the Serbian Air Force. The country's pilots hardly made their Western counterparts quake in their boots, but they did have a few functioning MiG29s at the air base nearest to Nis. If the Serbs deployed MiGs in pursuit, they could catch up quickly—and a trained pilot in an attack jet, flying in daylight, could take out the chopper.

"You couldn't have met this guy at night?" Alejandro yelled back at his former teammates. "This chopper is black! Stealth! During the daytime we stick out like Johnny Cash at an Indian wedding!"

Tom wondered how close he could get to the helicopter's red-line or VNE, "never exceed speed" of 222 miles per hour. The Black Hawk's standard top speed was about three miles a minute, and the Kosovo border and the end of Serbian airspace was forty-two miles away—about fourteen minutes. Gunning the craft to the cusp of the never exceed speed would get them there in less than twelve.

The sudden surge of additional acceleration thrust everyone back again, leaving them gripping the sides of the helicopter to balance themselves.

Alejandro started swearing in Spanish and English. "NATO Air Command confirms two MiGs launched from Ladevci air base behind us—those things can go Mach 2, they'll be on top of us before we know it!"

"Almost there," Tom muttered through gritted teeth. The terrain of mountains, forests, hills, and switchback roads offered some ability to hide, but not much. In those rare moments where they could spot villages before they flew past them, they appeared to be miniscule collections of homes in the middle of nowhere, with rarely more than a hundred people.

"After we cross the border, we flip them the bird," Alec suggested.

"That's assuming those MiGs stop at the border," Katrina warned.

The minutes ticked down. Alejandro sweat as NATO Air Command updated them on the position of the MiGs, once top-of-the-line Russian aircraft with a top speed roughly five times as fast as the Black Hawk helicopter. The two Serbian MiGs weren't even going their top speed. Alejandro did math in his head, and his finger traced out the numbers in the air. Alejandro turned around for a moment, looking behind them, and Katrina thought she saw his eyes bulge behind his flight visor.

He shook his head. "They're going to catch us three minutes before we reach the border! We'll be in the range of their missiles any second now!"

Katrina felt her adrenaline kick into a higher gear she didn't know it had. "Can we land and try to cross the border on foot?"

"Easy pickings for the border guards, who are probably on high alert already!" Ward shouted from the rear seats.

Raquel kicked the side of the helicopter. "I knew this mission was a stupid risk! I knew Stanko wasn't the client! Dammit, if Stern hadn't insisted we go—"

But Alejandro suddenly held up his hand and listened carefully to his radio headset.

"One MiG just broke off pursuit—seems to be experiencing mechanical difficulty," he relayed. He took another deep breath, and the lower half of his face registered shock. "Unbelievable!"

"What happened?" Katrina demanded.

Alejandro smiled. "Shortly after the first MiG turned around to return to base...the second one radioed that he's having an instrument problem. He's breaking off pursuit, too."

He looked up in a mix of a relief and confusion and saw the same expression staring back at him from Katrina, Alec, Ward, and Raquel. Tom seemed to be ignoring it all, obsessively focused on pushing the helicopter to its limits, hell-bent on getting across the border into Kosovo in one piece.

"Do we have the ability to jam them or something?" Alec asked.

Alejandro shook his head negative. "If we've got that ability, they've kept it secret even from us. NATO Air Command doesn't understand it, either."

Then after a few more minutes of listening, he offered an update.

"Serbian military frequencies are full of confusion and chatter ... Apparently"—he started chuckling in disbelief—"both Migs experienced system failures shortly after reaching cruising speed. I guess the Nis Air Base staff have been way below standards in the past few months. They were one of the last spots hit by coronavirus before the vaccine and maintenance crapped the bed since the new crews rotated in." He listened some more and after a few moments, started hooting and cackling. "I guess the current MiG crew is the bottom of the barrel, and now the entire Serbian Air Force command is screaming at each other over the inability to keep the MiGs ready for duty."

All six of them chuckled with relief and incredulity that the hated virus had just played a role in saving them as the Black Hawk crossed the border.

***

Less than twenty minutes later, the Cassowary landed safely at Camp Bondsteel, and NATO support staff quickly looked the team over for injuries. No one had been shot, no one had anything worse than bruises from jumping into the helicopter and maybe some lingering motion sickness from the wild ride. After the checkup, walking across the tarmac, Raquel seemed okay—then suddenly stopped walking, shuddered, and nearly lost her balance, then bent over on the tarmac.

"Raquel, what is it?" Katrina asked. After seeming fine a moment ago, her friend seemed to be turning green.

Raquel heaved, and suddenly deposited what remained of her most recent meal upon the tarmac. She coughed, and held up a hand, indicating she was all right.

"You're okay, you're going to be okay," Alec said, rushing to Raquel's side—and then recoiling from the scent. "Oh, man! That's the good stuff right there—prime *Exorcist* material!"

After a moment or two, Raquel recovered, taking a cloth to wipe her face.

"I'm all right," she said, taking a deep breath. "Dammit, I knew Stanko wasn't the client! I knew it in my bones, and I agreed for us to go out there anyway, and nearly got us all killed!"

The team—including the prodigal sons, Tom and Alejandro— formed a little protective circle around her.

"Hey, this is just another day at the office," Tom said. "Just like we remember."

Alejandro shrugged. "The shootout in Istanbul was way worse than this."

Raquel nodded in appreciation. "Thanks, guys." But after a moment, her simmering frustration just wouldn't cool. "But the clock's still ticking on us. We don't know where this guy is, when the virus will be ready—maybe it already is—or where he's going to release it. We just spent days hunting a false lead. We are screwed. And if we're screwed, then the world is screwed."

Katrina nudged the others aside and put both hands on Raquel's shoulders, coming face-to-face, her stance and tone as direct as she could be.

"What this tells us is that your instincts are right, Raquel," Katrina declared. "This isn't your first rodeo, and you've developed an intuition about this. Someone once told me your subconscious figures things out faster than your conscious mind, and that's why you have gut feelings pushing you in one direction or another. You and I liked the Dutchman from the moment we read his file. We're gonna find him."

Alec patted Raquel on the back. "You don't rack up a string of successes like we did unless it's meant to be! To quote Alexander Hamilton, 'what are the odds that the Gods would put us all in one spot?'"

"That was Lin-Manuel Miranda," Alejandro corrected.

Raquel nodded. "Oh, I know we'll find him. The question is whether it will be in time."

Everyone paused for a moment, inescapably contemplating of the consequences of Hell Summoner releasing a virus that could kill millions, and how the world would react when it realized a virus could target just one particular genetic group.

"However way this shakes out, our job's pretty much the same," Ward concluded. "If we can't stop him, we make him pay. Hague's too good for this guy. My vision of justice for Hell Summoner involves a wood-chipper."

Before anyone could react to Ward's particularly bloody vision of vengeance the phone in Katrina's belt clip buzzed. It was a text from Dee.

A moment later, Katrina's face broke into an expression that was one part satisfaction, one part determination.

"Dee says she found the Dutchman."

# CHAPTER FOURTEEN

SOMEWHERE BETWEEN CAMP
BONDSTEEL, KOSOVO
AND DULLES INTERNATIONAL AIRPORT
MONDAY, APRIL 27

The Serbian government reacted apoplectically to the reports
that an American team had launched an insufficiently covert
operation right in the heart of one of their biggest cities,
killed two Serbian intelligence officials, and in the process shot
up a solemn national landmark. They withdrew their ambassador to the United States, subjected the US ambassador to a furious, spittle-spraying diatribe by the Serbian president right in his
office at Novi dvor in Belgrade, and declared about a third of the
American embassy staff persona non grata.

The official explanation from NATO was that a routine
training mission involving a Black Hawk helicopter had come
close to Serbian airspace but had not entered it, and Belgrade was
wildly exaggerating. Unidentified military sources contended in
a handful of major European newspapers that a Russian mercenary team was responsible for the shootout. The entire diplomatic
ruckus could have been a major story in the United States, but
Kanye West and Kim Kardashian had a public spat in a restaurant that week, and the American news cycle simply didn't have
much room for claims that the US was running covert operations
in the Balkans.

Arguably even worse, the CIA's station chief in country had been given only the most cursory details before the operation launched, and he was caught flatfooted by the volcanic reaction from the Serbian government. Station chiefs tended to perceive their level of authority over what the CIA did within their country as ranking somewhere between Genghis Khan and God, and his tirade about the Dangerous Clique creating messes for other people to clean up resonated far and wide within the halls of Langley.

The Serbian station chief calmed down somewhat when CIA Director Barbara Stern told him that the team had been carrying out her personal orders. Raquel was pleasantly surprised when Stern admitted she had erroneously focused her suspicions on the Serbs too much because of that government's past efforts in "ethnic cleansing."

"I should have listened to Raquel and focused on Vinny the Dutchman," Stern quipped.

But as the director giveth, the director taketh away. Upon returning to the United States, Tom and Alejandro volunteered to continue their temporary assignment with the team. Unfortunately, Director Stern decreed that after the fallout from Serbia, the Dangerous Clique would need to use a much lighter touch in its continuing hunt for Hell Summoner. Tom and Alejandro remained on standby, but suspected Stern would not call their phones until the virus had been detected on the seventh floor of Langley.

After the team dragged themselves into the conference room at Liberty Campus—after yet another transatlantic flight, and yet another set of nasal swabs being uncomfortably jabbed up their noses—Dee started a detailed explanation of Vincent van der Groot's top-of-the-line encryption methods and efforts to stay off the grid, and then suddenly caught herself, observed that no one cared about the details, and moved on.

"Van der Groot is divorced and has a seventeen-year-old daughter. The daughter has a secret Instagram account with geo-location still on," Dee said with a chuckle. "Her pictures indicate last week she was on safari with her father in Kenya, at some lake with flamingoes." She held up a map. "Shompole Conservancy. She flew out of Nairobi yesterday, back home to her mom in Amsterdam. As far as we can tell, he's still there."

"Good alibi if you're going to start a worldwide pandemic—I was out in the middle of nowhere, far from civilization," Ward murmured.

"Much like being on a hunting trip when a Chinese embassy staffer gets shot by a sniper, not that any of us would ever do that," Dee sang.

Before Ward could object to the widespread belief that he had murdered Bao Fang Min, Katrina walked the group through what she had previously uncovered about Vincent van der Groot.

He was born in 1983, the only child of Ambroos and Beatrix van der Groot. One branch of the family's ancestry had employed Vincent van Gogh in the 1880s, and it is was believed that the couple named their son after the famous painter. The van der Groots had helped rebuild the Dutch sugar industries after World War Two and by the sixties had become one of the wealthier families in the country, although a fairly large and extended one. Ambroos and Beatrix were considered the eccentric couple of the family and rumored to have an open marriage.

Ambroos and Beatrix were killed on October 4, 1992 when El Al flight 1862 crashed into the Bijlmermeer apartment complex on the outskirts of Amsterdam. The flight had only four people on it but killed thirty-nine people on the ground and inflicted considerable injuries upon many others. This was not a wealthy or fancy apartment complex, and mostly housed immigrants. No one in the family or official investigation ever determined why Ambroos and Beatrix were in the complex at the time of the crash, but both public and private investigations speculated that they were engaged in scandalous sexual behavior there.

Vincent was nine and away at a boarding school at the time. He was raised by an aunt and uncle and lived with many cousins, and, as far as anyone could tell, adjusted about as well as could be expected to a terrible tragedy.

After graduating from the University of Amsterdam with a degree in finance, Vincent did a little work for the family company and then started investing his considerable inheritance. He married into the Heineken family, had a daughter, divorced, and somehow came out with alimony payments; the rumor was he was effectively paid to keep quiet about some sort of embarrassing matter. The estimate of his fortune by *Forbes* magazine made him not quite a billionaire—although some contended a portion of his wealth was hidden through complicated networks of offshore investments.

The divorce papers were sealed, but the Amsterdam rumor mill claimed that Vincent van der Groot had a hidden side, full of rage and paranoia, telling his wife that "the Jews" had lured his parents to the apartment complex and then deliberately crashed the El Al airliner to kill them and make it look like an accident. Shortly after the divorce, he vehemently denied the rumors and made several donations to the Anne Frank House—donations that, it should be noted, with his personal fortune, were the rough equivalent of spare change under the couch cushions for ordinary people.

But year by year, van der Groot became an increasingly vocal supporter of the Dutch Green Left party and the Boycott, Divestment, and Sanctions campaign again Israel. He attended BDS protests at Amsterdam's World War II monument, where the speakers' rhetoric often spilled out well beyond denunciations of Israel to furious tirades about what "the Jews" were doing. The Netherlands witnessed rising levels of vicious anti-Semitism year by year: desecration of cemeteries, assaults on the street, and a small group of Dutch soccer fans chanting "Jews burn best" on Holocaust Remembrance Day. When a Dutch rapper who resembled a blond *Playboy* centerfold wanted to use the stage name "Anne Frank," van der Groot sent her a supportive note.

Still, he hadn't lost his position in European high society; he still wrote large checks to charitable causes and showed up at the black-tie events. He was a man of the left—but one whose fervent opposition to Israel kept bringing him into strange alliances with right-wing anti-Semites.

"Should we consider Pretty Boy here to be armed and dangerous?" Ward asked. His photos suggested he could have been a model—a winning, confident smile. But Katrina noticed in one photo, his eyes weren't smiling. She noted he had fenced in college, listed hunting as a hobby, and the wife had described a temper. He might well be dangerous after all.

\*\*\*

Even without the options of military backup or Tom and Alejandro, the team briefly considered a nighttime assault on Shompole Lodge. Owned and operated by the Maasai, the camp only took one booking at a time, at either its lodge or in "luxury tents" that could rival those of fine hotels in world capitals. But they quickly concluded that even with every technological advantage, the odds of some lodge staffers getting hurt was considerable.

For several days, van der Groot had noticed the animals, particularly the flamingoes, periodically looking skyward. They could hear what he could not, a US Air Force RQ-4 Global Hawk surveillance drone, watching from sixty thousand feet above. After two days, the drone footage suggested a pattern of van der Groot's behavior at the camp since his daughter departed. He traveled with two bodyguards. The first was his longtime body-guard Camille, a blond human mountain and highly touted vet-eran of professional protective services, allegedly unbeatable in hand-to-hand combat. The second was Muthusi, who was former Kenyan military and a giant of a man; he appeared to be a tem-porary hire for this lengthy safari.

The day Vincent van der Groot's daughter departed back to Amsterdam, "Cali," a new "friend" of van der Groot's arrived, a blue-haired, tattoo-covered former fashion model; whatever natural beauty she had once had, she had now embraced "bet-ter living through plastics" to the point of ludicrous proportions. She had little interest in the wilderness, it seemed; she never left the camp.

Van der Groot would sleep late, have a late breakfast, check messages on a state-of-the-art secure satellite hookup, then head out to the farthest reaches of the Shompole wilderness, crossing the border from Kenya into Tanzania, to the strangely red waters of Lake Natron. He would return in the late afternoon; eat, drink to excess, carouse with "Cali" and then collapse into bed.

\*\*\*

On the long flight over the Atlantic, Alec insisted that van der Groot's fascination with Lake Natron had to do with tales that the lake could turn animals to stone. Katrina insisted there was no basis to the tales of the Medusa and other curses turning people into statues.

But Alec laid out that it was no curse. Lake Natron was a salt lake, comparable to the Dead Sea and Great Salt Lake in Utah—rainwater flowed in and gradually evaporated, but had no place to flow out. The lake's name came from the substance natron, a naturally occurring combination of soda ash and baking soda. Lake Natron was extremely alkaline, or basic, the opposite of acidic. While people think of acidic as dangerous and basic as safe, the water in Lake Natron could be as alkaline as ammonia. Throw in the blazing African sun and lack of shade, and the water could reach 140 degrees Fahrenheit. Most animals could not survive in the waters, or drink the waters, other than a select breed of fish, flamingoes, and salt-loving microorganisms that had adapted to survive in the harsh conditions. The microorganisms often turned the surface of the water pink or bright red, and their ample presence the diet of the local flamingoes contributed to their distinctive vibrant pink color.

The "turned to stone" stories stemmed from birds who would see a fish in the lake, dive into the waters to catch it, and then die from the water's chemical properties. Once the bird's bodies fell underneath the waters, the dissolved natron minerals would start to attach to the outside of the bodies, building up an even, calcium-like crust all around the bird.

Throughout the year, perfectly preserved "bird mummies" would wash up around the lake. (Natron was used by ancient Egyptians to preserve their mummies.) From this, it was easy to understand why any creature that failed to recognize the dangerous toxicity of the lake's waters could conceivably end up looking like it had been turned to stone.

***

If a CIA team needed to sneak into a country in Africa, they could do a lot worse than Kenya. The country's government cooperated with the agency in renditioning terror suspects to the notorious "black sites" used for interrogation. By the standards of the continent, Kenya was relatively prosperous, relatively stable, and relatively secure. It was also the current posting for a legend within the community of the agency's support staff, Ryder Rodgers.

Rodgers had the cheer, confidence, and charm of Geoffrey Holder, the giant Trinidadian-American pitchman who informed Americans that 7 Up was the "un-cola." Even by the standards of the agency, Rodgers traveled in a perpetual cloud of mystery and rumors and seemingly implausible tales. Katrina knew he had worked in Addis Ababa, Algiers, Amman, and Athens. Rodgers joked he was working through the world's most troubled cities alphabetically, and that Ankara fell just short of making the list.

Somehow upon arrival in a country's capital, Rodgers developed contacts and connections with the speed of a small-town mayor running for reelection. His position enabled him to do favors for everyone—local cops, government officials, black-market merchants, religious leaders, everyone from the sophisticated to the seedy. Then, when needed, he would remind his rapidly assembled network of sources and fixers of their debts with a smile. He seemed to be able to quickly obtain almost anything, almost anywhere.

Rodgers greeted Katrina and the rest of the team with a set of secure communications gear, firearms, two jeeps, access to a safehouse, GPS tracking equipment, night-vision goggles, first aid kits, zip-ties, gags, tasers, and a pair of jeeps designed to handle all kinds of terrain. He assured her that the Kenyan authorities had been notified that an American team was on a mission of the highest importance, and particular code phrases and phone numbers would get any local law enforcement off their back.

After a half-hour of consulting maps and detailing everyone's role in the plan, Katrina nodded. If van der Groot stuck to his habits, everything might just work out and they would get out of it alive. Still, the plan required Alec to stick his neck out in a particularly dangerous way.

Katrina kissed him and gave him one last reminder. "Remember, when we're out there, stick close to me."

"It's gonna take a lot to drag me away from you," Alec declared with such emphatic sincerity that Katrina knew he was up to something.

"Alec."

"That's something that a hundred men or more could never do," he insisted.

She rolled her eyes. "Alec!"

"I've blessed the rains down in—"

"That's enough, Alec!"

\*\*\*

Probably ninety-some percent of the rest of the humans on the planet would find the heat too much to bear. The air temperature in Tanzania was actually mild that morning, inching through the seventies and approaching eighty in Fahrenheit, but the noon-day sun just reached its apex and the surface temperature would climb rapidly now. As Katrina crawled, the grass, dust, and small stones under her arms and elbows, belly, and legs grew less and less comfortable. But the ghillie suit atop her body generated the most unbearable, heaviest, sweat-drenching heat.

The promotional advertising for the ghillie desert camou-flage suit described it as lightweight, and technically it met that threshold: five separate pieces of polyester, covered in light straw that reasonably matched the yellow grasses in the Gregory Rift valley.

Alone, moving slowly when at all, only hearing the sounds of animals and intermittent messages in her earbud, gazing through her binoculars, and hoping she didn't encounter a scorpion, spi-der, or snake. She had run into enough of those tracking down Atarsa in Brazil. Katrina had a reputation for being patient, but she didn't think of herself this way. Circumstances like this left her alone with her thoughts.

Moments like this were when Katrina Leonidivna, nearly-twenty-year officer of the Central Intelligence Agency, could be most uncomfortable.

She quickly corrected herself; almost two of those nearly twenty years shouldn't count, as she felt like she did nothing consequential as the coronavirus pandemic spread and burned around the world. The agency's overseas operations slowed down, and in some cases, ground to a halt. Maintaining cover while under quarantine proved impossible in some cases. Dead drops required leaving the house, case officers and agents in the field stood out walking down an empty street, and brush passes required violating rules on social distancing. Operations that depended upon face-to-face contact were suspended, first temporarily, then indefinitely. Back in the nation's capital, working from home wasn't an option for those whose duties involved classified information. All around the world, both allies and enemies stayed home for long stretches. Even ISIS warned its members, in its *al-Naba* newsletter, that Europe was not safe, and that "the healthy should not enter the land of the epidemic and the afflicted should not exit from it." Alec observed that members of ISIS followed quarantine instructions, but CNN anchor Chris Cuomo did not.

All of that left Katrina with plenty of time to think. After the operation in Cyprus that killed Gholam Gul and Sarvar Rashin, and effectively shut down Atarsa, she felt a newfound confidence in the woman she was, what she did for a living, and what it required of her. She was not becoming "just another scorpion," as she had feared. She was the modern successor to the "Onnabugeisha," or female samurai—fearsomely lethal but guided by a rigorous and righteous code of honor. She was the equal to any man—superior, arguably—but distinct, thankful to be born a woman. Alec accepted playing Steve Trevor to her Wonder Woman, and her longtime and tested bonds of friendship inside and outside the agency made the quartet on *Sex and the City* look like casual acquaintances.

But the accomplishments of Katrina's career could only be measured in terror plots disrupted, cells broken up, and terrorists captured or killed—all matters of subtraction, not addition. She did not create; she deleted. And for many years after 9/11, the work felt like whack-a-mole. Kill one terrorist, warlord, or illicit arms dealer, another one will take his place a short while later. The names and faces changed, but the circumstances rarely seemed to get *better*.

Katrina took pride in the fact that she was good at what she did—perhaps among the very best—but she found herself wanting to do something more, to enact some permanent change, something that would be standing and influencing the lives of others long after she was gone. And every now and then, she realized she couldn't continue this kind of work forever. She was in fabulous shape for her age, but the bruises, scrapes, cuts, and other consequences of her lifestyle didn't heal as quickly as she remembered. Some mornings, her body's joints liked reminding her of missions where she hadn't come through quite so unscathed—*"Remember that hard fall in Budapest? Or how about the shootout that went bad in Istanbul? Is this pain in your head from last night's wine, or a lingering effect of that concussion in Cyprus?"*

She knew she would have to move on "someday," and always pictured that day being far away. In these quiet moments of waiting, she realized maybe it wasn't as far away as she thought.

But move on to what? She knew she would hate a permanent desk job. She had thrived in the Dangerous Clique because both she and Raquel couldn't stand the sclerotic bureaucratic culture and office politics that had taken root in so many other parts of the agency.

Every year, Langley welcomed a new, young all-star team: honor roll and dean's list recent college graduates, former military veterans of Iraq and Afghanistan, as well as increasing numbers of mid-career transitions, almost all multilingual, off-the-charts IQ, elite athletes. The CIA recruited brilliant Wall Street analysts who had already made all the money they could ever want and hungered for a bigger challenge or to serve their country, Silicon Valley tech geniuses, chameleonlike actors who could slip on personalities as easily as clothes, and hard-charging adrenaline junkies of every kind whose resumes were so sterling they glowed.

The organization was filled to the brim with self-starters, eccentric geniuses, tough guys, prodigies, and every Type-A personality imaginable. But when you put thousands upon thousands of the best and brightest in one organization, all desiring to serve their country to the best of their ability ... friction happens anyway. Egos grow; the agency could make a Harvard alumni reunion look humble and self-effacing. Factions and rivalries form, toes get stepped on, grudges develop and grow like kudzu. Proposals get shot down, ambitious, bright rising stars get convinced they were unfairly passed over for promotion, and particularly ambitious types begin subtly stabbing each other in the back. (Only metaphorically, as far as Katrina knew.) The Central Intelligence Agency represented a massive gathering of extraordinarily bright people, all used to being the best, all with steely-eyed confidence that their ideas and methods are best, and many of whom had been trained to be effective manipulators and liars. In this light, it was a small miracle that anything got done at all. Somehow, each year, Raquel kept them free from the worst of the office-politics morass.

But from the CIA's Dangerous Clique to where? The State Department? Diplomacy appeared Sisyphean, even compared to counterterrorism. NASA? Exciting, but by the time she was prepared to be an astronaut she would be too close to collecting Social Security. The United Nations? That institution was noble in theory and venal in practice. The Bill and Melinda Gates Foundation seemed to be doing good work, and it certainly appeared financially stable for the long haul. Katrina chuckled at the thought of moving from one favorite of conspiracy theorists to another.

Every time Katrina contemplated this question, she ended the labyrinth walk with the recognition that a safer world was a precondition for a better world. Breakthroughs in fighting poverty, hunger, disease, or hatred were hard enough in prosperous peacetime; the climb became steeper every time someone crashed an airliner into a skyscraper or a dictator hanging on to power gassed his citizens with sarin or an authoritarian regime insisted a fast-spreading virus was not contagious. The world had agents of chaos, men and women who made the world worse, and until they were checked, humanity would be like crabs in a pot—so blinded by misery and resentment and bitterness that they pulled down anyone who seemed to be climbing to a new height.

Someday, Katrina concluded again, she would set the world right and create something important and beneficial to the world, something that would outlive her. But before that day, she had to track down a bioweapon that could set off so much ethnic bloodshed it would make mid-1990s Rwanda look like the "We Are the World" video.

***

The flock of flamingoes took flight all at once, briefly blotting out the sun. The sound of a rifle shot across the lake and valley startled them, spurring them to take wing to the other side of the lake.

Van der Groot had insisted that Camille and Muthusi give him some space on the day's walk around the lakeside. Muthusi had happily stood by the Land Rover; only professionalism prevented him from checking his cell phone. When the shot rang out, he instinctively reached for his sidearm—the rifle in the jeep, meant to deal with any larger dangerous predators, was too bulky. Within a few moments of creeping closer to where van der Groot had wandered, Muthusi saw a target, if not his target: a white man crawling toward their position.

Muthusi turned toward the crawling man and leveled his weapon. But he belatedly realized that the man he spotted had been bait; a woman with Eurasian features seemed to manifest out of thin air near him, shrouded in a cloak designed to look like the grasses nearby.

"Drop the gun," she repeated in English and then horribly mangled Swahili.

Muthusi nodded and gently put his gun on the ground. "English, please," he said. "Your Swahili hurts my ears more than your gun ever could."

Katrina smiled wryly. "We're not here for you, we're here for van der Groot," she said gently. "We just need some answers from him. We've got no quarrel with you, and won't harm you, unless you attack us."

Muthusi nodded, raised his arms, and interlocked his hands behind his head. He liked his reputation and would somewhat regret whatever these assailants would do to van der Groot, but he had found the Dutchman to be an insufferable client and wasn't going to take an insane risk to protect him.

Muthusi sighed as the white man approached to restrain him with zip ties. "Scuff me up a little before you leave, so I can say I did all I could to protect him."

The man rolled his eyes. "Hey, you *did* do all you could to protect him. Don't beat yourself up over it. Or, if you want, beat yourself up over it, because I'm not going to do it for you."

Muthusi raised his eyebrows. "Are you going to kill him?"

Simultaneously, the woman said "no," and the man said "yes." They exchanged an annoyed look with each other.

Muthusi shrugged. "No difference to me. He's an insufferable son of a bitch and I'm paid in advance with a no-refunds policy."

***

They zip-tied one of Muthusi's hands to the back of his Land Rover but left him with a thermos of water. They took his phone, knife, and the keys to the vehicle. Off on the horizon, a cloud of dust meant Ward and his jeep were approaching fast.

A few moments later, Ward picked them up, and they accelerated along the scarlet lake's edge to where their target waited. Along the shore, they passed the dead body of Camille. He had been shot in the head, an unlit cigarette in his mouth and lighter in his hand, and his head fell right at the water's edge, white bits of soda ash starting to clump around his hair.

"Nice shot," Alec observed.

"Big target," Ward shrugged.

"Yeah, tell us again how you couldn't have made that shot outside the Chinese embassy," Katrina observed, spotting their quarry. Farther down the lakeside, Raquel held Vincent at gunpoint.

***

Despite Raquel's seeming appearance out of nowhere, and the sudden murder of his primary bodyguard and the disappearance of his second, Vincent van der Groot had quickly adjusted to his situation. He had ignored Raquel's orders to put his hands above his head, sat back down in the folding chair facing the lake he that had been sitting in moments earlier, and calmly sipped from the drink in his chair's cupholder. Vincent concluded that if his assailants intended to kill him, the sniper who killed Camille would have shot him by now. He was an extremely wealthy European vacationing in a remote corner of Africa; the possibility of a kidnap and ransom was a risk he had learned to live with a long time ago.

A jeep with three more assailants arrived—two white men and a woman who looked like she was from Nepal, or Mongolia, or some country with "stan" in its name. Vincent removed a flask from a vest pocket and raised it to his captors.

"Let's get this over with, shall we?" he said with a smile, then taking a swig. "I am Vincent."

Alec leaped out of the jeep. "Do you believe this guy? He's lucky enough to be named 'Vincent van der Groot,' and yet he doesn't introduce himself by saying …'*I am Groot*'? Dude, if I had that name, that's the only thing I would ever say!"

Vincent seemed to recognize the reference and heaved a sigh of contempt. "I suppose if it isn't in a movie, Americans have never heard of it. 'Groot' is a Dutch word meaning 'big' or 'great.'"

"So far I'm finding him a groot pain," Raquel spat. "Vincent, we're going to ask you some questions, and how this goes depends entirely about how honest you are."

Vincent stared at them, particularly focusing on Raquel and then Katrina. He seemed to be intensely studying her features.

"Kazakhstan?" He guessed. "Uzbekistan?"

"Queens," Katrina answered.

A light bulb seemed to go off above Vincent's head. "Ah, I see," he chuckled. "I suppose here in the farthest corners of Africa, I should have heeded the warnings about running into the wrong… *lost tribe*." Vincent was now certain this was the Mossad assassination squad he had long feared.

Raquel and Katrina exchanged an exasperated look. Before they could respond, Alec closed the distance between himself and Vincent and flung his hand sideways across the bridge of

Vincent's nose. The Dutchman fell backward in his folding chair, tumbling to the ground.

"Hey, I make the jokes around here, Vanilla ISIS!" Alec reached down and lifted him up. "Now, let's start with what in the name of T'Challa you're doing out here!"

"I suspect an ignorant brute like you could never understand," Vincent sighed, getting his legs back under him and dabbing at his now-bleeding nose. He motioned to the alien-red lake before them.

"I am studying the marvels of evolutionary adaptation," Vincent declared. "This lake should not be able to support any life—far too alkaline. Put your bare skin in, it would burn layers off, and if you could bear that, the natron minerals would start encasing you in a white body cast. These flamingoes, the algae, the fish—they've all adapted to live in conditions all other species find deadly. Thus, they have shelter, protection. When you have the wealth I have, you are obligated to contemplate the bigger questions that face us as a species. Many people fear that somewhere out there is a bigger, worse virus, just waiting to jump out of some bat or other creature and wipe us out. We forgot we live with other species on this rapidly changing planet, all competing for survival of the fittest."

Katrina stood eye-to-eye with him. "Tell us about your bioengineered virus."

Vincent ignored her and pointed an accusatory finger. "I know why you're here. When you're done with me, you'll murder me, just as you murdered my parents," he declared, standing as tall as he could with defiant pride. "Whatever you do to me, it won't change anything. It's time to thin the herd of humanity, and we're starting with the ones that caused the rest of us the most trouble."

Katrina refused to let his bluster rattle her. "You're spending a billion dollars—"

"*We* are spending, collectively, a little more than four billion dollars, once you include all the transfer fees," Vincent corrected.

"Four billion dollars to build a virus?!" Alec raged. "Do you know what you could do with that? How much cancer research? How many scholarships? How many homes for the homeless? You could fix, like, three or four NFL franchises with that kind of money!"

"Or he could pay off, like two percent of the national debt!" Ward added.

"For that modest sum, we are altering the course of history!" Vincent beamed. "My daughter will grow up in a world where the surface of the earth has been scoured of the most repugnant. And you know just who I'm talking about," he said, smiling and pointing in particular at Katrina and Raquel. "It's as plain as the noses on your fac—"

Before he could finish the sentence, Alec drew his gun and slammed it against Vincent's ear, cutting the side of his head badly. Vincent howled in pain, and Alec's teammates shouted in shock and anger, but he calmly holstered his gun.

"A fly landed on him, and I was trying to kill it," Alec calmly insisted. Vincent now had a bloody ear to match his bloody nose.

Katrina shook her head in frustration. "Alec, we have better ways." She and Ward helped Vincent back to his feet and settled him in his folding chair.

She ran to the jeep and returned with a metal case, full of medical equipment. She opened it and handed Vincent a gauze, which he promptly pressed against his bloody ear. Katrina removed an IV drip from the case. She checked everything carefully, and then wiped his arm with alcohol.

"Oh, yeah," Alec said, rolling his eyes. "That's good. We're interrogating him, but make sure he doesn't get an infection! I hear they do the same thing right before a lethal injection."

Vincent winced a bit and insisted that the IV wasn't necessary, that the blood loss wouldn't be that bad. Katrina gently shushed him, noting that head wounds tended to bleed a lot. For a few minutes, Alec fumed, Katrina carefully ensured the IV was flowing, and Raquel and Ward watched Vincent warily as well. After a while, the Dutchman realized something was wrong. The questioning had stopped.

He looked at them suspiciously. "What is going on?"

Katrina reached out and held Vincent's hand.

"Vincent," she began. He realized Katrina's gentle look was not the naïve maternal sympathy he initially thought. He realized she was trying to suppress a calm smile, and it refused to stay completely hidden. She had him right where she wanted him.

"This IV infusion is gene therapy," Katrina explained. "It's a perfect irony, really, because we're using a virus as the carrier. Right now, all throughout your body, noncontagious viruses carrying Haplogroup J-M267 are in your bloodstream. They are integrating the new gene into your cells—and as your own cells replicate, they will surely and gradually create more and more of those genes within you."

Vincent stared in horror at the IV in his arm. "You're..."

"I'm not going to kill you, Mr. van der Groot," Katrina declared firmly. "I'm just going to put your fate into your own hands. If you tell us nothing, and we cannot stop Hell Summoner from releasing that virus, then at some point in the not-too-distant future, that virus will reach you, and it will kill you."

Vincent turned all kinds of new shades of pale.

"Welcome to the *tribe*, Vinny," Alec declared, with a wide-eyed manic grin. "You're probably not going to love the bris."

Vincent realized that Alec had hit him just so that Katrina would have an excuse to give him the IV. He found himself uncharacteristically stammering. "Y-you ... you can't—"

"I suppose you could try to quarantine yourself from the virus you paid for," Raquel said with a satisfied smile. "Lock yourself in some room with filtered air, never have visitors, never interact with anyone again. But that's … not much of a life, now is it?"

Ward leaned over and whispered into Vincent's intact ear. "If we were the kind of people you think we are, we would have threatened your daughter, but I've got scruples and a soul and I don't threaten kids. But you probably should think through what she'll think when she learns her daddy died of a virus that targets Jews and Arabs and North Africans, the very same virus he paid to build." Ward patted Vincent on the back.

Vincent had shifted from pale to pale green. He took a deep breath. "I'll—I'll tell you what you want, just give me the antidote!"

Katrina couldn't help but let out an embarrassing giggle. "You really don't understand the science part of this, do you, Mr. van der Groot? There is no antidote to gene therapy. It's already done. There's no way to go through your body and remove the infected cells—there are just too many of them. Your genes are already being rewritten."

Vincent sat back in his seat, horrified.

Alec raised his arms. "Ooh, wait! Maybe if right after we stuck in the IV, you had immediately cut off your arm, you could have stopped the virus from getting into the rest of your body, and if you escaped, you could have gone on to kill Dr. Richard Kimble's wife—"

Katrina snapped her fingers before Vincent's dazed eyes. "These are your options, Vincent: help us, or die from the virus you helped create."

He nodded.

"What is Shedim?" Katrina demanded.

Vincent smiled in a way that infuriated his captors. Knowing things that they didn't restored at least a fraction of his usual sense of superiority. "Shedim is just a social group, not a conspiracy. A small group of wealthy, bright minds, mostly Europeans, who grasped that the Original Sin of the postwar world was the creation of Israel in 1947."

"Shedim is a Hebrew term, referring to demons from ancient Kabbalism. Why do you call yourselves that?" Raquel asked. Vincent stared back angrily.

Alec piped up. "Let me guess, some other group of Nazis had already taken the name 'Hydra'?"

"The Jews think we're monsters, so we figured we should adopt the name of their nightmares," Vincent responded. He looked past the women and directed his comments to the men. "You're too blinkered and mesmerized to see it. No Israel in 1947, no Six-Day War, no Yom Kippur War, no Palestinian refugee camps! The Middle East never turns into a powder keg and chess board during the Cold War! The US never backs up the Shah, the Iranian Revolution never happens! Islamic fundamentalism never catches fire, no bin Laden, no 9/11, no invasion of Iraq, no ISIS! No waves of refugees flooding Europe, no Donald Trump! No new Cold War between the West and China, and no coronavirus pandemic!"

Katrina had heard a lot of twisted self-justifications from terrorists over the years, but Vincent van der Groot would take his place in her personal pantheon of the most warped.

"I think you skipped a few steps," Katrina murmured with bemusement.

Alec stared at Vincent, bewildered. "Your train of thought runs on rails designed by M.C. Escher," he blurted out.

Katrina leaned over Vincent, restoring her sense of authority. "Vincent . . . where is the virus and who's the Hell Summoner?"

"I don't know where the virus is," Vincent laughed. "I don't know who Hell Summoner is. I just know he had elaborate instructions for laundering the money that would be his payment so it could never be tracked, and that his fee is enormous. He wanted...in US dollars, about twenty billion at first. We talked him down to four billion."

Raquel felt her stomach tie itself into a knot. "But he can really do it."

Vincent chuckled again. "No one pays four billion dollars for something that might not work."

"Other than the Pentagon," Ward murmured to himself.

"You're going to tell us the names of every last Shedim member," Katrina declared.

"We're not Skull and Bones, we don't keep formal membership lists. Folks join, they drift away. When something big with Israel or Zionist politicians goes on, we get more people at our informal get-togethers—cocktail parties, private dinners. At any given time, we have a couple hundred people plugged in, all over Europe, a few Americans, a few Russians and elsewhere. Politicians, financiers who have been screwed over by the Bilderbergers. BDS is a first step for our crowd. A quarter of Europeans recognize that Jews have too much control in politics and finance—the Jewish lobby in your country."

Alec stepped over and pulled back for a punch, but Katrina turned and stopped him with a glare.

"Where's Hell Summoner going to release the virus?" she demanded.

"Wherever he is, it's going to be a big city that's an air travel hub. Health security screenings shouldn't detect the asymptomatic, and he'll get it all around the world fast before a quarantine can be put in place." He checked the gauze by his ear. "We thought of everything. The fact that I'm worried I'll catch the virus here, in a far-off-corner of Tanzania, should tell you just how certain I am that this will spread far and wide."

Katrina studied him. "You're not afraid to die. But you're afraid of dying in a way that will leave people thinking you're a Jew."

Vincent stared back angrily. "Yes. Are you happy? I detest the thought of being mistaken for one of you."

Katrina nodded. "Then how you get remembered all comes down to how honestly you answer this question: who is the Shedim member who's Hell Summoner's contact?"

Vincent's defiance started to crack. Katrina's stare seemed to burn into him.

"After you're gone, we'll bury you quick, no embalming, in keeping with Jewish tradition," Katrina declared with quiet, carefully calibrated fury. "We'll recite the mourner's kaddish, have everyone drop handfuls of dirt upon your grave and your ex-wife and daughter will stay at home for a week in mourning—sitting shiva. Vincent van der Groot, if you don't help me stop this virus right here and right now, I will personally ensure that you are forever remembered as everything you hate the most. I will move heaven and earth to ensure that your daughter converts, that she breaks a glass under the huppah when she gets married, and that every one of your grandchildren has a *brit milah* or *simchat bat*. Not only will you fail in your mission to exterminate people like me, I will use your own flesh and blood to ensure we carry on. I will turn everyone you love into everything you hate. Look in my eyes, Vincent, and see if you can find any reason to doubt that I will do this."

Alec shook his head and whistled. Poor Vincent van der Groot had no idea what he was in for when he angered his wife. Even Ward seemed startled by Katrina's just-barely-under-control white-hot fury.

Vincent first stared up at the sky, then looked down, sad. Katrina found something he needed even more than for his grandiose plan to succeed.

"Shakira Erikat," Vincent answered. "She's a member of the German Bundestag. Elected a few years ago, one of our youngest members. This was her idea. I think she heard about it from someone in—oh, it could have been Turkey, or Iran, or Syria, or someplace. Maybe one of the factions in Libya."

Katrina nodded. But behind her, Raquel pressed her earpiece to her ear, trying to hear what Dee was saying, listening in to the interrogation, halfway around the world at Liberty Campus. Finally, she relayed the question.

"Vincent, Shakira Erikat makes no sense," Raquel declared. "She's of Palestinian heritage. Her parents were immigrants. Why would she be creating a virus that would kill so many Arabs, Turks, North Africans?"

Vincent smiled. "She's just an angel," he declared. "She doesn't like them any more than I do—or at least, she recognizes the world has too damn many of them. We wipe out the Jews, take out a bunch of the Middle East with them." He let out a menacing grin, knowing it unnerved his captors.

"She and I thought of this endeavor as global... *spring cleaning*."

Vincent couldn't have known those would be his last words. Alec grabbed Vincent, yanked him out of the chair, and dragged him, kicking and screaming, until he could throw him, face-first, into the alkaline waters of Lake Natron. With a giant splash, he disrupted the scarlet-red layer of microorganisms, and ripples emanated out into the broader lake. It was barely eighteen inches deep, but it was enough—the water singed his skin and burned at all of his wounds. Vincent managed to get to his knees, and howled in pain, holding his face; it must have been like jumping into a swimming pool full of bleach. Everything burned—his eyes went blind, his nose and mouth were scalded, the hideous burning liquid searing his throat and scorching his lungs—and all of his wounds stinging as if lemon juice had been poured over torn-up knees. Overcome by pain, he fell backward and went under again … and he did not surface.

Alec watched him disappear under the water. "Hey, good news, Vinny, you don't have to worry about that virus anymore!"

He turned back to his friends. For once, no one was objecting.

"Ordinarily, I'd say we should try to avoid killing detainees, but that stance is really hard to uphold in the face of a genocidal maniac," Katrina murmured. "The man had a heart of stone."

Alec beamed with satisfaction. "Well, now the rest of his body will match!"

# CHAPTER FIFTEEN

APPROACHING JOMO KENYATTA
INTERNATIONAL AIRPORT
JUST OUTSIDE NAIROBI, KENYA
THURSDAY, APRIL 30

Katrina and the team relayed the name "Shakira Erikat" to Dee, who got it into the hands of Director Stern quickly.

Thankfully, the National Security Agency did not take long to determine that Bundestag member Shakira Erikat was, at that moment, on a flight from Berlin to Washington, continuing on to Los Angeles. The trip had originally been part of a long-planned effort to renew trade ties between the United States and the remaining member states of the European Union, but her Washington meetings had been canceled. Congress and the president were having their millionth showdown over what to do about the post-pandemic economic woes, with talk this could lead to yet another government shutdown.

Erikat was supposed to meet with "business and health innovation leaders" while in Los Angeles, but her public schedule had nothing specific listed. An NSA hack of her office computers found nothing. Her personal cell phone was unreachable while she was high above the Atlantic.

She had already lined up all the appropriate entry visas, and as her trip was part of her official duties, there was some argument within the CIA of whether Erikat was covered by diplomatic immunity. Arresting or detaining her was certain to create an international incident and cause the State Department to go bonkers—and they were *still* raging about the Dangerous Clique's work in Serbia. After Lars Egner-Baerwald's death, German politics-watchers noticed considerable buzz that Erikat could be the next head of the Social Democratic Party and perhaps even chancellor within the next few years.

Finally, when Erikat landed in Washington, she turned on her cell phone again. Within moments of being turned on and connected to various cell towers and wireless signals, the NSA hacked it and found one address in Los Angeles:

*HS Medical Supply, Suite 3100, Fox Plaza.*

Fox Plaza was a skyscraper in Century City.

***

In her office on the seventh floor of CIA Headquarters in Langley, Director Stern let out a long and slow sigh of dread. She was going to need the Federal Bureau of Investigation to set up surveillance on Erikat the moment she stepped off the flight in LAX, and she really didn't want anyone in the FBI beyond Elaine Kopek knowing why.

***

The prospect of another round of long waits and jabbing health security nasal probes filled Katrina with dismay as they pulled up to Nairobi International Airport. But Rodgers was waiting for them, waved them down, and then, almost by magic, escorted them through every conceivable checkpoint with ease. The Kenyans treated Rodgers like royalty. Only one security official—a giant of a man who appeared to be in charge of the whole airport—briefly opened and inspected the case for Ward's

Barrett sniper rifle. Upon seeing it, the security chief let out a long whistle.

"That's a fine piece of craftsmanship," he declared. "Good hunting this trip?"

"Only the most dangerous game," Ward responded with a smile.

He closed the case and waved them through. Katrina and the others were pleasantly surprised, to the point of befuddled, at how Rodgers seemed to motion his hand and the airport security and customs officials quickly moved to open doors and sign papers with only cursory glances.

"I wish I had you around every time I traveled," she marveled in disbelief. "How did you—"

Rodgers unleashed a deep rumbling laugh that James Earl Jones would envy. "The fine, fine professionalism of the United States State Department! Well, that and a couple hundred million dollars in foreign aid. And the fact that we signed a trade deal with them when we were putting up tariffs with everyone else. And the fact that we sent them a bunch of ventilators when we realized we had manufactured more than we needed. And my sheer persuasive natural charm. And there's a rumor that they're going to film the *Black Panther* sequel here, and—"

The last set of doors opened, taking them outside of the main airport terminal to a row of hangars.

"This is all great, but we're still looking at a long series of flights to catch up with—" Alec stopped when he saw the gleaming black jet awaiting them.

"A local mogul who made a fortune in exporting tea was kind enough to loan us his plane. Don't break anything, don't drink his booze, and use a coaster." He glared at Alec, who responded with a pantomimed "Who, me?"

Rodgers chucked and continued. "Top speed of mach point eight, you won't have to get off the plane for the refueling stops.

We should have you in Los Angeles in …" He checked his watch. "… nineteen hours."

The sharp-angled black Cessna Citation Longitude private jet looked like a giant mechanical raven.

"Thank you, Rodgers," Katrina declared. He wrapped his arms around her in a bear hug.

"Our friends in Washington didn't give me many details, only that you're trying to prevent the end of everything." His grin disappeared as he released her from the embrace. "So … don't let everything end."

She nodded. "Win or die trying," she promised.

"Not such a fan of that second option!" Alec grumbled behind her. He saluted Rodgers, walked toward the plane, then turned around before climbing the private jet stairs.

"Look at it this way, Rodgers … if we don't succeed, you're probably not gonna need the plane back anyway."

***

Ursula Aldana was a beauty from Spain, recently retired from that country's Military Health Corps. Just a few years ago, Ursula's friends would have described her as vivacious, fun, a woman who laughed easily, and inadvertently wrapped men around her little finger even easier. Good-looking since puberty, she had been determined to show she was so much more than a pretty face—that she, too, could be tough, and smart, and compassionate. And first in medical school and then in her country's military, she had.

And then the coronavirus arrived in Spain and unleashed a nightmare. She lost both parents and far too many friends and neighbors. She survived, but her friends described her as a different soul in the old body. Ursula Aldana's warmth was gone; she barely smiled anymore and never laughed. She spent a month trying to drink herself to death, and then crashed her car on purpose. Fate seemed to hate her so much, she survived with minimal injuries.

She turned cold, withdrew from friends and surviving relatives, and was looking for a new purpose when the man calling himself Hell Summoner found her.

Ursula's experience overlapped somewhat with Orso Veppi's, who had spent his career in Italy's Agenzia Informazioni e Sicurezza Esterna—*External Intelligence and Security Agency*—the country's foreign intelligence service. Italy's intelligence services didn't get nearly the amount of attention and fame or infamy of their American or British counterparts. When their work was acknowledged publicly—which was rare—it was vague references to arranging the release or rescue of Italian citizens kidnapped abroad or tracking terrorist threats against the Vatican. Veppi's work there was not glamorous; he knew that compared to the CIA or MI6, his organization was perceived as minor league. But he was smart and skilled, and he was among those who tried to sound the alarm to the Italian government about the reports of a strange virus in Wuhan, and the risk of travelers from China bringing it to Italy. Before the pandemic, 310,000 Chinese citizens lived in Italy, many working in the northern part of the country, in the textile industry.

Veppi's warnings were too late.

The pandemic extracted a horrific cost in lost lives, and his countrymen emerged psychologically battered and bruised. Veppi had never quit, but he found it hard to remain motivated. Like many, he suffered from depression and various forms of post-traumatic stress syndrome. He felt like he had already engaged in the grandest battle of his life ... and lost.

But then this strange man came to meet Veppi—God knows how he had run across his name and reputation.

The strange man had already recruited Wilhelm, a Berlin policeman who knew a great deal about how Germany and other countries handled potential biological weapons attacks. Ursula, from Spain, melded military experience with additional understanding of medicine and human health. The strange man asked Orso to complete his quartet, operating under his code name "evocatore dell'inferno"—"Hell Summoner" in his native language.

"Hell Summoner" ran an exceptionally small operation; fewer people, fewer possible mistakes. He explained that they were not terrorists, although the world would see them as such. They were businessmen, providing a service and a product, meeting a demand with an extremely limited supply. Their actions would involve handling and manipulating dangerous biological material, be indisputably illegal, and leave them widely hated. The deaths of innocent people were inevitable. But their firsthand witnessing the passing of so many of their loved ones, among the deaths of hundreds of thousands around the world, had left them numb to the thought of more.

They would walk away from the operation having enacted a terrible vengeance upon an unjust world, and wealthy enough to simply disappear and live however they wanted, wherever they wanted, for the rest of their lives. Whatever the world thought of them, they knew they were heroes—instructors of the harshest, most-ignored, most-denied truths. A world that had turned "never again" into a casual, meaningless empty slogan needed a brutal reminder of the evil that lurked in the hearts of men and just how catastrophic the powers of science and technology could be in the wrong hands.

Their equipment was easily obtained and relatively inexpensive, indistinguishable from any one of the thousands of new small businesses, institutions, schools, and groups studying genetics, immunology, and virology. Wilhelm obtained them firearms, but really he was mostly needed as protection as they quietly reached out to a long list of potential clients and began negotiations. They started with the governments of Iran and North Korea. When both seemed unable to pull together the mind-boggling sum, Hell Summoner moved on to virtual and in-person meetings with representatives of the governments of Turkey, Serbia, Myanmar, and Equatorial Guinea. Orso thought he already knew every form of human evil under the sun, but he was horrified to learn that Equatorial Guinea's dictator, Teodoro Obiang Nguema, had reportedly eaten the brains and testicles of rivals he deemed a threat to him.

None of the world's most detestable governments outright rejected Hell Summoner's offer; they merely dawdled and complained the price was too high. Hell Summoner moved on to nongovernmental organizations—one of Libya's militias, then the Dinka tribe in South Sudan. Hell Summoner was certain that someone would feel tempted enough to start trying to accumulate the funds. The twenty-first century had already seen no less than twenty-six separate ethnic cleansing campaigns—most of them relatively small-scale and easily ignored on page A22, the "world news" section of the newspaper, in the communities where people still read newspapers.

Hell Summoner was only mildly surprised when he heard about this "Shedim" network of wealthy anti-Israel and anti-refugee ideologues. Europe's aristocrats and wealthy elites had always liked their secret societies—the Black Hand in Serbia, the Thule Society in Germany, the Order of the Solar Temple in France. European society had been shaken to its foundations by the war on terror, waves of refugees, the United Kingdom leaving the European Union, the rise of populist leaders and protest like the yellow vests—and then the coronavirus hit on top of all that. Anger, paranoia, and fantasies of bloody revolution had taken root in the cracks that the pandemic exposed.

And now one of the Shedim's youngest members, Shakira Erikat, had somehow persuaded the wealthy network to pay Hell Summoner his exorbitant sum and follow his elaborate money transfer methods, to make their money truly untraceable. She would be in Los Angeles tonight. And after their meeting, the world would never be the same.

\*\*\*

Flight records indicated Shakira Erikat traveled with a companion, Marwan Mabarek, believed to be a bodyguard.

Undercover FBI agents would tail Erikat and Mabarek from the moment they stepped off the plane at LAX. If the agents saw either one taking possession of something before she arrived to Fox Plaza—even something as seemingly innocuous as a shopping bag from a store or café—they were to move in and inspect the package. CIA Director Stern said that if they failed to find any bioweapon, the FBI agents should apologize and act like it was a case of mistaken identity.

"She'll probably claim it's racial profiling," the FBI director grumbled.

"Well, thankfully, you guys have spent several decades establishing a good cover explanation," Stern deadpanned. "With any luck, she won't think we're onto her, she'll just think your people are racist."

\*\*\*

"Our enemies get younger every year!" Alec fumed. "Look at her, Raquel. Just look at her! Madam Pouty-Lips here looks like she belongs on the cover of *Maxim*!"

He threw the folder across the private jet's interior.

"You gonna pick that up?" Ward growled.

"Bats! Monkeys! What, is she waiting for us in LA with a swarm of murder hornets?" Alec raged. "I was ready for this to be the work of some old Nazi! Give me Belloq, give me the Red Skull, give me Colonel Klink! I am used to sickos and psychos like Gholam Gul and Espino and van der Groot! Did you ever notice that you almost never see any young terrorist leaders? Bin Laden, Baghdadi, Zawahiri! It's always some old man sending young men out to die in his name! Fearful, bitter old men who couldn't cope with a world changing—" Alec paused, and wondered how much his description applied to himself. He looked at his hands and wondered when they stopped looking like young men's hands.

He shook his head and switched back to his rant: "—a world changing underneath their feet. But some young political rising star? Somebody who's got every advantage and a bright future ahead of her? Somebody who's already got power, and a voice in society? And at such a young age? If somebody like that can be driven to do something like this..."

He picked up the picture. "And a woman?" Alec was utterly befuddled.

Katrina reached up and put her hand on the back of Alec's neck.

"Kipling observed, 'the female of the species is more deadly than the male,'" she said. In her mind, this was as self-evident as water being wet or deserts being dry. Alec sat down next to her.

"I know you can keep it together," she told him.

She knew her husband well. He desperately wanted to be perceived as dangerous as Ward and herself. And apparently, between the warping long-term stress of the pandemic and the revelation of the threat of Hell Summoner's virus, Alec had unlocked some psychological vault of adrenaline and aggression and a creative, inventive vindictiveness toward their foes. But this wasn't really him.

She just needed him to keep it together until Los Angeles. And with his tantrum complete, Alec reclined his seat and lapsed into a deep sleep.

***

The black Cessna Citation Longitude had just crossed into American airspace when Katrina felt the need to wake the others. She needed her teammates well rested for whatever confrontation the City of Angels would bring, but the news Stern had just relayed to her over a secure line was terrible and altered the calculus of what they were about to face.

"There's been an outbreak," Katrina gravely informed the others.

Alec nearly leaped out of his chair and asked where.

"Mexico City, but something doesn't make sense." Katrina looked at Raquel with concern. "It's reportedly a strain of Influenza B, which…isn't that deadly compared to other flus. And the other thing is that it's clustered around the city's Kehila Ashkenazi community."

"Mexico has Jews?" Ward asked in surprise.

"Their food must be *amazing*," Alec gasped.

"Wait, wait, wait," Raquel said, wiping the sleep crud from her eyes and trying to get her head around what she was hearing. "Ashkenazi Jews don't have that gene, JN-8675309 or whatever it is. We're—I mean, they're not supposed to be vulnerable to the virus that they're cooking up."

Katrina nodded, brushing her hair out of her face. "Precisely, they *don't* have that gene, meaning either this is a coincidence, or…or maybe it mutated. Or maybe the Shedim ordered a second virus to take out the other half of the world's Jews."

Raquel slammed her fist on the armrest and muttered profanities that would make Dave Chappelle cringe. Ward looked at her in concern, unsure if the outburst represented bubbling rage or whether she had just slammed her hand down so hard she had injured herself. Katrina checked for an update on the emergency flash message from Stern.

"But it doesn't make sense," Katrina muttered when she read the addendum. "Influenza B isn't likely to kill people as long as they get treated. It's most dangerous to the elderly or immuno-compromised. Why in God's name would the Shedim pay four billion dollars and then just get a bad flu season that starts in Mexico?"

The quartet looked at each other in confusion and apprehension. Alec's manic glee had disappeared. The news had drained all of his tantrum-spurring anger.

Then his face lit up with realization.

"It's a test run," Alec muttered. "Hell Summoner is refining his creation through trial and error."

# CHAPTER SIXTEEN

THE PRIVATE SUITE TERMINAL
LOS ANGELES INTERNATIONAL AIRPORT
SUNDAY, MAY 1

Shortly after landing in Los Angeles in the early evening hours, Katrina and Raquel reacted to the update from Special Agent Elaine Kopek with the same words, simultaneously: "What do you mean, the FBI *lost* her?"

"Relax!" Elaine emphasized. "The surveillance teams lost her, but then we found her again—she and her bodyguard took an Uber to Fox Plaza. They just arrived and went inside."

Elaine introduced another FBI special agent, Joseph Mills, who looked stocky and seasoned, a head full of salt-and-pepper hair and posture that Joe Friday would envy. "We'll be driving you to Fox Plaza."

"We're in hurry, Mills, so please tell me you drive a Maserati on weekends," Alec quipped.

Mills shook his head. "Nope. The most fuel-efficient highest-safety-rating minivan on the market."

Ward and Alex exchanged a skeptical look. "At least he won't be taking unnecessary risks. You do know we can use the car-pool lanes, right?"

Elaine and Mills escorted them through the airport, arriving to a secure parking lot with two black Chevy Suburban SUVs with government plates.

Raquel sighed. "Not exactly inconspicuous."

Elaine sighed. "What do I look like, Carmax? When the director of the CIA calls and says, 'catch the next flight to LA, we need some FBI vehicles and weapons and gear to raid the offices of a medical research company, and everything has to be kept completely quiet and off the books until further notice'... This is what we've got! If you don't like it, call an Uber!" She wondered if the ride-sharing companies had ever worked out their dispute with the state government.

Alec and Katrina had furiously argued the last hour of the flight about whether she should even be present when they raided what they believed was the operating laboratory of Hell Summoner. Alec insisted Katrina should be coordinating their raid from some secure location, far from the presence of any viruses designed to devastate her genes.

As they climbed into the SUVs, Alec started it again. "You should be nowhere near that site! Don't tell me about Mexico City! That bastard can hit Ward and me with as much of that stuff as he wants, and I'll heal like Wolverine! I'm bioweapon bulletproof! For once, you're the vulnerable one, and you just refuse to see it! You're just as helpful a mile away—"

"Yes, and what happens if you catch it?" Katrina asked. Alec paused, realizing the risk of speading the virus to his wife.

Katrina clenched and unclenched her hands.

"This virus is designed to sideline people like me," she fumed. "If I sit this one out, they win. I'm very impressed with this"—she waved her hand at his head—"obsessively driven maniac persona you've adopted, but I know that's a mask you're wearing, honey. It's an adaptation," she observed. "This is what I do, and this is what I am best at. For two years, I have been desperately searching for some way to help everyone climb out of this muck and mess, to help us build something better. That 'something better' can't happen until Erikat and Hell Summoner get taken out of commission. In about two hours, we will have either taken a big step to fixing this world, or nothing we've done will have mattered. Nothing *I've* done will have mattered! If you think I can sit on the bench or run comms from a mile away, you're nuts." Her eyes were wide, and her tone was adamant.

Alec looked away in frustration. From a row behind them, Ward cleared his throat.

Alec laughed, and Katrina realized his laugh was to hide the building tears.

"Sweetheart, you think I'm nuts now?" Alec laughed. "You're the thread that's keeping me tied to—well, anything. I have lived, for almost twenty years, with the girlfriend and wife who's running down alleys in Wherever-the-hell-istan and sneaking through windows in East Armpit–ville! And I'm fine with it! But not this! But not a virus! It's just … it's …"

She put her hand on his.

"It's too much like the fear you thought we just put behind us?" she asked.

He nodded. "I just got over this."

"I know what you need," she said firmly. "And you know that I need to do this. I *need* to do what I can. If I sit on the sidelines … you might as well ask me not to breathe."

Alec turned. "Is that an option?"

"Yeah, as a matter of fact, it is!" Ward declared from the third row of seats behind them. He had been rooting around a crate in the trunk carriage behind his seat and removed an FBI hostage rescue team twin-port protective mask. "Somebody got the message that we're dealing with potential biological weapons."

"Get out of those crates!" Special Agent Mills shouted from the driver's seat.

Alec exhaled and nodded. The mask should keep Katrina from inhaling the virus, he concluded.

Emphasis on *should*, he thought.

"We've all got to wear those," Alec declared. "Otherwise, we might spread the virus to her."

\*\*\*

In the black SUV ahead of them, Raquel's phone rang. The number indicated it was Director Stern.

"We are really pushing it trying to keep this away from other agencies," Stern declared, without any greeting. "The FBI director is calling me every five minutes, and I can't even blame him. His teams have already been instructed to monitor, seize, and detain two foreign nationals if either one takes any package, and to look for potential biological weapons or biohazardous material. This isn't going to stay under wraps for long. If you don't want to get every other law enforcement agency in LA involved, you've got one minute to convince me otherwise."

Raquel winced. "She's in Fox Plaza. We think she's getting the virus now. If she sees LAPD swarming on her, she's just gonna release it and hope it gets airborne ..."

Stern realized that this decision would probably define her time as director. There was little reason to think that van der Groot was lying about anything he said. Shakira Erikat was, at this moment, probably in the offices of some mad virologist, finalizing the payoff and picking up a custom-designed bioweapon. Raquel and her team *might* catch her and neutralize her in Fox Plaza in time ... or maybe not.

"What if I just asked the city to shut down LAX?" Stern mused aloud. "If she wants this to go worldwide, that's the easiest vector."

Raquel understood Los Angeles reasonably well; a long time ago, work with In-Q-Tel had brought her to California's tech companies regularly. "If we lose her, she could just turn around and go to Ontario International, or Burbank and John Wayne or

Long Beach. She could just take a car and go to San Diego or San Francisco. Or she just releases it in the city and hopes it spreads far and fast enough. Anything we do that suggests we're onto her will probably make her move up her timeline for releasing the virus."

Stern swore. "Okay. Okay, how about I ask the mayor of Los Angeles to enact a curfew for the night?"

Raquel looked at her phone in confusion. "Madam Director, viruses work in both daylight and nighttime."

Stern raged that she knew that, and that she wanted to keep people off the streets.

"Look, in about an hour, it's probably not going to matter," Raquel said. "If we have the virus, people can be on the streets all they like. If we don't have the virus … a curfew's not going to make much difference. Gotta go, we're pulling up now."

Their destination stood before them like a menacing, ancient tower: Fox Plaza.

***

Fox Plaza is a thirty-four-story, 493-foot skyscraper in Century City, Los Angeles.

The building site was once part of the backlot of 20th Century Fox movie studio. Billionaire Marvin "Wildcatter" Davis, who owned Fox from 1981 to 1985, wanted a signature skyscraper on the company's property. He wanted, and received, a classic of 1980s symbolic architecture straight out of the dreams of executives from the alleged "decade of greed"—tall, powerful, and, some argued, phallic. With odd corners sticking out of each side, the result was sixteen corner offices on every floor. Built in the late 1980s, the *Los Angeles Times* praised its "pink-toned granite and gray tinted glass and tilted and angled at the upper floors to subtly reflect light" and the lobby's "granite and Moderne-styled light fixtures," but lamented "the columns blocking the natural light cast a pall over the space and makes it feel oddly claustrophobic."

Most of the office space was used by 20th Century Fox or rented by a variety of law firms, but Davis was a friend of the soon-to-retire President Ronald Reagan, and let the president know that prime office space would be available for his friend. Reagan agreed, and answered the phones himself on the day he moved in because his new receptionist wasn't available yet. Because of Reagan, the building had hosted visits from Mother Teresa and Margaret Thatcher. Reagan's office moved to a different location in 2001.

Many Los Angeles residents believed the skyscraper had been originally built by a Japanese corporation and that it had been the site of a terror attack in 1988, although no official records could confirm the wild stories of die-hard believers.

The recent pandemic-driven economic collapse shut down a slew of once-thriving businesses and opened up rental space in even the most sought-after addresses in Los Angeles. About two months ago, a small medical research startup put down a deposit and set up shop on the thirty-first floor. The rent had been paid on time, and the neighboring tenants had no complaints. Building managers and the security team noticed that other than a flurry of activity moving lab equipment into place in the first few days, the space was particularly quiet, with no one entering for weeks at a time.

The two black SUVs rolled up to the large, somewhat ostentatious twin-circle brick driveway that led to the lobby. One FBI man stood by the lobby entrance, doing a terrible job of appearing inconspicuous. The Beefeaters standing guard at the Tower of London stood out less.

Katrina, Alec, Ward, Raquel, Elaine, and Agent Joseph Mills hopped out. Mills popped the rear hatch.

Ward examined the selection of Glocks the FBI had provided and grumbled that suppressors would have been useful. Alec recommended using water bottles, but Ward scoffed at that trick often depicted in the movies. Shooting through a water bottle offered only a minimal reduction in sound at considerable cost of accuracy—and that was presuming some piece of the water bottle didn't fly back and hit the shooter.

***

Thirty floors above them, five figures met inside a conference room adjacent to a biosafety-level-2 laboratory.

On one side of the table sat Shakira Erikat; her tall, lean bodyguard Marwan stood by the doorway, hands free, watching everyone carefully. The other side of the table featured Hell Summoner and the remaining two members of his four-man team.

Ursula Aldana sat next to him; Orso Veppi stood beside him, mostly watching Marwan. Hell Summoner removed a laptop from his briefcase, flipped it open, and gently pressed a few keys, ensuring that the payments from the Shedim network had continued to transfer according to his plan.

Hell Summoner required a complicated payment process. He had studied the laws requiring increased transparency associated with transferring funds through US banks and "money services businesses," along with the tales of the almost unparalleled NSA snooping in the financial systems around the world. He concluded that the only truly untraceable form of money was cash. The only way to move money from one account to another and evade law enforcement and intelligence agencies was to take a sum of money out of one account in cash, give the cash to another trusted individual, and then have that trusted individual deposit a slightly different amount in the second bank account. This meant investigators didn't have a particular sum to look for in transaction records; a withdrawal of $9,987.65 from one account in one bank would turn into $9,890.90 in the next, with no record of the money moving from one person to another. All cash deposits of more than $10,000 in US banks had to be reported to the Internal Revenue Service.

For the past month, the roughly one hundred members of Shedim had taken cash out of one account, given it to a trusted business manager, lawyer, personal assistant, or family member, and had that person deposit the cash into one of the dozens of accounts Hell Summoner owned. The amounts changed each day, and the accounts changed each day. There were no nice even sums in the money transfers for the Treasury Department or other investigators to spot, no patterns for any algorithm to recognize. On average, the transfers were nine thousand dollars. Each day, about nine hundred thousand dollars moved into Hell Summoner's accounts; every few days, he then transferred small sums into a Swiss bank account. He and his team had accumulated nearly twenty-seven million dollars so far.

To the Shedim, this made little sense; the bioweapon-maker wanted the ungodly sum of more than four billion in increments of about nine thousand; this was like an NBA star asking for his multimillion dollar signing bonus to be paid entirely in rolls of nickels. What's more, Hell Summoner seemed strangely trusting; once the Shedim had their bioweapon, they could theoretically stop the payments, instead of continuing the cash transfers for every day for the next twelve years. But they recognized Hell Summoner's system was likely to outwit the world's governments and financial authorities and were somewhat impressed with the creativity of the method. No government would be able to prove the Shedim members had paid him without cooperating witnesses.

Satisfied that all of the payments were on schedule, Hell Summoner rose, headed to an airtight refrigerated biohazard safety cabinet, and unlocked it. He removed two stylish but functional pouches with shoulder straps and returned to the table. He demonstrated how the virus was in a series of small vials, and how the vials would be easily hidden in in the bottom of the pouch. He explained that the vials could be easily opened; they didn't need to be unscrewed but could simply pop off with sufficient pressure from a thumb. But he warned that they should not open the vial until they were ready; once exposed to air currents, the viruses within would disperse fairly quickly.

"Haplogroup J-M267 is sometimes referred to as J1," Hell Summoner explained. "I have engineered what I call 'absumovirus.' The term 'absumo' is Latin for 'annihilate.' To a person who does not have that gene, a sufficient load of virus should produce an effect comparable to the common cold. To the person with Haplogroup J-M267, this will hit them on a level comparable to the influenza of 1918."

Shakira nodded with satisfaction.

Hell Summoner continued. "I would recommend LAX for release. Even with the reduced flights since the pandemic, it's still the second busiest airport in America and third busiest in the world. The infected should be asymptomatic for days. The health security checks won't be able to detect it. El Al flights to Israel, Emirates to Dubai, Etihad to Abu Dhabi, Qatar Airways to Doha, Saudi Air, Turkish Airlines to Istanbul. If, as I suspect, you are returning to Berlin, you may want to do the same before the security check for departures on the other side. This will ensure the virus spreads around the world, faster than governments and health systems will be able to cope. As you requested, this will cut through the targeted populations with considerable fatalities and minimal effect on other populations, barring the risk of mutation."

He noticed her eyebrow raise at that.

"Listen, I know you've checked your genes, and you're certain that you don't have Haplogroup J-M267," Hell Summoner said after a pause. "It should have no serious impact to your system, but without doing a complete review of your DNA, I cannot guarantee that your exposure while dispersing it would not put you at any risk. If my creation inadvertently harmed you, after you and your friends have paid such a considerable fee, it would be … bad for business. So in the interest of maintaining our good business relationship, I strongly recommend that you first take this broad-spectrum antiviral as a precaution."

Shakira examined it. "You said this virus couldn't harm anyone who didn't have the gene."

Hell Summoner sighed. "To the average person without the gene, no, it would feel like a case of the sniffles. But if you are the one handling it at the point of dispersal, you could easily get a heavy viral load—enough that your immune system would have a challenge fighting it off. Anything in sufficient dosage can kill you. If I had you eat eleven thousand oranges, the overdose of Vitamin C would kill you. I'd recommend both of you take this. All of us took one before we started engineering the virus and have taken regular boosters since."

Marwan and Shakira exchanged a look, and then nodded.

\*\*\*

Once inside the ornate lobby of the Fox Plaza building, Katrina and her team met with the seemingly competent but increasingly unnerved building security manager, Craig Cortes. Katrina asked how many civilians were still in the building.

"At this hour, a few tenants working late, my team is trying to quietly knock on doors and evacuate all of the lower floors," Craig responded. "Are they at risk for some outbreak?"

"No," Katrina said as Alec said "yes." They exchanged a look, and Craig gulped.

"How many people work at HS Medical Supply?" Katrina asked.

"Normally, three," Craig responded. "Earlier tonight we signed in two visitors...a...boy, they scribbled their names here. Their photo IDs were passports," he said, bringing up the scanned images. "Mayada Arwan and Amir Haddad."

"Fake IDs," Katrina declared. "The woman is Shakira Erikat, a member of the German parliament. I don't know who the guy is, but I'll bet he's a bodyguard and armed. Tell us about the three at HS."

Craig brought up the building's ID and entry and exit records for that office.

"Jonas Meiner, Anastasia Roness, and Otto Eindringling, US passports. They have a few delivery guys come and go. They have accents. She's Spanish, the other guy's Italian. Meiner, I don't know, British but it sounds kind of fake."

Alec chuckled. "Eindringling" was German for "infiltrator."

Katrina studied the photo of Jonas Meiner. "I've seen him somewhere before. Not in person."

They gathered around Raquel, who placed a tablet on the counter and displayed the blueprint of the 31st floor.

"Wait, how did you get those blueprints?" Craig asked, recognizing the image.

"Totally not from the National Security Agency," Raquel answered quickly. She moved on. "Okay, we've got three men, two women. We don't know who has the virus. We presume at least one of the five has the virus in a secure transportation container."

Elaine shook her head. "Let's call in LAPD and all the backup the Bureau can muster. We have a man at every exit, but they could try to blast their way out. We establish a perimeter, keep their virus contained right here."

Raquel rejected that idea. At the moment, the only advantage that they had over Erikat and Hell Summoner was the element of surprise, she contended. At the first sight of FBI helicopters or an LAPD SWAT team rolling down the street in an armored vehicle, any of their targets could high-tail it to the roof or an open window—and if the virus was aerosolized, they could just spread it out from the top of the skyscraper, letting the wind and gravity disperse it upon the unknowing Los Angelenos below. The Fox Plaza tower was in the middle of Century City, near shopping malls, supermarkets, a recently reopened public movie theater, and gas stations. Whichever way the wind blew, a lot of inhaling noses and mouths were below—Santa Monica Boulevard to the north, Beverly Hills to the east, Rancho Park to the south, and Westwood to the west.

Elaine briefly argued that the virus would probably disperse too widely, but quickly relented, recognizing that they simply didn't know enough about the virus Hell Summoner had cooked up.

Craig, Katrina, and Ward completed a review of all of the security cameras and concluded there was no sign that anyone else was on the thirty-first floor. Alec got excited.

"Raquel, how quick could we get a fuel–air explosive over here?"

"I'm sorry, what now?" Craig asked, doing a double take.

"We take the fuel–air explosive, rig it to a remote detonator, put it on the elevator, send it up to their floor—*ding!*—elevator doors open—'now I've got a Hellfire missile, ho-ho-ho!'—and burn them, and their lab, and all traces of the virus back to hell," Alec said excitedly. "No muss, no fuss, no risk of accidental release of a virus designed to kill her"—he pointed to Katrina—"and after going Conan the Thermo-barbarian on their asses, we all get to go home and drink."

Craig cleared his throat. "I would really rather not have *The Towering Inferno* on my watch."

Alec sighed. "*Someone's* never made an omelet."

Craig stared back in disbelief. "Wow," he groaned.

Raquel shook her head. "Even if I thought blowing up a whole floor of a skyscraper was a good idea, that would take … at least an hour, minimum. Maybe Camp Pendleton would have one. That's not gonna get here in time."

***

Right as Hell Summoner had administered the antiviral shots to Shakira and Marwan, Orso received a message on his phone and left the room. He returned a moment later.

"Someone's downstairs. Either FBI or cops," he said gravely.

Weeks earlier, Orso had tapped into the building's security systems and built his own piggyback monitors. He displayed a tablet that showed video footage. Several men in dark suits who stood out like *Men in Black* were dispersing through the lobby, while a small group was huddling around the lobby desk, including a Eurasian woman and some sort of commando lumberjack.

Hell Summoner looked irritated, but not frightened. He studied the video footage from the lobby; he counted maybe a half-dozen FBI suits and then the oddball group breaking up their huddle. He looked up at his teammates. "It's time." Orso nodded and opened his laptop and started typing furiously.

Fear gripped Shakira. "We've got to get out of here!" she insisted.

Hell Summoner turned to his clients. "We have prepared for this eventuality and can get you out of this building. In just a moment, Orso will execute his countermeasures against their communications. This building has six elevators and four stair-wells. Your man is trained? Good. I recommend he engages the FBI, in order to draw them away from other ways down, leaving you a clear escape route. Besides the two main entrances, there are four emergency exits on the ground floor and the driveway up from any one of the six levels of the garage. You could also break a window on the second floor and jump—just don't break an ankle because you'll need to move quickly once you're outside. Do you need a weapon?"

Shakira looked shocked and shook her head. Hell Summoner pushed the two strapped packs across the table.

"Remember, you're carrying a deadly virus, which is lever-age. Carry one vial in your hand."

Orso nodded and led them toward the office door. A moment after the door closed, Ursula turned to Hell Summoner. "And when do we leave?"

He put a reassuring hand on hers. "Orso will create a racket, and our idiot clients will likely do the same." He then gave her hand a squeeze. "I'm counting on you to protect me."

She nodded. They had grown surprisingly close these past few weeks.

"I can do it," she said. "I just wish I could count on a little luck."

"You want luck, Ursula?" Hell Summoner chuckled. "It's only the FBI."

***

The original plan was to take the stairs, but Alec pointed out that time was of the essence, and they would be exhausted after thirty stories. "Didn't you see *Ghostbusters*?" he asked.

Alec and Ward split into one team, and Katrina and Elaine the other. They double-checked their masks. The city's hazmat teams had been instructed to be on alert, and a group of special-ists from the CDC were on the way, but no one had any guaran-tee when they would get there.

On the twenty-ninth floor, they stepped off the elevator, split up, and ascended the last two floors up the east and west stairwells.

*** 

"Slices of the pie, bottom to top, quick and thorough," Ward reminded Alec in a gruff whisper, one hand on the stairway door handle. "You ready?"

"Oh, I'm ready!" Alec whispered with manic glee. "I'm com-ing through that door like Jack Torrance! Hey, Hell Summoner, here's Johnny!"

"Just shoot straight, my friend. We move on three … One … two …"

Ward opened the door—and his hand flew off the handle as a sudden loud BUDDA BUDDA BUDDA barrage of gunfire ham-mered the door. One or two ricochets bounced into the stairwell before the door closed, sparking and embedding into the wall above them. The door closed, but they could still hear more gun-fire, and see little indentations forming in the metal door.

Ward swore loudly.

"Gee, do you think they knew we were coming?" Alec asked.

"Better hope no ricochet hit their containers with the virus!" Ward muttered. He pulled his microphone closer to his mouth. "Katrina, Elaine, they know we're coming!"

But they heard no answer. "Katrina? Hello? Hello?"

Alec tried his. "Comms are down. Jamming our signals somehow?"

The gunfire had stopped. Ward reached up and tried to open the door a crack. The gunfire started up again.

Alec laughed.

"What is so damn funny?" Ward demanded.

"If they had jammed us before they shot at us, I could have asked you, 'how could they be jamming us if they don't know we're coming!' Just like Lando!"

Ward chuckled. He and Alec looked at each other.

"It's a trap!" they shouted at each other simultaneously, breaking into a long and continuing burst of laughter. Alec was suddenly overcome with the ludicrous absurdity of how they had managed to track down Hell Summoner from Berlin to Puerto Rico to Serbia to Tanzania to Los Angeles, only to get stuck in this stairwell.

"Will you look at us?" Alec said between convulsions of laughter. "You with the MPK, me with the Glocks, ready to kick ass and take names... years of experience, the slayers of Atarsa, and we can't even get past this door!"

Ward wiped a tear from laughing so hard. "I think the stress is getting to us."

\*\*\*

Down in the lobby, Raquel and Agent Mills could get no signal.

"Is your phone working?" he asked. Everything had seemed to go out at once—the operations comms, their walkie-talkie backups, and even their cell phones had no signal.

"These are state-of-the-art comms," she fumed. "They're not supposed to be able to do this! Dee? Dee, can you hear me?"

\*\*\*

Back in Liberty Campus, Dee smashed buttons on her keyboard in an apoplectic frenzy.

"Somebody tell me Century City in Los Angeles didn't just get nuked!" she shouted. Everything in Fox Plaza had just done dark: Internet, cell towers, phone lines, and both the CIA and FBI secure radio comms on all frequencies. It was as if a shroud had just been pulled over the entire skyscraper complex. Dee finally could pick up a traffic camera a block away, and then another. No indication of an explosion or other disruption, no indication of problems on LAPD communications.

No, this was no explosion, no earthquake, no natural disaster. Dee realized she had finally found the hacker Moriarty to her Sherlock. She straightened her back, cracked her knuckles.

"Oh, game on, punk!"

*** 

Once they had stopped laughing, Ward and Alec formulated a plan. Alec would go up one flight and try to descend from another stairway and come around behind whoever was firing at them.

On the stairwell entrance of the thirty-second floor, Alec opened the door a crack and checked for trip wires or other signs someone had been here. He opened the door very slowly and quietly, hearing another round of gunfire on the floor below him. He entered the hallway and noticed one office complex had its entrance door slightly ajar.

This office suite was much more luxurious and elaborate, with a Japanese motif and what Alec hoped were replicas of antiques. Creeping further inside, he guessed it was an architecture or engineering firm. One table had a scale model of a vast, curving bridge project, with a small plaque indicating it was built in Indonesia. Another table offered a model of the Fox Plaza skyscraper itself; a small plaque next to it declared, "And when Alexander saw the breadth of his domain, he wept, for there were no more worlds to conquer."

Alec wondered what kind of stuck-up snob would run around comparing himself to Alexander the Great when he heard a door close. He scrambled to the most poorly lit corner of the office suite lobby, away from the windows, and froze.

A moment later, Alec saw her: Shakira Erikat, trying to sneak toward another stairway. She glanced around, moving almost silently and regularly looking behind her, cradling a small case with a shoulder strap.

*God is good*, Alec concluded. He rose, stepped out, both hands on his Glock 17, arms extended, and at shoulder height, Erikat's head square in his sights. One squeeze of the trigger, and this could be all over. But Alec realized Katrina would disapprove of him not giving Erikat even the tiniest chance to surrender. He would give her just that—the tiniest chance to surrender.

"What's up, danger?" he called out.

Shakira looked up, saw Alec, and froze. Alec couldn't help but break into the widest and most satisfied of smiles. Then she slowly raised both hands... one of which held a plastic medical vial, her thumb in position to flick the vial open.

She smiled back. "What's that line?" She held the vial before her. "You have to ask yourself, 'do you feel lucky?'"

Alec felt an overwhelming compulsion to pull the trigger. Put a round through her skull, there's no way she would be able to open the vial in time—even if her muscles spasmed as she died. Right?

But... if he was wrong... if it took a second shot to finish her... and that vial opened... what if that virus got out? How close was Erikat to the building's ventilation system? How aerosolized was her virus? How potent was it? He looked at the ceiling and noticed an air conditioning vent uncomfortably close to where she was standing. It was probably blowing *out*, not *in*... but viruses rode air currents more easily than the seeds of a dandelion.

Alec grappled with the darkest thought: what if his decision to pull the trigger would get Katrina killed?

"This is the wrong day to dare me, Pouty-Lips," Alec declared. "Let's try truth instead of dare. Remember Shakira, hips don't lie, and neither should you. Why did you hire Doctor Mindbender down there to create a virus?" He choked back his emotions. "Out of all of the twisted, sick-in-the-head things to do, why this? You're a German-Palestinian swarthy centerfold! What on God's green earth could make you think you've got some reason to lash out at the world like this?"

"I'm not lashing out at the world," she scoffed. "I'm cleansing it. What do you think will happen when Haplogroup J-M267 is scoured from the face of the Earth? Yes, the Arabs, Turks, and North Africans will take a hit. But Israel will collapse. Half the world's Jews," she snapped her fingers. "Gone in a matter of months. I will share in the celebration of the Shedim. But they are my tool, not my master."

Alec nodded slowly. "Well, I agree that they are a bunch of tools."

She laughed. "Really, you thought those bitter old men could manipulate me? I'm manipulating them," she said with a smug, seductive smile.

"Yeah, yeah, Fox of Pox, just put down that vial and the whole container, or your family's going to need the closed casket option."

Shakira stood defiantly. "You really think you can stop me, Mr. American policeman? I'm—"

Alec moved his gun over a fraction, pulled the trigger and shot so close to her head that the round passed through her hair, missing her ear by less than inch. Shakira tumbled to the ground from the collective shock of the gun and looked up in horror and rage, breathing heavily.

Alec offered a satisfied smirk. "I love it when people mistake me for a cop, they always think I'll never shoot first," he declared. "Now put the virus down, Greedo, or I'll paint the wall behind you red."

But she held it up defiantly, like a talisman that could repel him. He could tell her thumb was pressing against the lid. One more bit of pressure, and it would pop open—releasing Hell Summoner's virus.

He stood over her; the pair remained frozen in their desperate standoff.

\*\*\*

Marwan knew he would need to reload soon. He fired his remaining shots, alternating directions in the hallway, then used the last round to break a glass door. He disappeared into an office suite.

\*\*\*

After a few moments of silence, Ward used a hand mirror to peek around the corner at one end of the hallway. He saw a quick, small, flash of light—not where the broken door was, but down by the other corner.

Another mirror?

"Alec?" Ward called out. Then he remembered he probably should have used Alec's code name, but it was too late now.

"Ward?" It was Elaine's voice. Apparently, no one was using code names tonight.

"He's inside one of the offices," Ward yelled. "I think it's Marwan, the bodyguard."

Ward heard movement in the hall and peered his head around the corner. Elaine was already advancing down her end of the hallway, gun level, just as the Bureau tactical training instructed while sweeping an insecure site. He was impressed. Elaine might be a little by-the-book for his tastes, but she didn't lack any courage.

He rose from his position and swept to the other side of the door.

He assessed the situation. "I'm remembering this floorplan correctly, right, that there's this entrance and a rear door down that other hallway to the west?" Elaine nodded agreement.

He peeked down inside the entrance to the office suite. "The broken glass is to make sure he hears us coming."

She nodded again and pointed down the hall. "You watch that back door. I'll try to bring him out this way. If he runs your way... try to take him alive."

Ward smirked and shook his head. "No promises."

***

"The world from South America to Africa to Asia will see the victims of this virus as victims a genocidal and malevolent West," Shakira seethed from the floor. "As cruel in its dark heart since the days of smallpox on blankets for your native tribes. The world will see America and Europe as irredeemable as the Nazis."

"Look, Ilsa She-Wolf, *you're the actual Nazi here*," Alec fumed.

Somehow, through sheer will, Shakira backed up toward a wall and got her feet back under her, rising to a crouch.

"And in the aftermath of the second straight worldwide pandemic, the collapse of the old regimes will be complete," she predicted, grinning madly. "We will build a new world upon the ruins of the old one—first a unified Europe, then a unified globe. We will wipe all the chess pieces off the board—nation-states, corporations, political parties. A true New World

Order…under my leadership. I will eliminate all of the petty differences that divide us. We can implant health-monitoring devices into each one of us, constantly tracking us and giving us early warning of any new outbreak—merging ourselves with the best advantages of technology. We will prove that the weakness of any one of us—like the way a stick can be easily broken—can be overcome by bundling us all together in one form, working for one purpose, the way a bound collection of those sticks becomes unbreakable. We will finally overcome our worst human instincts—greed, selfishness, racism, hatred—and achieve the unification of everyone toward one goal that serves us as a collective!"

Alec was unimpressed. "Sounds delightful," he scoffed. "Maybe we could all live in a giant cube in space."

Shakira stared back in confusion. "What?"

"God, everyone's culturally illiterate these days," Alec said, shaking his head in frustration. "Look, Queen Bee Wannabe, the world is broken enough without you trying to assimilate everyone into serving your Looney Tunes collectivism. Put the virus down or I will f—"

She interrupted him with a raging cry: "The world isn't broken because we've killed too many—it's because we haven't killed enough!"

Alec froze. "What did you say?"

***

Elaine heard Ward shout that he was in position.

She didn't even step through the threshold.

"Marwan Mabarek!" she shouted. "I am a special agent of the US Federal Bureau of Investigation! There are only two ways this situation ends, and please believe me when I tell you that coming with me is the good one."

She heard no answer from within the office suite. She wondered how well anyone could understand her, shouting through her chem-bio protection mask.

"We know you are Shakira Erikat's bodyguard, and you were not involved in the production of this biological weapon," she continued. "There is no need for you to pay the ultimate price over someone else's crimes."

Frustrated, Elaine took her first steps through the shattered glass doorway. It crunched underneath her feet.

"The building is surrounded by the FBI, there is no escape," she continued. "There are some people here, Marwan, who want you to make the wrong choice, so they can use deadly force that will kill you. I don't want that to happen, Marwan. As I see it, you're a professional bodyguard who just got stuck in the wrong place at the wrong time. I don't know what you've heard about the American criminal justice system, Marwan, but I will ensure that you get a fair trial. You're just a man who tried to do his job, and whose client got him mixed up with some really bad people."

Elaine thought she heard movement somewhere in the darkness. She took a calculated gamble.

"We took Shakira Erikat into custody a few moments ago," she declared to the darkness. "There's nothing left to protect. Your duty is complete. Come on out, and we will sort this all out."

An object flew out of the darkness. Elaine resisted the impulse to fire her weapon at the space the object emerged from—and then she realized it was a semiautomatic pistol like her own.

Marwan emerged, hands raised, and Elaine realized he had been crying.

"Marwan, keep your hands up," she said evenly, keeping her gun on him. "Everything is going to be okay."

"No, it isn't," he said quietly. "I accidentally broke one of the vials."

Elaine looked at him in horror and called for Ward.

***

Once Elaine and Ward realized the virus had been released and might be dispersing through the building, Elaine stayed with Marwan while Ward ran to find Katrina and warn her not to take off her mask under any circumstance. They both pulled at the straps holding their masks to their heads, wondering if the airtight seal was genuinely airtight.

Ward had run to find Katrina, and when turning the corner had literally crashed into Orso, who had been frantically running himself after being seriously wounded by some woman in a mask, blood running from one of his shoulders. Guns and gear tumbled everywhere, and the two exchanged punches, kicks, and slaps while trying to not get entangled in each other's straps, belts, ammunition bandoliers, and other gear pouches. Ward had wondered what Alec had meant on the elevator when he said, "you look like Rob Liefeld drew you."

The two men scrambled for handguns, knives, tasers, anything to alter the balance of power in their messy, desperate wrestling. Orso had a baton, but finally Ward just got his arm around Orso's neck and squeezed. Enough pressure on the carotid artery would stop the flow of blood to Orso's brain and make him pass out. Ward managed to get his other hand behind Orso's head and pressed it forward, trying to maximize the pressure. Orso's limbs thrashed, and he slammed the elbow on his non-wounded side into Ward's ribs over and over again. Ward grimaced, feeling like his ribs were about to be smashed into balsa splinters and turn his lungs into a pincushion.

Just when Ward thought he himself would pass out, Orso suddenly went limp. Ward threw his body aside, held his aching side, and scrambled to put handcuffs on Orso's body.

\*\*\*

After several rounds of gunfire, Ursula left Hell Summoner in the lab, locked the door behind her, and went to check on Orso. Apparently Orso hadn't done so well, because within moments, Hell Summoner heard two gunshots and then the sounds of an intense struggle. Either Ursula was throwing someone against a wall, or someone was throwing Ursula against a wall. A woman exclaimed in pain, and Ursula let out a series of war cries.

He heard glass breaking, someone's head being slammed into drywall, then something heavy—a piece of furniture?—being picked up and thrown down on someone. He was tempted to unlock the door; he felt like he was listening to an epic throwdown between two extremely skilled fighters—Ali vs. Frazier, Tyson vs. Holyfield, or the planned Ronda Rousey-Gina Carano fight that never happened. Finally, he heard a woman's—not Ursula's— agonized cry. Something spectacularly heavy—a bookcase?—tumbled to the floor.

He heard tired, heavy footsteps coming, and Ursula jingling keys. He exhaled. She had just won the fight of her life.

And then the door opened, and some other woman, wearing a broken respirator mask, entered, leveling a Glock in his face.

\*\*\*

"Hell Summoner, I presume?" A thoroughly bruised but triumphant Katrina Leonidivna exhaled.

He quickly backed away.

"You better be careful with that," he warned her. Katrina's fight with Ursula had been so brutal, it had cracked the eye visor on her protective mask. "If you are a wise woman, you will put the gun away, because there's a lot of biomaterial in here, some hazardous, some harmless, and breaking the wrong container could mean a painful death for all of us."

She lowered her gun only slightly, pulling off her broken mask, concluding the crack had made the imposition on her peripheral vision and breathing no longer worth the cost. She stepped a little closer, out of the shadows by the doorway, and took her first good look at Hell Summoner's face.

She froze in confusion. "Wait, I know you...you're that British doctor!"

Dr. Allen Pittman chuckled.

"I suppose you want an autograph?"

Katrina was speechless, but only for a moment. "How...why..." Then she raised her gun higher. "Hands where I can see them! You have no idea how much you're going to pay for your crimes."

But Pittman just smiled and shrugged.

"My crimes? Oh, you mean Shakira and those vials of the common cold I just sent her off with?" he said, raising his eyebrows. "Assuming your colleagues haven't caught her, she's about to open vials of a particularly mild rhinovirus and, if she's really lucky, give many flights full of international travelers a case of the sniffles."

He couldn't help himself; the thought of Shakira's disappointment left him laughing like he was enjoying Monty Python.

Waves of relief and confusion crashed over her. "Wait, you...you *conned* her?" She slowly lowered her gun...somewhat.

Pittman laughed so hard he started coughing. "Dammit, woman, I'm a doctor, not a monster! I have secretly, carefully, and securely recorded her half of our conversations from the start. I have been swindling her and her repulsive colleagues in Shedim from our first meeting. I will expose her and the whole Shedim cabal to the world, ensuring they all get taken out of commission. But I'm taking a lot of their money first."

He turned on his tablet and held it up to show Katrina. "I've scammed almost thirty million dollars from them. But the money is simply the side benefit. My colleagues and I set out to expose the group most likely to pursue an ethnic bioweapon, and we've done it. We will anonymously expose the lot of them, after Shakira Erikat goes to sprinkle some common cold around Los Angeles airport—"

"—that assumes my teammates don't shoot her before she leaves," Katrina observed.

"Oh, that would be unwise," Pittman said. "That could turn out quite badly for them. See, for this to work, I needed evidence that she had been working with a genuinely dangerous virus, one mildly contagious. If she's caught with common cold, there's a chance she walks because of some hot-shot lawyer or idiot judge. I needed to create evidence that she and Shedim were working with a genuine bioweapon."

"What kind of evidence?" she raised her gun again.

"When I gave her what she thought was an inoculation, I injected her and her bodyguard with Bundibugyo ebolavirus," he declared with a smug smile.

"*Ebolavirus?*" she screamed.

"Relax, it's the mildest form of Ebola, barely a thirty-five percent death rate," he scoffed with a tone of exasperation.

"You just put ebolavirus into someone and sent her to go to the airport?!" She felt an extreme temptation to put a bullet through his head now.

"She's going to spread cold viruses around the airport departure gate, and then get on her flight back to Germany, convinced she's immune to her designer absumovirus. What she won't know is that Ebola is currently in her system, and when she meets with the rest of the Shedim, she'll probably give it to all of them, too."

"And anyone else she meets with along the way!" Katrina exclaimed.

"Collateral damage," he shrugged. "Like I said, this is the least contagious, least-deadly strain of Ebola. Worst-case scenario, she spreads it to, oh, fifty, maybe a hundred people." He thought for a moment. "Maybe a few hundred."

She suddenly realized that Allen Pittman, once-distinguished British virologist and doctor, had completely snapped at some point during his Herculean efforts and had built up his own antibodies against the moral consequences of his actions.

"I swore I'd move heaven and earth to find a way to not kill anyone," Katrina murmured. She suddenly aimed her gun.

BLAM!

A round tore through Allen Pittman's left foot.

*"Dear God!"* he cried and yelped in pain. *"What are you doing?"*

"An oath to avoid killing anyone doesn't mean I won't shoot someone," she declared. "That's to make sure you don't run away while I try to find my partners and Shakira and make sure we don't have an ebolavirus outbreak—even your so-called least contagious, least-deadly ebolavirus outbreak—in the middle of Los Angeles!"

She shook her head. She tried the comms, but they continued to be jammed. She took one last furious look at Pittman.

"What the hell is wrong with you? You were one of the people who was trying to save us!"

He winced from the pain and scowled at her. "Do you really think I'm that much worse than anyone else? How many American companies do work for the Chinese government, the Russians, the Saudis? Google helped the Chinese censor the Internet. Chevron made deals with Chavez and Maduro in Venezuela. McKinsey Consulting helps Russia's state-run companies and banks that are basically extensions of the FSB. It's perfectly fine to work with demons with blood on their hands if you're big and famous enough. Some of the biggest names in Washington made tons of money representing unsavory regimes—Manafort, Podesta, and that's not even counting all the retired lawmakers who become lobbyists for foreign governments. Lots of 'respectable' people have made fortunes working for the world's worst monsters. I spent my career saving people. Why can't I get my share?"

She shook her head in contempt.

"Stay here, or you won't like where my next shot goes."

Katrina departed, frustrated that Dee hadn't restored communications yet. Everyone needed to know that any vials of biohazardous material were no longer the primary threat; Shakira and Marwan were, with the Ebola virus now flowing through their bloodstreams. One bad gunshot could splatter Ebola-infected blood everywhere. All of the FBI personnel and any remaining civilians needed to be kept away from them, and whether Shakira and Marwan were killed or captured, the personnel handling them would need to be in protective gear. And right now, the only person in the building who knew this was Katrina.

She had just gotten to the stairwell when she heard another series of gunshots.

***

Alec's struggle with Shakira had not gone well. As dramatically as his emotions had overwhelmed him in Spandau Citadel, hearing that the engineered virus could kill Katrina, Shakira's declaration that the world was broken because she hadn't killed enough ripped out his heart. He realized he had just said those words days ago, and that his self-justification was not all that distinguishable as her self-justification. And he felt waves of guilt and horror reverberating through his body.

His hands started shaking, and Shakira saw it as an opportunity to run. Alec had pulled himself together and fired a shot, but it had gone past her, shattering a window on the thirty-second floor, sending glass down to the street outside Fox Plaza. The shot was enough to make Shakira freeze in place … and then she slowly drifted over toward the giant hole in the wall, where the floor-to-ceiling window had been a moment ago. She still had the vial and the case around her shoulder.

She was contemplating jumping.

Alec realized her temptation to end her own life and holstered his gun. Kind of moot now, he realized.

Their eyes met. Shakira Erikat, genocidal maniac, looked awfully small and scared at that moment. And Alec, who moments earlier felt overwhelming excitement and anticipation at the thought of sending her to Hades, suddenly realized he didn't want her to jump.

"Look … I am the last guy who should be right here, right now, trying to get you step away from that ledge … but you don't have to do this," he said, wiping sweat from his brow. He frantically tried to think of what he should do or say in this situation, but all he could envision was Mel Gibson handcuffing himself to a ledge jumper—a plan that would not work here. Finally, Alec blurted out, "Think of your family!"

"That's why I want to jump," Shakira answered.

Alec looked skyward in frustration. "Will you please work with me here? This is my first suicide intervention!"

\*\*\*

Across the country, Dee realized the jamming system assembled by Hell Summoner's team left her with no choice. She could restore the communications system used by the FBI and the Dangerous Clique with the most basic reboot of all: turning the whole system off and then on again. The hard reboot would allow her to restore the communications on a rarely used frequency that would probably be outside the range of the jamming equipment on-site. She began the process and sent an update to Stern.

The CIA director, who have moved to monitor the situation from the agency operations center, stared at the message in confusion. "What, are we running our comms through my home cable box?"

***

In the lobby, Raquel sighed relief when an elevator opened, and Elaine pushed a mostly cooperative, handcuffed Marwan through.

"Ward has the Italian subdued and handcuffed on the thirty-first floor, but he's hurt," Elaine reported, as two FBI men approached to get ahold of her prisoner. "Marwan here said he broke a vial so the virus might be airborne." The FBI men froze in their tracks.

Raquel threw up her hands in frustration. "Where the hell is the CDC team? What, did they stop for drive-through along the way?"

Elaine continued. "I don't know where anyone else is, the comms are down—"

And both Elaine and Raquel she heard a familiar sing-songy voice in their ears. "The comms are back! The comms are back! They thought they could stop me, but the comms are back!" Dee pronounced proudly.

"Great, now hush," Raquel declared. "Alec! Katrina! Can you hear me? What's your status?"

After a moment of silence, the three women heard Katrina's breathing.

"Situation's changed," Katrina's voice said in between deep breaths. She was running somewhere. "Hell Summoner is that British doctor, Pittman. He says the virus is a fake—repeat, the virus is a fake, minimally harmless. I think he's telling the truth—"

"All right!" Elaine's arms shot up like she was signaling a touchdown, and she pumped her fist. The two FBI men each grabbed an arm of Marwan.

"But the reason I think he's telling the truth is because he also said he injected both Marwan and Shakira with Ebola," Katrina continued.

Both FBI men holding Marwan suddenly let go of his arms and took two steps back. Marwan's jaw dropped in shock and horror.

"Close that mouth!" Raquel ordered. "Go sit in that corner. Everyone keep six—eh, let's make it ten feet away." She turned to Agent Mills. "Get LAPD hazmat teams here immediately! And anybody else who knows how to respond to an Ebola infection!"

She turned to Elaine. "Wait, I'm trying to remember if you can catch Ebola by breathing. Did you exchange bodily fluids with this guy?"

Elaine looked at Raquel if she was crazy. "No," she declared emphatically.

Raquel exhaled in exasperation. "I don't mean did you make love in an elevator, I mean did he sneeze on you, cough on you, bleed on you, anything like that?" Elaine shook her head negative.

Raquel pressed in her earwig. "Katrina, we've got Marwan. That just leaves Shakira."

Craig, the building's security manager, ran to the desk frantically. "I just heard from a client we evacuated out from the top floor—he said he heard a gunshot on the thirty-second floor on the way down."

"Alec went to that floor to sneak around behind them," Ward's voice groaned.

"I'm on my way," Katrina answered.

***

Alec's earwig was on the floor, knocked off when he had tried to grab Shakira moments earlier. His gambit hadn't worked; Shakira wriggled out of Alec's grasp and managed to put her foot deep into his crotch. By the time Alec had slowly and agonizingly gotten back to his feet, muttering that he had still hoped to be a father someday, Shakira was now standing with her toes right at the edge of the building. The only upside was that during their struggle, he had torn the bag of vials so hard that the strap snapped, and he had placed the dropped package at the other end of the room. Now he just had the one vial in her hand to worry about ... and his newfound sense that if she jumped, it would be a tragedy he could have and should have prevented.

Alec found himself inching closer, almost within arm's reach, as she stood and contemplated an irreversible decision.

"Please don't do this," Alec pleaded. "You still have things to live for. You seemed so happy a moment ago, playing soccer with my testicles."

Suddenly, the doors to the thirty-second floor architectural firm flew open, and Katrina burst through them like a compact wrecking ball. She had heard talking through those doors, and when she emerged through, she was shocked to see Shakira Erikat standing near an empty space where a floor-to-ceiling window was supposed to be, standing right at the precipice.

And Alec was about a few feet behind her, one arm outstretched, seeming to hope she would take his hand.

"Alec!" she screamed frantically.

Alec turned, realized his wife was there. "What the hell are you doing here? She's got the virus! Get out of here! Where's your mask?"

Katrina waved her arms. "The virus she's got is harmless, the common cold!"

"WHAT?" Shakira screamed in shock and disbelief. Alec's face burst into a relieved grin.

But Katrina kept waving her arms. "But she's got Ebola in her blood!"

"*What?*" both Alec and Shakira exclaimed at once. Katrina kept approaching. Alec and Shakira's minds raced, calculating the new variable. All three of them kept moving, and all three leaped at the same time.

Shakira leaped for the ledge.

Alec leaped for Shakira.

Katrina leaped for Alec.

Shakira felt the pull of gravity as she went over the threshold—and then some other force, an arm, latching on to her and yanking her backward. Alec had a grip on her belt and the back of her pants and was hoping and praying he wasn't about to reenact an old Coppertone advertisement. He got his other hand's fingers on her shoulder, then neck, and latched on to the neck of her shirt and jacket. Meanwhile, Katrina nearly crashed into him, wrapping her arms around his waist and digging her fingers into him, desperately clawing for a grip. The trio of bodies wobbled and stumbled for a few moments...

... Alec tried to hoist her up with her belt, released his grip on her shirt and jacket and then put his meaty paw around part of her neck and he frantically wished his fingers had been longer. Katrina spread her feet, trying to spread her meager weight over a wider area, hoping it would provide enough leverage, with her whole squirming body trying to get traction against the office carpeting... After a moment of screaming, and grunting and pulling...

... the trio finally tumbled back into the Fox Plaza's thirty-second floor conference room.

"Don't breathe on me!" Alec shouted frantically at Shakira. "Don't breathe on her! Don't touch her! Don't—"

As Alec screamed instructions that Shakira would surely ignore, Katrina sat up, pulled back her arm—accidentally elbowing Alec in the side of the head—and threw her an open-palm punch right into Shakira's forehead. The Palestinian-German saw stars, and slumped down, groaning. Alec scrambled away, wondering if Shakira was exhaling or otherwise shedding Ebola viruses at that moment, and yanked Katrina with him.

Once they felt a safe distance away, they looked at each other, and Shakira. Her eyelids were fluttering, and a thin stream of drool ran from the side of her mouth to the carpet beneath her.

Katrina and Alec embraced, then he pulled back.

"Wait!" He recoiled in horror. "If she gave it to me, then I could give it to you!"

Katrina laughed and shook her head. "Alec, Ebola isn't a respiratory virus, it's not spread by breathing." He looked startled. "Bodily fluids. Mucus from coughs and sneezes. Blood and spit, which means stay away from that drool running from her mouth … If you had shot her, we would have been in much more danger."

When Alec thought about how close he had come to shooting her, he grew so dizzy he had to put his head between his legs.

# CHAPTER SEVENTEEN

FOX PLAZA TOWER
LOS ANGELES, CALIFORNIA
JUST AFTER MIDNIGHT, MONDAY, MAY 2

**"N**o, there is no risk of anyone being accidentally exposed while I was working in my lab," Pittman fumed indignantly. "This isn't Wuhan!"

*\*\*\**

When Elaine sent a message up the chain that the Dangerous Clique had arrived, the FBI Los Angeles office sent an urgent but cursory three-sentence message to the Los Angeles Police Department that a Bureau operation was about to begin at Fox Plaza, and that the FBI needed all LAPD units to remain a safe distance away. Emergency services should be prepared for casualties, including the possibility of biohazardous material.

It was a cursory message that prompted a lot of cursing on the other end. The LAPD dispatched every available plainclothes detective and non-uniformed personnel to the Avenue of the Stars, Olympic Boulevard, Galaxy Way, and the West Olympic Boulevard parking lot. Whether or not the FBI *wanted* a secure perimeter, they were going to get one, or at least the ingredients to rapidly form one. LAPD choppers altered their course. Uniformed units and SWAT were instructed to assemble by the

Intercontinental Los Angeles a block away. The hotel's skeleton staff was just thrilled to have someone coming through the door.

By the time the on-scene detectives reported shattered glass falling from a thirty-second-floor window, the LAPD's deputy chief Alden Powell gave the order to form the perimeter, regardless of what the FBI's instructions had been.

Within a few minutes, social media lit up with reports of some mass LAPD operation outside the Fox Plaza, and shortly after that, the news choppers, news vans, and several hundred cell phones congregated to the scene like ants on drippings from an ice cream cone on a summer's day.

The FBI's Assistant Director in Charge and head of the LA office, Robert D. Johnson Jr., second-generation FBI, addressed the assembled reporters after about an hour.

"Tonight, acting on information gathered by other federal agencies, the FBI conducted a raid of a small laboratory involved in research using biohazardous material in violation of regulations from the Occupational Safety and Health Administration and the Environmental Protection Agency." Johnson's strategy to handle the public fears about dangerous threats was to make everything his office dealt with sound as boring as possible. His official jargon made the gunfight sound like an IRS audit.

"The lab was staffed by three foreign nationals who entered the country legally on work visas. One from Britain, one from Spain, and one from Italy. Two German nationals including a visiting member of their ... parliament?" Another aide stepped and whispered in Johnson's ear. "A member of their legislative body was in the building at the time of our operation and they have been taken to Cedars Sinai as a precaution for risk of exposure to biohazardous materials."

The shouted questions began. No, the FBI had not yet determined precisely which biohazardous material. No, there was no risk to the surrounding community. No, the teams working in full hazmat suits with bottled air now visible behind Johnson should not alarm anyone. That was a routine precaution.

\*\*\*

The Department of Justice was preparing charges against Pittman, Veppi, Aldana, Erikat, and Mabarek for violating 18 US Code § 2332b—"acts of terrorism transcending national boundaries" and 18 US Code § 175—" knowingly developing, producing, stockpiling, transferring, retaining, or possessing any biological agent, toxin, or delivery system for use as a weapon."

Despite being foreign citizens, by committing their crimes on US soil, all of them were subject to American laws and would be tried in US courts. Some prosecutors in the Department of Justice were licking their lips, eyeing a career-making case.

But not everyone was brimming with confidence. In their small huddle outside Fox Plaza while Assistant Director Johnson was taking his victory lap, Raquel asked whether the world would be better off not knowing about what had just transpired.

The world had just been through a nearly two-year ordeal, where life and death frequently came down to the public's willingness to trust the advice of medical experts, and to cope and adapt as medical experts changed their assessments based upon new information. Far too often, vocal pockets of people who needed to believe in a convenient devil contended that the virus was spread by 5G cell towers, that masks were worthless and a con, that the virus was less deadly than the flu, and that Bill Gates was behind some sinister global effort at population control. (More egalitarian conspiracy theorists contended that Bill was the figurehead, and Melinda Gates was the true mastermind.)

Now the US Department of Justice was about to indict a British doctor—not quite the Anthony Fauci of the United

Kingdom, but a good more reliable and trusted than Dr. Phil McGraw—on cooking up bioweapons. The respected virologist who had just helped the United Kingdom grapple with the epidemic had psychologically snapped and launched his own con and sting operation, recklessly endangering innocent people along the way. Katrina argued that the world deserved the truth, no matter how ugly it was. Elaine pointed out that a criminal trial of Pittman—the eloquent, history-citing professorial medical researcher who was widely seen as a heroic doctor until a few months ago—would create a circus on par with the O.J. Simpson trial, with a potential similar outcome.

"If we can't change the facts, we can change the speed," Elaine thought out loud. "If we get him thinking we've got an open-and-shut death penalty case, he might accept a deal for life in Supermax. Guilty plea, quick sentencing, let him spend the rest of his life with El Chapo, the Unabomber, the Shoe Bomber, and Little Brother Tsarnaev."

"He confessed to me!" Katrina pointed out.

"Yes, except we can't exactly put you on a witness stand, now can we?" asked Elaine, mimicking a defense attorney: "Ms. Leonidivna, please explain to the court how many times you and your CIA team have straight-up murdered someone in the name of American counterterrorism policy? If you don't have a precise figure, give us a sense of the number by comparing it to the seating capacity of a particular sports arena or venue. Are we talking Staples Center, or Los Angeles Colosseum?'"

"Oh, it's at least the Colosseum," Ward muttered behind them.

"I can get him to say it again," Katrina insisted. "You, me, some DOJ lawyer, all in a room with him, recording. I don't even have to say anything. He's an arrogant man, Elaine. We've seen his kind before."

\*\*\*

Allen Pittman scoffed when the terms of the deal were put before him.

"I'll take my chances with an American jury," he said coolly. "I'll be tried in here in Los Angeles, correct? I don't think they've convicted anyone here since Manson."

A defense attorney sat next to Pittman. The head of the counterterrorism section of DOJ and the Los Angeles District Attorney were watching through one-way glass; Pittman periodically shot a contemptuous look at the mirror, then returned his gaze to the three women on the other side of the table: Katrina, Elaine, and Geraldine Murphy-Fitzal, a Department of Justice prosecutor who Katrina had worked with many years earlier on the indictment and prosecution of a handful of captured jihadists.

Other federal prosecutors kept spreading the rumor that Geraldine Murphy-Fitzal's maiden name was because she was related to Edward A. Murphy Jr., the US military engineer credited for "Murphy's Law," the declaration that everything that can go wrong will go wrong, but Geraldine denied it.

But it was not difficult to see why she had that reputation. Inside the courtroom, Murphy-Fitzal was cool, calm, methodical, meticulous; she could positively shred a witness's account without raising her resting heart rate. Outside the courtroom, she was something of a mess, sleep-deprived, perpetually stressed and running late, a working mom of two daughters who tried to devote her entire life to several top priorities at once. Many defense attorneys had sized her up in pretrial meetings or negotiations and scoffed that Murphy-Fitzal had to be the bottom of the barrel of federal attorneys, easy pickings. They marched into court, confident of a quick dismissal ... and then, as soon as court was in session, Murphy-Fitzal's verge-of-a-nervous-breakdown stressed-out persona disappeared like she had a split personality.

Once proceedings began, Murphy-Fitzal would beat up the opposing counsel, pull down their pants, give them a wedgie, and take their lunch money. She could argue complicated law with the best legal minds or go straight to a jury's hearts with a homespun I'm-just-a-simple-woman-from-tiny-Eastport-Maine-so-far-north-I'm-almost-Canadian routine that could rival Matlock. She could beat you on the facts, she could beat you on the law, or both; she had yet to come to the point where she couldn't win on either and had to resort to pounding the table or histrionics.

Judges and juries loved Geraldine Murphy-Fitzal, and some prosecutors joked that if she had handled the bribery prosecution of Lori Loughlin, she would have convinced the jury to bring the electric chair out of storage just so they could watch Aunt Becky fry. It took a long time for other attorneys to realize that maybe Murphy-Fitzal had exaggerated her disorganized, frazzled, chaotic perpetual-calamity image and she was steadily building an exemplary career, a throne atop a metaphorical mound of skulls, as a seeming unending line of opponents, mostly men, kept underestimating her until it was too late.

"Okay, then," Murphy-Fitzal said, exchanging looks between Pittman and his attorney, a criminal defense lawyer so respected and feared that she didn't even have to make television commercials where he sounded like pitchman Billy Mays. "I guess the upside is this means we will have an extra doctor around at your lethal injection."

Pittman's lawyer, a little uncomfortable with his client's confidence and seething hostility from the meeting's start, gestured for everyone to wait. But after a moment, Pittman looked at the three women before him and scoffed that the greatest prosecutorial minds in America were coming after him with Charlie's Angels.

His eyes kept sliding over to Katrina. "Then there's the matter of being shot in the foot by her."

Katrina gave a little shrug, and then leaned forward with a smug grin. She noticed Pittman's eyes darted low, where she had deliberately left one less button buttoned than decorum would expect. She reclined back, folded her arms behind her head, and smiled with satisfaction. She didn't have to say a word, her message was clear: *It was worth it.*

Pittman scowled. "All your arrival did was disrupt a well-laid plan. My aim was to determine who in this world would be willing to pay the highest price to obtain and use an ethnic bioweapon, and we succeeded. I figured it might be the Iranians or North Koreans, but go figure, it's some network of wealthy European anti-Semites, one that I suspect no one in your government even knew existed until now."

"I think you should stop talking now," Pittman's attorney said, putting his hand on his client's hand. Pittman shot him a look of pure contempt for interrupting him, and the lawyer withdrew her hand. Katrina and Murphy-Fitzal noticed that Pittman was not brimming with respect for his high-priced lawyer.

He returned his attention to Katrina. "If you had never arrived, Shakira Erikat and that evolutionary missing link she calls a bodyguard would have walked through LAX, spreading mundane viruses around, doing little to no harm to anyone. But within a few days, as she kept checking the news for reports of an emerging pandemic that would never arrive, she would have started running a high fever herself. She would have contacted her Shedim colleagues and then they would have realized she herself was infected with something serious—and with any luck, Shakira would have spread it to her own coconspirators."

"Because you infected her with Ebola," Elaine prompted, hoping Pittman would take the bait.

"I think you will find it difficult to prove how she caught it," Pittman said, with a confident smile. "You certainly won't find any Ebola in my lab. All you will find is samples of the common cold."

"How did Lars Egner-Baerwald die?" Elaine asked.

"I heard he contracted a rare virus from India," Pittman replied. "I suspect you'll have a very hard time proving any particular vector of infection."

"What about the outbreak among the Kehila Ashkenazi in Mexico City?" Elaine asked.

"A mild influenza strain, as I heard it. Anyone who died from that one was already on his deathbed," he shrugged. "Surely you haven't found any evidence of genetic engineering on that virus or you would have confronted me with it. Cases of the flu occur everywhere, even outside of the usual season. Sure, someone who knew what he was doing could develop it and mail it overnight to members of the community in the form of, oh, I don't know, gift cards or something. The virus lives for forty-eight hours on plastic. But if that occurred, tracing the origin of the virus would be impossible. Certainly not within a reasonable doubt."

The women fumed. A confession without a confession.

Pittman leaned forward, his voice soft and gentle with condescension. "You can tear apart my lab, and maybe if you're lucky you'll find minor violation of obscure OSHA regulations. If you want a deal, I'll accept a minor fine."

Murphy-Fitzal turned and momentarily gave a look of concern to Katrina. Pittman knew what he was doing. Katrina's participation in the interview was supposed to make Pittman come unglued, but he seemed as cool and confident as ever.

"Otherwise, if you take your chances in a trial, I will go on at length in a public forum about exactly how someone goes about engineering a virus to target one ethnic group, ensuring that any radical group that has the roughly eighteen thousand dollars to buy a CRISPR machine and the expertise can, within a matter of weeks, cook up their own viral ethnic cleansing programs."

The skin under Elaine's eye twitched, and Pittman knew he had hit a nerve. He grinned and continued.

"Then I will explain, under oath, to the jury about the US government's bioweapons programs that lasted until 1969. The secret release of bacterial spores in San Francisco in 1950 and use of fungal spores on black employees at the Norfolk Naval Supply Center in 1951. The US army spraying zinc cadmium sulfide over the skies of Saint Louis and Minneapolis in 1953 because their climates matched that of Moscow and Saint Petersburg. The CIA spraying whooping cough bacteria over Tampa, Florida in 1955. The army releasing Bacillus atrophaeus in the New York City subway in 1966 to simulate an attack and never bothering to check if anyone got sick. I will point to enough real-life history to make the US government look like the most reckless and amoral monster that ever lived. Then I will contend that I am being railroaded and scapegoated to distract from your government's recent stumbling and bumbling through a global pandemic. And trust me, young ladies, someone on that jury will have a reasonable doubt."

He smiled like a devil. "As you can see, ladies, I have all of the leverage here. You had best find some face-saving counteroffer and fine me, put me on probation or something. Slap my wrist. Because nothing I did out there represented a true threat to anyone. But if you put me on trial, I assure you ... I will indeed summon Hell to overtake the earth."

He could see nervousness in the eyes of Murphy-Fitzal and Elaine Kopek. They saw the logic of his arguments and deemed his threats serious.

But for some reason that maddening silent woman Katrina just smiled back.

Katrina removed a folder and put down five photographs—mug shots of Pittman, Veppi, Aldana, and Elikat, along with an old photo of Wilhelm Ballett. She removed a red pen.

She took the photo of Shakira and wrote underneath, "client, doesn't understand science."

Pittman nodded. "Finally, someone sees."

She took the photo of Wilhelm and wrote underneath, "muscle."

He nodded again. "Wilhelm, may he rest in peace, was not a stupid man, but yes, he was there for the possibility that our work could get rough."

She took the photo of Orso and wrote underneath, "operative, intel/tech, not scientist."

He looked over. "Indeed, I think quite well of Orso, he's a very reliable and professional man, but his expertise was in our potential clients, not in what goes on in a lab."

She took the photo of Pittman and wrote underneath, "lab technician."

He looked at her, wondering what she was doing. "You and I know I'm a lot more than a mere technician."

She ignored him and selected the mugshot of Ursula Aldana. Underneath, in bright red letters, Katrina wrote: "MASTERMIND."

Pittman stared at her in incredulity. "You cannot possibly believe that."

Geraldine Murphy-Fitzal shrugged. "Works for me. Spanish military doctor snaps from the pandemic, organizes all of this, nearly sets off an Ebola outbreak by hiring some British henchman—"

"I am not a henchman!" Pittman shouted angrily. "Ursula Aldana is a brilliant woman. Resourceful. Probably everything the three of you wish you could be. But no one—and certainly no jury—will believe that she orchestrated all of this."

Murphy-Fitzal stared back and shrugged. "The needle goes into the vein of a woman just as easily."

For the first time since Katrina shot him, Allen Pittman looked shaken.

"We can tell the jury that she put the Ebola in Shakira Erikat, or that you did," Elaine declared. "You'll be smooth on the witness stand, but will she? Will a jury believe her? Nah. They'll be looking for someone to punish. The virus just made everyone on earth put their lives on hold for more than a year. People are angry, Pittman, and your lover will make a really good scapegoat. You've gotten really comfortable with killing people, doc. Why not kill just one more by letting Ursula take the fall?"

He sat silently, weighing his options.

***

For a long time, Pittman believed his plan was foolproof, and that there was an infinitesimal chance the police or intelligence agencies would catch his team. Once Shakira Erikat had what she thought was a genetically engineered virus, Pittman and his team intended to shut down the lab and move on to some other location. They each had about nine million in untraceable funds, already, and should be gaining roughly nine hundred thousand each day. Within a few days or a week, after Shakira and Marwan began to suffer the effects of Ebola—and ideally, the rest of the Shedim as well, in addition to some unlucky Germans—Pittman would release excerpts from her side of their phone conversations. The Shedim would become some of the world's most hated criminals, Shakira and Marwan would likely be dead, and the remaining members of the team would be enjoying life as multi-millionaires under new identities.

They had originally planned to all go their separate ways, leaving the identity of "Hell Summoner" a mystery. Their legacy would be a world suddenly awakened to the danger of genetically engineered biological weapons, and the never-caught lurking menace of "Hell Summoner" would force governments all around the planet to take dramatic efforts to improve preparedness for another pandemic—massive investments in antiviral research, a worldwide crackdown on the exotic animal trade, new international inspections regimes of all BSL-4 laboratories. Pittman knew that after a threat passed, the desire for normalcy would allow naivete and blissful ignorance to return. After Osama bin Laden was killed, people stopped worrying about terrorism as much—until ISIS took advantage of the complacency. For the world to remain forever vigilant against the menace of new contagious diseases, they needed to fear some perfect villain, forever out there and capable of striking at any moment.

Even if law enforcement caught up with Pittman, he believed he could escape conviction at trial as he had just threatened. He had put the last of his Ebola samples into Shakira and Marwan and bleached the rest of his equipment, meaning the government had no concrete physical evidence he himself had handled the dangerous virus. Americans were in a suspicious and paranoid mood, and Pittman would just need one juror to believe that the American government was railroading a noble and internationally respected doctor to cover up its own failures. With any luck, a QAnon believer would end up on his jury.

But over the past few months, Orso Veppi had become a good friend, and Ursula Aldana had become so much more than a short-term operational partner. When he invited Ursula to join his plot, he offered her a chance to channel all of her rage and grief and despair into a defiant, audacious scheme for vengeance. He wasn't surprised when she kissed him, and he welcomed her sudden burst of sexual affection. They had already privately decided that they would not, as originally planned, go their separate ways after the operation.

Pittman knew Ursula and Orso deserved happy endings. And while he might have confidence in his ability to charm an American jury, he had less faith in theirs. No, these women sitting across from him—and in particular, that smug, silent Eurasian one—had maneuvered him into a perfect trap. He was familiar enough with the barbaric American practice of lethal injection; autopsies of several executed prisoners suggested they had suffered from pulmonary edema before death—a rapid accumulation of fluid in the lungs. It would be a terrible, painful death, similar to the way so many of Ursula's patients died during the coronavirus pandemic.

There was only one way to ensure Ursula's life didn't end that way.

Katrina—this bitch—had found his lone weak spot.

"Bring me the papers. I'll sign a confession and accept life in prison. But no death penalty for Orso or Ursula."

Katrina reached into her bag, removed a blank writing pad and pen, and slid it across the table with an enthusiastic shove. She reached for the mug shots of Pittman and Ursula. She crossed out MASTERMIND on hers and wrote COCONSPIRATOR, and under his photo she crossed out TECHNICIAN and wrote PRINCIPAL—the legal term for ringleader.

Katrina and Pittman stared at each other across the table, brimming with mutual contempt. She had beaten him, and she hadn't even said a word. Her name would not appear in the official transcript. Her voice would not occur in the audio recording. She had sat, strategically just out of the range of the surveillance camera focused on Pittman. The world would never know what she did during Pittman's interview and confession.

"You stupid woman!" Pittman sneered as he wrote. "I was about to use the world's fears against its own worst impulses, to force it to become better, and safer, and more secure place for the next generation. The pandemic gave us a once-in-a-century chance to learn from our mistakes, to build something better, and you sit there, so smug, so confident that you've done the right thing, by preserving the exact status quo that got us into this mess in the first place. Sometime soon, you will awaken in the middle of the night and realize what you've done by stopping me." He looked up at her with barely contained rage. "I hope at that moment you are overcome by a wave of regret and despair so powerful that you can never truly feel happiness or hope again for the rest of your days!"

Katrina just stared back at him for a moment. Then she stood up, picked up her bag, and walked out the door.

***

Several months later, Allen Pittman began his sentence at ADX Florence in Colorado. Ursula Aldana and Orso Veppi were each sentenced to thirty years in federal prison without parole. Aldana was sent to the high security unit of the Federal Medical Center Carswell outside Fort Worth, Texas. One of the other thirteen women in the facility was Fabrice Vuscovi, a recruiter and leader of the Atarsa terrorist organization.

Shakira Erikat and Marwan Mabarek recovered from Ebola, helped along by a new treatment developed by a joint research team at the University of Cologne in Germany and the Weizmann Institute of Science, a public research university in Rehovot, Israel. They both pled guilty to conspiracy and terrorism charges. She was sentenced to thirty years and joined Aldana as the fifteenth woman imprisoned at the high security unit at FMC Carswell. For his cooperation, the judge sentenced Marwan to fifteen years in prison.

The German government opened up a new inquiry into the death of Lars Egner-Baerwald and months later ruled his death "suspicious." While German prosecutors concluded they could not definitively tie Baerwald's viral infection to Shakira Erikat's conspiracy, she was effectively convicted in the court of public opinion in Germany. Her former colleagues in the Bundestag insisted, in interview after interview, that they had never liked her and always thought her ideas were nutty.

After several months, Iraj Khansari managed to remove his subdermal tracking device. The CIA did not know whether he remained in Flam, Norway.

Renaldo Alberto Pablo Espino was found alive, locked inside his estate in Puerto Rico, suffering from fever and aches and pains that were diagnosed as Herpes B, likely contracted from one or more of the hundreds of monkeys found in cages in a building on his estate. He recovered with treatment but was subsequently charged with conspiracy to violate the Lacey Act, which banned moving or trading wildlife across US borders.

The Serbian government continued to insist the United States had launched a commando raid that killed two intelligence officials at the Tower of Skulls. But they learned that no one outside of the country was all that upset to hear that Stanislav "Stanko" Radic had been killed.

The Russian mercenary team, the Iron Wolves, disappeared after the shootout in Nis. American intelligence believed they continued to do off-the-books dirty work for Vladimir Putin's regime.

Vincent van der Groot disappeared during a vacation in Kenya, and his body was never found. A sketchy "News of the Weird" column that ran in the country's few remaining alternative weekly newspapers claimed months later that the mysterious waters of Lake Natron, Tanzania had turned a man to stone.

***

Compared to the victory lap that the US government took after the slaying and capture of several key Atarsa leaders, the response to the "Fox Plaza Incident" was fairly muted. The president referred all questions to the Department of Justice, and the attorney general referred questions about the case to the prosecutors. As Pittman and his coconspirators all pled guilty, there was no public trial and only a terse news release from the DOJ. Longtime watchers of the judicial system found prosecutor Geraldine Murphy-Fitzal unusually tight-lipped about the case. Even US Attorney John Durham remarked that Murphy-Fitzal seemed extremely reticent to talk to reporters.

The hallways at Langley buzzed with rumors that Director Barbara Stern had actually smiled, moments before restoring her usual grim visage and assigning several teams specializing in European politics and finance to track down the full membership of the Shedim. Erikat had mentioned a few names during interrogation, but the CIA consensus was that she was protecting perhaps a hundred other well-connected and wealthy figures.

Several weeks after the filing of the guilty pleas, the *Wall Street Journal* and *Washington Post* reported in separate investigative articles that the Fox Plaza Incident was part of a multi-agency effort to hunt down a reported "ethnic bioweapon" that was never recovered. This set off one news cycle of near-panic, as millions of Americans heard of the concept for the first time, and hastily booked "medical experts" squared off on cable news like Rock 'Em Sock 'Em Robots, arguing whether some diabolical genius could engineer a virus to target a particular ethnic group.

The news cycle of panic took a dramatic turn when an unknown hacker sent a message to millions of American cell phones, e-mail, and social media accounts: "An ethnic bioweapon could never cripple America. E Pluribus Unum."

\*\*\*

No one could prove that Dee was behind the hack that sent that mysterious message. When Ward said she had left her fingerprints all over it, she responded that she had done extensive research and run computer simulations and concluded that Ward couldn't possibly have made the shot that killed Bao Fang Min. Pleasantly surprised, Ward remarked that he suddenly found her denial of that hack suddenly much more plausible.

The FBI Director invited Elaine to lunch, mentioned he was impressed with her work as liaison to the CIA's Dangerous Clique team, and asked her if she wanted to be groomed for assistant director of the counterterrorism division. Elaine answered that she would like a raise, but otherwise had no desire to get sucked into the office politics of the bureau's highest levels of leadership.

Raquel seemed much calmer in the weeks after the Fox Plaza Incident. When Katrina remarked upon this, Raquel said that her good mood had nothing to do with that, and everything to do with the fact that her husband Vaughn had gotten her parents and his mother moved out of the house, to adjacent rental apartments up the street—close by, but thankfully no longer all under the same roof.

Ward spent less and less time in the office in the weeks after the Fox Plaza Incident. He told Raquel that if needed, he would come running—but that recent experiences made him want to maximize his time with Marie and the kids.

"If I'm away from them long enough, I start to feel like a psycho," he chuckled.

Raquel looked at him with appreciation. "You looked pretty cool under fire out there."

He shrugged. "It's easy to look cool when I'm standing next to Alec having a nervous breakdown."

***

Alec and Katrina did not host a party this time, as they had after Atarsa's defeat. As summer arrived, Alec found himself sipping a bourbon on their back porch. Katrina joined him, having spent a portion of the morning in the bathroom.

"Are you feeling better?" he asked.

"Yes, probably just something I ate," she responded, wondering what part of Friday night's dinner could possibly have left her kneeling at the porcelain altar in their master bathroom in the wee hours of Saturday morning. She did find herself hungrier than usual; perhaps the multiple near-death experiences in hunting down Pittman had stirred all sorts of neglected appetites.

"How are you feeling?" she shifted the conversation away from her. "From Berlin to LA, you were like a different person. If there's some dial hidden on your body that can adjust your mood and personality, I'd really like to find it." She chuckled. "I mean, besides the one I already found that can make you more agreeable."

Alec smiled, but then looked pensive.

"I think learning the virus could kill you more or less ... removed my guardrails," he said. "Part of me I didn't necessarily want to let out ... I know my part. Comic relief while you and Ward cut through bad guys like Ginsu. I guess maybe all these years watching you two, I picked up a few things—"

She interrupted. "Oh, I never threw anyone into an acidic lake, even if he deserved it."

"An extremely toxic *basic* lake, not acidic. The point is, at that point, my life felt like ... a video game or *Lethal Weapon* or something where I could mow down mooks without a second thought. I didn't want to just be the consequences to someone's bad actions. I wanted to be hyper-karma, the terrible swift sword, the sommelier serving the finest vintages from the grapes of wrath. But the problem is that it's almost impossible to be ruthless and merciless and just a wee bit bloodthirsty and still remain someone who cares about other people. Play at being John Wick long enough, you become John Wicked."

She nodded. "Yes, but you can't fool me. You kept Shakira from jumping. The real you was always in there. All that inner panic, all that hunger to lash out with violence—when you saw someone who didn't have to die, life hanging in the balance … you managed to keep her alive."

"Yeah," he murmured, staring off into space. "But I'm still a little freaked out. If I had shot her or let her jump, she would have become a giant exploding marinara stain of Ebola blood. God knows what would have happened."

"We've both seen a lot. We're not the same people we were when we started this. Neither one of us has any illusions anymore that we can kill our way to a better world. The world's seen more than enough people die in the past few years. You're ready for a change. I'm ready for a change. We're going to have to find some role that demonstrates that we can create something better."

Alec's eyebrows shot up in curiosity. The concept appealed to him.

She let out a little laugh. "I'm still working on that part of the plan."

And she kissed him deeply.

***

Several days later, in the wee hours of a Wednesday morning, Alec groggily heard a noise from the bathroom. Half-asleep, he first slammed his hand into his alarm clock, and then when he realized his alarm wasn't making the noise, he swept his arm across his bedside table, looking for his charging phone, knocking a glass, a book, and the phone to the floor with a clatter. He groaned.

"Alec!" Katrina's voice, from within the bathroom.

The synapses in his brain gradually and stumblingly reintroduced themselves to each other, and began to receive and interpret the sensory information coming in. After a moment, they rejected all of the incoming sensory input and screamed at the prefrontal cortex that they refused to do any further work until their demand for coffee had been met. Alec's prefrontal cortex yelled back that first he wanted to know if Katrina was calling his name out of concern, fear, or excitement. His first guess was that she had seen a bug, as the woman who was fearless in the face of terrorists, cults, snakes, underwater tunnels, and deadly viruses absolutely hated the sight of spiders, particularly if she was on the toilet.

But as he sat up and stumbled out of bed, he realized she was calling his name out of a sense of excitement.

The bathroom door opened, and Katrina emerged in the doorway in a bathrobe, beaming, simultaneously ordinary and somehow utterly transformed, as if all of the problems in the world had been temporarily put on hiatus.

"I'm pregnant."

# ACKNOWLEDGEMENTS

Many thanks go to Matt Carlini at Javelin, the team at Amazon, and to Scott Bryan Wilson for his copy-editing. Any errors that are still in there are my fault.

Thanks to Rich Lowry, Charlie Cooke, and everyone at National Review for the best political writing job in the world, giving me an exceptionally long leash to dig into information about research labs in Wuhan, China, as well as virology, epidemiology, and any other topic that was important during the early months of the pandemic. As you can probably tell, a lot of that nonfiction research ended up shaping my fictional scenarios. Thanks to the readers who made that all possible.

To Allison, C, and A, putting up with me, in all ways and forms.

# ABOUT THE AUTHOR

Jim Geraghty is an award-winning senior political correspondent at *National Review*. His work has also appeared in *The Philadelphia Inquirer* and *The Washington Examiner*. He spent two years in Ankara, Turkey working as a foreign correspondent and studying anti-Americanism, democratization, Islam, Middle East politics, and U.S. diplomatic efforts and has also filed dispatches from Great Britain, Germany, Egypt, Italy, Israel, Spain, and Jordan. In 2019, Jim made presentations about foreign disinformation campaigns on social media and tools to counter propaganda to the Austrian National Defense Academy, the Organization for Security and Cooperation in Europe, the University of Vienna, and the U.S. Embassy to Austria. He is also the author of the first book in the Dangerous Clique Series *Between Two Scorpions,* the novel *The Weed Agency,* which was a *Washington Post* bestseller, and the nonfiction books *Voting to Kill* and *Heavy Lifting* with Cam Edwards.

Made in the USA
Monee, IL
21 June 2021

71931233R00155